Tales of the Black Arts

a

Sword & Sorcery
Anthology

ISBN-13: 978-0692223451
ISBN-10: 0692223452

Published by Hazardous Press

Copyright 2014 by Hazardous Press
Cover Art Copyright 2014 by Luke Spooner

Table of Contents

The Blood of God
by Aaron J. French

Religion has become a terror to the shining city of Ethrika. Many flock into its incorporeal arms, that is true, but many the same stay fervently away. I have heard voices in the wind whispering about murder and contrivance. Trouble is brewing right under the king's nose. And he permits it—why? Because he is not a real king. No real king would take handouts from these finely adorned folk who dwell in great halls and shout from podiums about the death of the gods and the birth of the One God. A real king would balk at such ridiculousness. Sair-in, the old king—*my king*—would have filled these streets with their blood. That is why I have no king. I have only the blade. And the Order.

***

The day came when this whispering finally took shape in the form of a lovely young woman. She approached me outside a tavern where I sat drinking mead and reading a book on spellcraft. She glanced at the book, glanced at me, then, smirking, said, "Strange book for a warrior."

I looked at her. She was pretty in the way flowers and flocks of birds are pretty. *Natural.* Not a rugged, quest-worn beauty.

"Warriors do not only carry blades," I said.

She lifted her brows at me, then sat in the adjacent chair. Before us, the bustle of Market Square, stalls adorned with crafts and weapons, venders touting vegetables and meats, was like a dream of motion and bodies. Voices called back and forth, mixing together indistinctly, and men in heavy armor trundled with authority through the crowd—the king's guards against chaos. The guards commanded most of my attention, for if any were to recognize me there would be blood.

She giggled. "I know you are no mere warrior. I know *exactly* who you are, Atreyous, son of Talfon. I come in search of you."

My eyes darted to her. I closed the spellcraft book. "Only a select few know my name in this shining city. Only those in the Under Region, and those of the Silent Order. Both areas of avoidance to the likes of you—such a young, unspoiled beauty. You had better explain yourself or you may find a knife sticking into your breast."

It is unsettling how quickly a woman can turn from magnificent to wicked. I've seen it on a number of occasions, this being one of them. Her face contracted, grew hard around the edges, in whole less round and less appealing. Her eyes glowed red.

"Your arm wouldn't make it back across the table," she hissed. "But if you allow yourself to remain calm, I will gladly explain."

I nodded.

She softened and said, "My father is Regeous Phen. You have heard of him?"

After thinking about it, I said, "I believe he operates the large church on Houl Street. The one with the gold dome, the glittering turrets, and the brass steeple."

"That's right. I am Nuvena, his only daughter, and since I was a child I've lived with him in various cities, helped him erect various churches, but none have lasted aside from this one. My father adores your city, your shining Ethrika. He bought into it. Your king has accepted his view of the One God. Soon it will be the only religion in Ethrika."

"Half of the Ethrikans would perish in blood before I let that happen," I replied angrily. "But tell me, why do you call it *my* city and *my* king? Is it not also your city and king?"

She gave a wry smile. "It is not. I honor no man and no place other than God. That is why I want to hire you to kill my father."

Her words cut through the din of the crowd. I glanced about, certain someone had heard. "Are you mad?"

"Either we discuss this here and now, or you take me to someplace where you feel safe. To me it matters naught. But something tells me you are interested. I have lots of money. The followers of the One God are generous, indeed."

"You mean you rob them of their earnings."

She shrugged. "A matter of opinion."

I was interested. *Very* interested. A chance to get paid for lopping off one of these flailing arms of religion, that creature which was pulling Ethrika down into an abyss . . . yes, I wanted in.

"Come," I said, pocketing my book and getting up from the table. "Keep close. We must move fast. If you lose me—"

"I won't lose you."

I darted into the crowd, moving between the stalls and the admiring patrons. I avoided the soldiers, taking different routes to stay clear. Smells of meat and smoke assaulted my senses. I could hear music in the distance and the sound of people dancing.

We escaped Market Square into a matrix of huts and buildings. Ethrika is divided into three quarters based on class. There are the most rich who live in the Upper Region—in marble houses cut to perfection—and the Middle Region where the working-class Ethrikans abide, and lastly the Under Region, which the degenerates and delinquents call home. The Under Region is also the location of the Silent Order.

I led Nuvena farther down through the descending levels of buildings until we reached the mudflats of the Under Region. We passed by a sickly peasant asleep on the side of the street, and another, blind, ringing his empty bell for coins. I stopped and dropped a single silver into his cup.

At the very bottom of Ethrika, in a section known as Hell's Landing, we entered an alley. At the end of a long, brick-flanked corridor, the alley came to a dead end, where a single section of wall sat inconspicuously. I knocked thrice on the bricks, and we waited.

"I find this section of Ethrika disgusting," Nuvena commented. "The peasants here are diseased, and they are without God."

I glared at her. "Perhaps it is *you* who is diseased."

One of the bricks in the center of the wall evaporated. Dark eyes appraised us. At length we were permitted by a strange ghostly hand into the dwelling of the Silent Order. The wall, which is really only the illusion of a wall, was breached quite easily.

Friends of mine, great silent men trained in the arts of death and stealth, greeted us with nodding heads. I noticed that Nuvena was apprehensive as we made our way down the winding stone stair, deep into the bowels of the earth. Perhaps this was due to the many bricks that were so often made into nothing, and through which many dark eyes examined us.

At the bottom of the stair, where the air was most black, we passed through another of the illusory brick walls. Here was the chamber of the head of the Silent Order, Caesius Clianthus. He was sitting behind a grand marble desk; to either side stood his guards, men wearing black hoods and black chainmail—the demon monk assassins. They are the ones who protect the head of the Silent Order with dark secret magik and daggers made from the bones of demonic men.

Caesius glanced up from his writing as we entered. Sturdy and muscular, he is among the largest of all men. His eyes, those strange gems that shine out like twin moons, regarded us in all their inquisitive glory. Employing a monocle, he inspected the blonde lady, and his lips quivered with lust.

"Atreyous," he said, "have you brought the Lady Madonna herself? Such rarefied beauty is a blessing to my eyes. Tell me, is she mine to employ as I see fit?"

I did not tell him. Instead I informed him of her personality and recounted the proposal she had put forth outside of the tavern. He listened carefully, nodding, never taking his eyes from her. I have known Caesius for more than eleven years. When he gets his sights on a woman, the worst will usually happen. I recall many cases in which he raped some young beauty all the way to her grave.

When I had finished, he said to her, "Why should such a lovely, *God-fearing* lady such as yourself seek the death of her father?"

"Because he is polluted by demons, much the same as you. He can no longer see the face of the One God, and worse he is not even aware of his falling by the wayside. Money and power have blinded him. It is time that I take over his position as leader of the church. I shall declare the One God religion as being the only recognizable religion in Ethrika."

Her words seemed to amuse Caesius. "What will the king have to say about it?"

She turned her head slightly, as if in shame. "The king will say nothing, for he is already aware of my plan. He even knows about hiring Atreyous of the Silent Order."

These words put fear and anger into my heart, but Caesius laughed bitterly. "And how on earth did you manage that?"

Nuvena turned her head more and said nothing.

"Come on," Caesius insisted.

But she turned until she faced the wall, her skin flushing bright red.

Caesius suddenly lifted his brows. "Aha, I have just picked the answer out of your mind. Did you know that I can read minds? Did you know that minds are readable?"

She shook her head.

"Well they are, and I have just read yours. And now I know that you have sacrificed your innocence, your body, and your purity to the king. That is how you got him to agree to all this."

"Is it true?" I demanded. "Have you shared your body with the king?"

She flushed with embarrassment and shame. "It is true. I make no excuses for my actions. There was no other way by which to sway him."

"You are playing a dangerous game, Nuvena, daughter of Regeous," I said.

She turned on me. "You know nothing of my life, Atreyous, son of Talfon. You could never understand the mystical revelations the One God has shown me. For these truths, I would gladly sacrifice my body a thousand times. And you . . . you are nothing but a common criminal. What know you of divine visions?"

"I know that religion is a deceiver of men. First the pantheon of gods held the world in its grips, and now your One God strives to do the same. But it'll never make a slave of this man, for I shall forever be my own master."

She laughed. "Such arrogant words! Indeed, you shall receive the harshest of punishments come judgment morn!"

"This is all quite fascinating," Caesius cut in. "But the Silent Order cares little for religion and redemption. What we care about is money and deathblows. Your proposal has intrigued me. Perhaps you could illuminate us as to your plan, so that we might get on with it." He grinned at her, his face like a porcupine.

She then proceeded to tell us everything she had in mind. When she was through, Caesius leaned back in his chair, hoisting his boots onto the marble desk.

"Now *that* is a daring endeavor," he said. "Wouldn't you agree, Atreyous?"

"I do not like it," I replied. "I am interested in the money she is willing to pay. Everything else reeks of a familial vendetta and power-seeking."

Caesius chuckled. "Indeed it does, my old friend. But speaking of money, we cannot take this upon our shoulders until we have received payment."

"You shall have your money by the end of the day," Nuvena said.

"When is Regeous's sermon to take place?" I asked.

Her eyes flicked to me. I could see she was growing weary with the lot of us. "Tomorrow, at sundown."

"Where?"

"At The Great Speaker's Shrine."

I considered this. "He will be preaching for several hours?"

She nodded.

"And where will you be?"

"Watching from the crowd."

I considered yet again, then finally I agreed. "Provided you come through with the money, as you have promised, then I shall deliver the deathblow tomorrow evening toward the end of his sermon."

Her face brightened. "Excellent!"

I sensed an underlying emotion in her, something akin to the rage she had exhibited at the tavern. Whatever tricks and wiles the woman had up her sleeve, they were fueled by pure, callous evil—of that I was certain.

Caesius cleared his throat. "Eh. Just one more thing before we make all of this official."

Fear usurped her expression and she turned to him. "What is it?"'"

Her mouth twisted with rage. "You filthy pig. And why should you be equal to the king?"

"Well, are we not both just as essential to all this? He at one end of it, and I at the other?"

She balled her hands into fists. "Perhaps. But still . . . "

"I'm going to tell you now that Atreyous will not receive my permission to go ahead with the deathblow unless I get what I want."

She was quiet. Then: "If your demons require my body in addition to the amount we agreed upon, so be it. I ask only that you make it quick."

Caesius grinned and his face became a little orb of sheer wicked delight. "You heard her, men," he said. "She's so eager for this that she wants to begin forthwith. Leave us," he said to his demon monk assassins. Then, to me: "Atreyous, you have your orders. Return once the job is complete to receive your percentage."

I bowed, turning to leave. But before I could escape onto the stair, Nuvena caught my attention with her eyes. There was a desperate plea in the look she gave me, and despite my repugnance I wanted to assist her, to free her of the horrific situation into which she had placed herself. But I knew I could not.

The sounds of her screaming hastened after me up the stair.

***

The next day was heralded by an unexpected rain shower. Water fell from the sky all morning in great gray sheets, and the streets were awash with puddles and mud. When it let up, a bank of the whitest fog moved in, encroaching through the cracks of the buildings like a silent deadly spirit.

I betook myself to cleaning the equipment I would need for dispatching Regeous. I sat on the roof of my stone dwelling, located in the higher quarters of the Under Region, and sharpened my blade, cleaned the lenses of my eyepieces, and even shined my stalker's boots. I readied the Veil of Unconsciousness, secured my set of poisonous darts and my blowgun, and equipped the blackjack Caesius had given to me upon joining the Silent Order.

The peasants were on their way to work, a teeming mass of them shuffling up the street. I wrinkled my nose at the combined smell of them—though I was quite used to it—and watched as they tromped through the mud toward Middle Region, where Ethrika's labor and commerce takes place.

Later, when afternoon was dawning, I adorned my things, dressed accordingly for the kill, sheathed my blade, and descended through a hole in the center of my floor. This deposited me in the vast system of tunnels that make up the sewer system of Ethrika. Once down, I leaped off the ladder into the darkness, my stalker's boots splashing in a puddle of fetid water.

Lighting my fire-resistant wax candle, I crept through the foul stone tunnels, as the flame flung my misshapen shadow across the walls. Things moved in those dark stinking waters, which extended from wall to wall save a single pathway, which I traversed toward my destination.

Colossal surfacing bodies broke into view, then vanished back down equally as silent. Small creatures, rodents and the like, plus clouds of fattened insects, also moved in the black air. Whatever of these creatures took interest in me I flattened with my boot heel or discouraged with a wave of my candle.

I have killed many people in Ethrika. I often use the sewer tunnels to move about unseen, to reach a destination during the daytime when the cover of night is absent. I spent years mapping the layout and committing it to memory, thus I have no trouble navigating the harsh foul rivers of our shining city's waste and refuse.

When I came to the area underneath The Great Speaker's Shrine, I stopped. I heard a commotion overhead: the crowd had already gathered. I knew one of the upper entry holes led to the alley. After a bit of searching I discovered this particular hole and emerged from the womb of excrement into fresh city air.

Luckily no one was around to witness my emersion; the alley, littered with broken crates and old pots and pans, was deserted. At once I heard the babble of the crowd and the din of many persons gathered. I took a moment to adjust myself, then located the nearest ladder and ascended to the rooftops.

I approached The Great Speaker's Shrine from the north, making use of the hidden wood platforms that the Silent Order has suspended all around Ethrika. However at one junction I was forced to leap like a cat from rooftop to rooftop. In the old days, King Sair-in used to give his powerful speeches at The Great Speaker's Shrine. But those days are done. The new king doesn't orate; only the religious fanatics and zealots employ the shrine now.

Secreted high above the teeming crowd, made up of both peasants and wealthy Ethrikans, I observed everything from a bird's eye view. There is a large stone fountain in the center of the square, shaped like a dragon, round which the people thronged. Their faces were directed to the shrine itself, a basalt platform with marble railings and a great sheet of green jasper erected in the rear. Here was the stage from which the grand king once orated. I took notice of the fat pompous figure presently stalking back and forth— Regeous preparing to give a sermon. My blood boiled. It felt, to me, like sacrilege.

Regeous approached the front of the basalt platform, calming the crowd with his gestures. He wore a gaudy red and gold fur-lined gown with split hanging sleeves, and a red feathered hat. His face was round and pale, his jowls like bread dough, and he was short. It was hard to imagine that he had sired the beautiful woman, Nuvena. But for his eyes, which possessed the same fierce cunning and wickedness as that woman's did.

"The days of the pagan gods are over," he said, voice booming, reaching, echoing through the city. He spread his hands as he spoke. "Too long have we suffered in the name of these awful abominations, who amuse themselves by observing idly our despair; who indeed inflict this despair upon us for their own enjoyment. The beasts that dwell in the sun, in the sea, in the sky, in the forest, they are devils, I say. They desire only that you fall, as they themselves have fallen."

It was the usual ridiculous rhetoric, the same corruption of speech, designed to influence, to overtake, and ultimately to befool the listener. I let the words pass unheeded from my ears and scanned the entranced masses for the sermon-giver's daughter. It wasn't long before I spotted her toward the side of the shrine, where she stood dazzling dressed in white and lace. A group of men clustered about her—the king's guards against chaos—bearing cutlasses and other hooked weaponry. Nuvena had a look of utter revulsion on her face.

More of these armed men loomed about the rear of the platform, standing stock still, their hands on their hilts. I would have to somehow bypass them to get at Regeous. I examined closer, noting the various entryways and alleyways, all the nooks and crannies, windows and rooftops, and the marvelous places where shadows of the buildings fell across the ground.

The sound of his orating faded into the background of my mind, became like a mad jabbering there, an indistinct drone. I swept down the side of one building, landing softly in a pile of plucked chicken feathers. Staying in the shadows, I sidled up on the wall, moving through the alleys until I reached the empty space behind the jasper wall.

Here a man surprised me by suddenly turning out of an alley and appearing before me as though from thin air. He was only a peasant, whom I realized had been urinating in that alley, but he could not be allowed to leave having seen me.

With a lightning-fast sweep of my right arm, I brought him to my chest, clutched him, and covered his mouth. He stank of mead and stale sweat. His eyes grew wide as I withdrew the Veil of Unconsciousness and draped it over his head. At once he was out, slumping in my arms, and I gently laid him back in the alley.

Two of Regeous's guards took notice of me as I swept through the shadows; curious, they approached, and I let them come.

"What the 'ell is 'at?" one said. "Some measly cat?"

The other shook his head, drawing his blade. His face waxed into a grin. "It's a damn fool assassin, I believe. But who'd be dense enough to stalk the prophet of the One God on this day?"

I stepped from the shadows, validating his suspicions. "I would be—" and then, drawing my blade, I cut swiftly through both their necks. The sharp edge passed through their skin, heads plopping to the ground. Moments later, their bodies did the same. They had not even the chance to alert their comrades before perishing.

I dragged their bodies, and their heads, into the alley with the other. But for the blood and gore staining the ground, there was no evidence of the kill. I kicked dirt over the blood then crept back into the shadows.

Regeous was still giving his sermon. His words seemed to elicit an eerie silence from the crowd as he prattled on about original sin and the One God and the solitary chance at redemption.

Three guards were posted by the rear of the jasper wall. Sticking to the shade engendered by that wall, I disabled the first two with the Veil of Unconsciousness. The third got wind of me, and I was forced to club him on the head with my blackjack. I left their bodies stacked behind the stage.

It was fortunate that Regeous orated so deftly, for it allowed me to go about my work unheeded. Everyone present at The Great Speaker's Shrine was mesmerized by his religious rhetoric. I had no trouble arresting the majority of the king's guards—all save three. Then I perched in the black crevice underneath the stage and waited for the sermon to end.

He continued speaking for almost an hour, and by that time he had worked the crowd into an utter frenzy. With his last sentence, which was indeed a call for action, everyone went berserk. Their applause boomed through the city, and their raised voices split the sky.

They sounded more like an army than a gathering of civilians. They began chanting his name—*Regeous, Regeous*—and the name of the One God, and I feared they were fit to die for that short, fat, pompous man.

Secreted in my cramped space, I listened to his footsteps overhead. He reached the rear of the stage and I heard him calling for his guards. When they didn't come, I heard doubt enter into his voice. I withdrew my blowgun, inserted three of the deadly poisonous darts, and crept toward the sunlight.

I paused by the edge of the stage, where he stood glancing about in confusion. The roar of the crowd was deafening, yet I managed to secure his attention with a whisper—*"Hey you, down here!"*

He looked down and when his eyes betook me, first alarm then terrible fear passed across his face. "What the devil are you doing under there?" he said, but it was an unconscious question, because he knew full well what I was doing under there.

"Give the gods my regards," I hissed. Frightened, he turned and began to flee, but I spit all three darts straight into his back. The poison entered his bloodstream directly. He took a few steps, then hit the ground like a bag of stones. His feathered hat tumbled away, and I then sent a final dart into his exposed forehead, just for good measure.

The crowd, too absorbed in their feverish chanting, did not appear to notice the falling of their idol. This was good, for it ensured me a safe escape. I crept out from under the stage, then, skulking through the shadows, rounded the jasper wall and headed for the nearest entrance to the sewer system.

Nuvena was waiting for me in the alley behind the stage. When I saw her I stopped, and I almost drew my blade, but something about her expression stayed my hand. She appeared to be . . . giddy with delight.

"Well done," she said. "It appears you live up to your reputation after all."

"I appreciate the kind words, but I am trying to make my escape at the moment."

She laughed. "No need to worry. You have covered yourself most effectively. Come tomorrow there will be a new voice of the One God in shining Ethrika, and it will be the voice of a woman, no less. I wanted to thank you in person before you vanish the way all thieves do."

"I am no mere thief."

"I would say that much is evident."

"What of Caesius and the king?"

Her expression became most foul. Her skin pulled taut. Her eyes glowed. "The king will remain on my leash indefinitely, as he is vital in my overtaking of the city in the name of the One God. As for your leader, the wretched Caesius . . . once I render payment tonight for the services of the Silent Order, he and all others of his sect will become my sworn enemies. That goes for present company."

I grunted. "I should've known it would turn out like this. The One God and His followers are nothing but trouble, way I see it. Consider yourself equally opposed by myself the rest of my brethren. Now, get out of my way."

"As you wish." Smiling, her features returning to their normal comeliness, she moved out of the alley and into the space behind the green jasper wall. I gave her a final look before opening the hole to the sewer tunnels and dropping down into darkness. The sun had broken free of those overhanging clouds and a column of light had centered itself upon her. She resembled a beautiful angle standing there. I reckoned I had not seen the last of Nuvena, daughter of Regeous.

With the thunderous noise of the crowd still in my ears, I dropped into the darkness below the shining city of Ethrika and splashed my way through the muck toward Under Region. I hoped to seclude myself in my stone dwelling for the rest of the evening, until the comforting fingers of night pulled its blackness across the land.

Only then would I feel safe enough to lay claim to what was owed me.

Rules of Combat
by Jacqueline Seewald

"T-they are c-coming, my lady!"

As usual, when Bothgard was excited, his words lacked clarity.

"Take a deep breath. Good. Now *who* is coming?"

Bothgard ran his hand through the shock of white gold hair, which had loosened from its tie. "I do not know who they are, but they are warriors for cert. They wear armor and carry weapons. They approach us. I hurried to give warning."

"You did well." Cathra smiled at the young man and watched his cheeks catch fire. "Alert our people. Tell them I wish them to prepare our defenses with haste."

Cathra sensed the old woman's move beside her. "You heard?"

"This may be the one of prophecy."

She turned and met the old woman's gaze. "I do not believe in prophecies."

"You should." The old woman smiled at her. "But you are still young to understand such things."

Cathra pulled thoughtfully at her blond braids and bit her lower lip. It was always best to heed the old woman's words. She had the power of knowing. Cathra herself felt something important was about to happen. However, if those coming represented evil, she was prepared. She had her own powers and had fought and won against dark ones before, those who would greedily devour her father's domain.

***

The warriors stood before the gates of the stone keep. Cathra took her place at the top of the battlements. The old woman took a place beside Cathra on her right, Hargar, the garrison commander, on her left.

"Identify yourselves," Cathra called out in a clear, strong voice.

The warrior, who appeared to be their leader, rode forward. He sat tall on a large dappled gray stallion, a warhorse that looked tired and dusty.

"I am Ronwith of Feth. I fought with your father in the king's army. I bring you news of him. Will you allow us to enter your gates? We come in peace."

Cathra was dubious. Others had claimed they came in peace. Each time, they arrived because they heard an heiress ruled a rich land ripe for the picking. She never trusted the honesty of those she did not know. In her experience, strangers brought nothing but problems. Their motives were at best questionable.

"What do you think?" Cathra asked, turning her gaze to rest on the old woman.

"You should hear him out."

"Very well." Cathra allowed herself to be guided by the old woman's wisdom and second sight. Everyone knew the old woman practiced the black arts. But she would still use her own judgment and exercise caution. She called out, "Ronwith of Feth, you may enter, but alone. Your men must remain outside our gates. They can make camp for now."

"It will be as you ask," the leader said. "May I bring one other with me?"

"You can do so. However, you must leave your weapons behind as a show of good faith."

She watched as Ronwith exchanged wary looks with the younger man beside him. The young one spoke in an excited voice, obviously arguing against Ronwith's decision. Cathra waited. She knew how to wait.

Finally, the two men dismounted leaving horses and weapons behind. Cathra gave orders and her people allowed the two men entry. They were led to the great hall where guests were received.

"I bid you sit and break bread with us." Cathra's manner was polite but distant.

When they were seated at the long plank table, Cathra signaled and food was brought out as well as ale. The men were offered cheese and crusty bread slathered with fresh butter. They ate with the relish of the hungry.

She studied them thoughtfully. Ronwith had surely seen no more than thirty winters. He was dark of complexion like her father. This did not surprise her as the king's warriors were all of his kind, men who came from the southern provinces. They had conquered many with their efficient weapons and strong organization.

Ronwith had strong features, an aquiline nose, a square jaw, hair black as a raven's wing. He exuded strength.

"Please give me the news you promised of my father," Cathra requested once she saw that the men were sufficiently revived.

Ronwith gave her a sharp look. "I must tell you that your father was a brave warrior. He led his men well. I fought beside him many times. Unfortunately, I was not with him when he and his warriors were caught in an ambush, a trap, and died nearly to the man. My brother, Narth," he indicated the young man beside him, "found your father and his men while on patrol. We did what we could for him and the others. Your father gave me this as a token." Ronwith reached into his shirt and pulled out a ring that Cathra recognized immediately as having been worn by her father.

"He asked me to bring it to you. His last words and thoughts were for you." Cathra noted Ronwith had a deep, voice that rumbled in his chest. It was a strong voice but not unpleasant to the ear.

"I thank you for your trouble," Cathra answered solemnly. "You have come far to honor a dying man's request."

"But there is more to it than that, is there not?" The old woman stared knowingly into Ronwith's eyes. Her light blue orbs were sharp with insight.

He met her gaze with directness. "That is true." He turned back to Cathra. He paused for a moment and then spoke with intent. "Your father wished for us to marry."

Cathra's breath caught in her throat. "Why would he wish that?"

"Your father said that it was time for you to marry, that you had seen more than twenty winters, that you have held this land and keep for him. Now he wishes that you have a husband to do for you. He trusted me with the honor."

Cathra frowned. "How thoughtful of my father. However, in the years that he has been gone I have learned the ways of the warrior for myself. I hold these lands not just for my father or myself but for my people. Other men have come here seeking an advantage. They learned differently."

"I realize you do not know me and therefore cannot trust me, Lady Cathra, but I am an honorable man. I seek to woo you."

Cathra could only laugh at his tactic. "I am not a romantic young girl to be swept away by foolish notions."

Ronwith studied her with cool gray eyes. "What would win your affections, my lady?"

"Why I would have to know you much better, Ronwith of Feth. My life is one thing, the lives of my people are quite another. I take no risks where they are concerned. I have a duty to these people. I take my responsibilities seriously."

Ronwith gave a short nod of approval. "I would expect no less from your father's daughter."

"We will talk again tomorrow. Come in the morning when the garrison trains. You and your brother are welcome to work out with our warriors."

"We will do as you request," Ronwith said, his gray eyes solemn, his head bowed.

After they left, Cath turned to the old woman. "What do you think?"

The old woman shrugged. "It is hard to tell his exact intentions from so brief a meeting."

"I agree. That is why he will train with the garrison. A great deal can be learned of a warrior's character in such a manner."

"Will you marry him?"

Cath did not answer.

"Will you kill him?"

Would she? A great deal depended on what she learned on the morrow.

"For now, I make no judgment."

The old woman cackled, her eyes bright with unnatural light. "It will be decided in blood."

***

Ronwith sat down beside his brother and several of the other warriors. They warmed their hands and feet near the campfire.

"Ronwith, I think we should leave this place," Narth said.

"Why do you suggest such a thing? I intend to win the lady's love and respect. We will finally have a home, a real home. You see the lands beyond the keep? They are rich and fertile. It will all belong to us. Finally, we will be men of substance, of property."

Narth shook his head. "Lady Cathra's father is dead and cannot force her to marry you. There is something about the lady, something that makes me uneasy."

"She is a strong woman."

Narth frowned. "It is more than that, though I cannot explain what." Narth leaned closer. "I have heard rumors that Lady Cathra is a witch. That old woman, her advisor, most assuredly is one."

Ronwith gave his brother a pensive look. Narth had never been as brave or bold as his older brother, but Ronwith knew Narth was no coward. Narth had an awareness that Ronwith had come to respect. They shared the same sire but not the same mother. Narth's mother had charmed the king with her intuition and insight while Ronwith's mother had been a young girl of great beauty and vivaciousness. Each had served the king's lust. Each had given the conqueror a son. Both bastards, as he called them, had ended up cleaning out horse stalls, until the day the king had seen Ronwith's potential as a warrior. But serving his father had brought Ronwith only wars to fight. He was weary of that life, tired of the killing. He wanted land of his own, a life of prosperity, a woman to love, and children of his blood. For that, he was willing to fight to the death.

"Where is the boy, Dendar?" Ronwith asked. "Bring him."

Dendar was the only survivor of the massacre that had taken the lives of the lady's father and his warriors. Ronwith realized that he must learn as much as possible about this place if he were to have any chance of winning the lady.

If all else failed, he would consider taking the keep by force or laying siege to it. But as a seasoned warrior, he recognized that acts of desperation were not often the best alternative. Besides, he realized that Cathra would never truly accept him if he acted in a ruthless manner. He must find a way to convince her of his integrity or all would be for naught.

"You sent for me?"

Ronwith studied Dendar. The boy had a broad back, blue eyes and white-gold hair. He stood tall and carried his quiver of arrows and bow at all times.

"Sit with us and share some ale. I wish to know about you and this place. Do you have family hereabouts?"

The boy nodded his head. "My parents' portion feeds a family of six. When our lord came looking for archers, I was the oldest, strongest son and so was chosen. I thought then only of the excitement of adventure. Now I wish to go home to my family."

"On the morrow, I will bring you with us," Ronwith promised. "How is it that you survived the enemy attack that killed Lord Carn?"

Dendar bowed his head. "I confess my shame. My lord and his warriors rode ahead. I was to the rear of the archers who were all on foot. When the attack came, we archers shot our arrows and hit some of the enemy. But the fighting was fierce. The men were being killed all around me. I-I ran off into the woods. I let my fear best me. I returned only to find that it was too late to help. They were all dead or dying, like my lord. That was when your brother arrived and found us."

"I cannot condone cowardice," Ronwith said, his mouth set in a grim expression. "But I understand fear."

"Forgive me, Ronwith, I never wished to be in battle. To look death in the eye is a horrifying thing. I want only to help farm our land."

"You may yet redeem yourself," Ronwith said. "Tell me about this place. Who are its people?"

"Lord Carn, Lady Cathra's father, was the son of one the king's warriors. They came here and conquered our lands and built the keep which is as you see a great stone fortress. Lord Carn's father was killed by Grendar who ruled here before. Lord Carn swore vengeance and killed both Grendar and his son. Then Lord Carn took Lady Cathra's mother to wife much against her will. She was Grendar's daughter."

Ronwith nodded, encouraging the boy to continue. "Who is the old woman who advises Lady Cathra?"

"That is Wendra, Lady Cathra's grandmother. She was Grendar's wife. She is said to be a sorceress of some talent. Some say when Lord Carn took her daughter, Wendra cursed him, said that he would never father a son."

"And Lord Carn sired no sons?"

The boy shook his head. "No, he had no children after the birth of Lady Cathra. Her mother died in childbirth and he took no other women after her. Some say the curse destroyed his desire. But he did love Lady Cathra and treated her as if she were a son."

The boy spoke in a whisper. "It is also said that Wendra put a second curse on Lord Carn, that he would die a violent and horrible death."

"You have explained much that I needed to know," Ronwith said. "Sleep in peace. On the morrow, you will go home."

Ronwith fervently wished that this could be his home as well. His bones ached as did his old wounds. He was weary, tired of soldiering.

Narth turned to him again. "Wendra is a witch. The boy has confirmed it. We should leave this place, brother before you too are cursed by those who practice the black arts."

Ronwith raised his chin, squaring his jaw. "I wish to claim what has been promised me."

"Take heed of the danger."

Ronwith shook his head. He was a warrior. That meant he would not cower in fear of man or magic.

***

It was a spring day and the grass smelled sweetly of new birth. Surely not a day to die, Ronwith reflected. In the courtyard of the keep, two dozen warriors were dressed in battle gear, helmets and armor, swords and shields. Ronwith carried his own which were as battle-scarred as he himself.

The garrison commander approached him. "It is Lady Cathra's wish that you spar with her chosen champion."

So the lady wished to test his mettle. Well, he had expected as much.

"I request a blunted sword for I do not wish to harm anyone with my blade."

"Very well." He was handed a blunt-edged sword.

The champion arrived moments later. Lady Cathra's grandmother followed close behind, but the lady herself was not anywhere to be seen.

It must have been a trick of the sunlight, but the champion's armor glowed with an eerie light as did the sword the champion held. It had not been blunted.

Ronwith turned to the garrison commander. "The champion takes unfair advantage," he said, nodding toward the sword.

The commander did not look him in the eye. "You may change your mind and use your own sword."

Ronwith frowned in stubborn determination. "I do not wish it. I desire to hurt no one. This is a friendly practice, on my part at least."

The champion did not wait but challenged Ronwith directly.

The move, a strong, bold one, drew first blood since he was not prepared to block it.

Ronwith, a seasoned warrior, could not easily be intimidated. He lunged forward using all his considerable strength to disarm his adversary. The champion, although shorter and much more slender than he, did not budge, surprising Ronwith. Blinding light came shooting through his adversary's sword toward him. The next thrust caught Ronwith in his forearm. Searing pain shot through him. He was forced to drop his weapon. Before Ronwith knew what was happening, he lay on the ground disoriented and confused, a sword pointing at his throat.

"Will you admit defeat and leave this land now?"

Ronwith felt dazed. He wasn't certain quite what had happened. He'd heard Lady Cathra's voice but did not see her. How could that be?

"You have me at a disadvantage. Yet I know I would rather die here than walk away in defeat. I still wish to marry Lady Cathra."

The helmet was removed from the champion's head, and before him stood Lady Cathra, she of sun gold hair and sky blue eyes.

"You are the warrior I faced?" His eyes widened in amazement.

"I am trained to defend these lands. But my grandmother cast a spell with her sorcery and put magic into my sword and armor to make me stronger."

Around him the other warriors removed their helmets. Ronwith stared in surprise. At least half of them were women as well.

"Most of the men went off with my father. But I was trained to protect my home and saw to it that other women were as well. I will never be conquered or subservient to any man. Knowing all of this, do you still want me for a wife?"

"More than ever," Ronwith said truthfully. "I may not be worthy of you, but I would honor and respect you if you would have me. Yet I fear you have mortally wounded me."

Ronwith's wounds flowed freely. He felt his life's blood leaving him. Soon he realized he would die. He showed no fear. He was not a coward. He would die the death of a true warrior remaining stoic to the end. However, Cathra's grandmother touched him and moments later to his shock and amazement the bleeding ceased and the pain disappeared.

"How is that possible?"

"I am both healer and destroyer," the old woman said. "Sadly, neither my son nor daughter was born with such gifts. But you will find my granddaughter has much of my talent. Her strength is already legend, though she be still young."

Ronwith held out his hand to Cathra and she took it. Light and energy charged between their joined fingers. The old woman smiled and nodded her approval, knowing a magical bond had forged that would be unbreakable.

Heart of the Southern Isles
by Lon Prater

It came to pass that Roderick Kingman and his companion Jack Dante left the soiled lands of Nefer-ha on a threefin galleon heading farther yet to the south; their stay among the Neferi had done nothing to further their shared quest for revenge against the mystery man who had stolen Kingman's lands and title, ruined half of Dante's face with a deforming wash of acid, and left the man without his memory. In the end, the Neferi shaman had thanked the pair for ridding them of the Dwellers in the Soil and whispered rumors of a great empty city on an island far to the south, an island also said to shelter one of the lost tribes of Squensheherra.

"When I was pressed to serve on a Druvinian privateer, the sailors spoke of this lost tribe," Kingman had said, somber in his close fitting brown traveling clothes. He wore an unsheathed rapier, recently blooded, on a plain leather belt into which was also tucked a pair of wide mouthed muskets. "The Squensheherra possessed great power of old, even the power over men's minds. Perhaps these descendants of theirs retain some of their forefathers' weirding ways?"

Jack considered this, hefting the blessed scimitar he had received from a grateful Kaffir sultan for the safe return of his dibbuk-stolen daughter. He wore green breeches laced Mazjan-style down the sides in silver and a sleeveless skin shirt. The lower half of his face was tied a brilliant yellow scarf, which did much to hide the acid-scorched landscape of his left cheek and jaw. "Perhaps we shall find at last a cure for my lost recall, and soon after, some clue to the identity of the scoundrel we seek."

Kingman eyed him dourly, saying nothing for a long moment. The firelight flickered about them like a possessed thing. "Perhaps," he finally said, before standing abruptly and moving to retire for the night.

The ship's master, a one-eared man with blue dye in his hair, stepped up behind Kingman. Thinking better of clapping his morose passenger on the back, he let one heavy hand fall onto the rail beside

Kingman, clearing his throat as he did. Kingman turned his long spare frame to face the ship's master; his expression as sharp and cold and sour as shards of broken limeglass.

"Sirrah, we putting in on the morrow but we cannot remain." He jabbed one finger aft, toward a low mass of iron-grey clouds that had taken up position a dozen leagues off the threefin's starboard quarter. "I'm not made to weather a gale like that."

It was a custom of the Southern Waters that a ship's master refer to his ship and himself as one and the same; the same custom made it disrespectful to refer to a ship's master by any title other than the name of his vessel.

"Aye, Gintle Rynthar, I have kept one eye upon that storm these last two days. She will be upon us before another two have passed. Will you return for us?"

"I will," he said, tugging at the stub of his right ear. "But I am getting short of supplies, and must travel west to Ibis to trade and replenish. Tonight the moon is fullest. I will return in one month for you, and will wait no more than three days before I set sail, with you or without."

"That is fair, Gintle Rynthar," Kingman said, breathing in the clean sea air. "I suspect if my companion and I haven't completed our business here in that time, we're likely beyond need your services."

The ship's master ground his teeth together. "From the sea tales of this island, you may be right, sirrah. You may be right."

***

Dante reluctantly paid Gintle Rynthar with the ebon tusk of a Neferi trunknose rat, and at Kingman's urging vowed to give over the other when they were safely back aboard. As the pair waded from the gig onto a blinding white shore, some of the sailors made catcalls about winning back their money in a month. Jack Dante laughed and shouted back at them, but the wind stole his riposte.

Kingman strode ramrod straight to the edge of the lapping sea, scanned the wall of solid rock before him. It stretched from one end

30

of the narrow beach to the other, just a stone's throw away. A half-day's careful climb would have them atop the cliff by dusk.

Jack splashed his way to the dry sand, still calling rude comments out to the sailors as their oars dipped and rose in the warm sea. Finally he turned to his grim-faced companion. "We have to climb that?" he asked gamely.

Kingman nodded. "How light are your packs?"

"None too heavy with you giving away my every souvenir. I can get them up that face, if we must climb. But look!" Jack dashed ahead of Kingman, his bare wet feet already crusted with sand. He stopped a short distance from the base of the rocky cliff, one finger pointing at a stony outcropping. "There's a cave opening there. Shall we see if it saves us a climb?"

Kingman stepped close to the outcropping and saw what Dante's sharper eyes had detected from the water's edge. Indeed, a gaping shadowy mouth beckoned the travelers from behind the shiny fist of sea sprayed stone. Cool air crept from the dark opening, chilling the sweat on Kingman's brow.

"It is an ill-feeling place," Kingman said. "But if some fell thing resides within, let us face it and be done. Have you any light?"

"Just the thing," Jack said, snapping his fingers. He unburdened himself of his pack and scavenged within. In short order had a coral oil lamp lit. He held it before him in his dirk hand, dangling from a bronze ring. In his right, he held the scimitar.

Dante ducked into the cave quickly, with so little caution it near took Kingman's breath. The taller man had to bend almost in half to fit into the small opening. "Careful," he said, as if uncertain of his own words. "I should hate to see you gutted and dead before you've regained your memory."

"Indeed." Dante smiled at Kingman. He had taken down the yellow scarf once he was alone with Kingman. In the unsteady lamplight, the scars and craters on his face would have made Kingman shudder, were he the sort of man given to shuddering.

They trudged along the curving path of the tunnel, trying to squint into the blackness at the moving edge of their light. Kingman held one of his muskets pointed skyward, ball and powder already loaded. One long finger tickled the trigger's curve. With his other hand, he lifted and dropped his rapier in the ring of metal that served to keep it attached to his belt. Something about the repeating <u>snick</u> and <u>click</u> comforted him.

"The smell of the unnatural is strong in this place," he said to Dante. His voice was low and steady.

"I lack your sense for such things, Rodder, but I know those markings up ahead do not bode well."

Kingman scowled at the familiar jocularity of that nickname but said nothing. He had long ago given up attempts to cure the man of it.

They stopped in front of a series of slashes and curlicues carved into a smooth section of the tunnel wall. Flakes of ochre and crimson indicated that at some time in their history the markings had been painted in. Jack was unlearned in his letters and so asked Kingman what he made of the strange writing.

"I have seen many kinds of word symbols in my travels, and learned half a dozen languages over the course. But these marks are unfamiliar." He shook his head. "They look most like Arvad-script here and here, and this is similar to the Kittorran sign which means both 'person' and 'flaw'. . ."

His sure voice trailed off as he set his lips together. "I suppose this could be from a language that later splintered into many different languages, perhaps even the tongue of the Squensheherrans." Kingman shrugged and cast his eyes ahead of them into the darkness.

Jack nodded then marched ahead, the point of his scimitar bobbing and glinting as he went. The narrow passage took several more sharp twists before depositing them in a chamber too large for the lamp to illuminate. "Left wall or right?" Jack asked.

Kingman pointed to the right, as ever he chose when given no reason to pick the left. The two men began working their way around the nearly smooth, nearly circular wall counterclockwise. About half way around, a shadowy form came into view at the bouncing edge of the light. Both of them stopped cold. Jack adjusted his grip on the scimitar even as Kingman leveled the wide mouth of his musket at the unexpected thing on the floor.

Neither breathed for a long moment; when the shadow made no move toward them--no move at all--they ventured toward it.

"It's a stone chest of some kind," said Dante.

Kingman was peering at the wall just above the queerly carved chest. There were more of the odd markings here, as well as on the floor surrounding the chest.

Jack sheathed his scimitar and began prying at the lid with the tip of one of his curved dirks.

"You truly have the heart of a rogue," Kingman said. The faint light made the angular lines of his face seem sharper, more severe. The tone in his voice was one of measured control, as if the tall man were expending great effort to only allow words to escape him, but not emotion.

Jack grinned, recognizing this tone as the one Kingman assumed whenever Jack was engaged in something questionable. His blade slipped into the fine line between the body of the chest and its lid, forcing them gradually apart.

"Sometimes I have a useful skill or two, though I know not what I did in my past life to come by them."

Kingman leaned close to look over Dante's shoulder into the chest. A fetid odor arose, stirred by the motion of the lid. Dante made a choking sound even as Kingman's eyes began to water.

"What foulness is this?" Kingman asked, glaring at the shriveled black thing that lay twitching within the stone chest.

Jack, who had recoiled slightly from the stench, now leaned forward again to look once more upon the strange artifact, his yellow scarf pulled snugly up to cover his nose. "I've no idea, Rodder. It would seem to be a heart, though how it continues to beat is a mystery."

"Dark magic," Kingman said, drawing himself back up to his full height. "Best we not disturb it."

Dante agreed and set the heavy lid back into place. He picked up the flickering coral oil lamp and continued around the room, looking back uneasily at the stone chest and the arcane markings that surrounded it as if he feared the thing might drag itself along the floor behind them.

Near to three quarters of the way around the chamber, the wan yellow light revealed a second tunnel angling steeply upwards. The pair made their way cautiously up the crumbling path until, just past a sudden sharp turn, they emerged into a green lit chamber much taller and wider than the one which held the stone chest and its curious contents.

This chamber proved no less peculiar. Far above them, beyond the range of the lamp's weak light, a plant-covered hole filtered the tropical sunlight, giving the chamber its viridian hue. Squarely in the middle of the cavern reared a monstrous black four-sided pillar, so tall it seemed to nearly reach the yawning hole above.

"Do you see? There on the pillar?" Jack asked.

Kingman grunted, striding closer to it. "Rune-carved like the chambers behind us, and the wall of the tunnel. These stand out in relief, though; unlike the engravings out there." He put one hand upon the side of the black pillar closest to him, traced part of a curling rune, then jerked his hand back with a sharp intake of breath. "It's freezing! And the stone--it stinks of an evil only the soul can smell."

Jack Dante knew himself to be tone deaf to such emanations. But here in this chamber even he could sense the palpable aura of some ancient, restless malevolence. Despite the warmth of the air, he shivered, turning away from the monolith and the long lean form before it.

As he did so, his eyes alighted on a series of jutting stone shelves that spiraled around the wall of the cavern. Jack gasped. "A staircase!" he exclaimed, "Though a mighty narrow one." He began to ascend as Kingman circled the pillar below, still absorbed in his thoughts.

It was tricky work, balancing on the slender shelves of stone. More than once, one of Jack's feet went astray, sending a shower of rubble to the cavern floor. Recovering himself, he would cleave to the step and the wall beside him until his breathing slowed and his heart quit racing so madly in his ears. About four times around, he could make out a section where the green sunlight played upon the pillar. There were no runes here, only large representations of things with rows of teeth devouring something that could only be meant to appear human. Behind it, embossed flames seemed to dance as the wind played upon the greenery surrounding the uppermost hole.

The sight made Jack's blood run cold, and would have robbed him of his will to climb, had he not seen a more material reason to abandon his climb. "The steps end here, Roderick," he called, "Though it appears they resume some distance above."

Kingman pointed one thin finger at a pile of stone blocks. "These would likely be the missing steps. We couldn't see them on first entering, as they were against the opposite wall, hidden by this"--he grimaced--"monument."

"I'm coming down now," Dante shouted down.

"One moment," Kingman replied. "Can you see the top of the thing from there?"

"Some of it. The top's at least four times my height above me. From this angle, it looks like it's capped by a four-sided pyramid."

Very well," Kingman said, and turned his attention back to the parts of the pillar which he could see.

Step by ginger step, the scarred man descended the treacherous steps. As he made his way down, he described to Kingman the horrific image he had seen in the shaft of light. A few steps from the bottom, Dante leaped to the floor. He rolled and sprang to his feet with a flourish.

Kingman's face remained sober, betraying no amusement at the younger man's antics. Jack cleared his throat. "Must you always be so sour, my friend?"

Kingman glared at Dante with hard eyes that gradually softened, if only minutely. "So long as there is evil roaming free and unavenged, I can know no sweetness," he said. Kingman adjusted his twin muskets in his belt and looked away. "Let us return to the beach. We have wasted much daylight, and I want to be atop this cliff by nightfall."

***

After an exhausting climb, the pair pulled themselves over the ledge and onto a boulder-strewn plain. A valley stretched out before them, ripe and lush with vine covered palm trees, thick dank underbrush, and a dusting of bright flowers scattered amidst the sea of green. Off to the west, the setting sun was smudged by a haze of smoke.

"A village, perhaps?" Dante asked.

Kingman scowled. "Or a hell pit opened up. Either way, most like we shall find some trace of the living by seeking the fire. The moon is already risen, and that squall from the sea draws near. We should make haste toward the flames, whatever their origin may be."

With that they set off, dodging low hanging vines and limbs and listening--always listening--for the sound of company, whether it be of the two-footed or any other kind. Near moonset, the clouds were rumbling close and there was a heaviness in the air that made it nearly as difficult to breathe as the sulphur-thickened air of Teo, which this place faintly reminded Jack of.

When the first fat drops of rain began to assault them, they found shelter in the space between the mountainside and a jut of granite and stopped there for the night. The winds shrieked a horrible tune as the storm rolled across the island, every lightning strike accompanied moments later by a cannonade of thunder.

In the midst of it, Kingman swore to Jack that he could hear demonic roaring and the wail of innocents in the distance. Jack could not hear anything above the boom and crash of the weather. Kingman rose to leave the shelter nonetheless, unwilling to let something as yielding as air and water prevent him from taking up arms against evil.

But the howling rush of wind and rain proved too strong even for a man of his iron will. Not three steps from the enclosure,

Kingman leaned almost horizontally into the tempest. His close-fitting brown outfit ruffled and rippled madly against his gaunt frame. He stumbled once, then twice in the blackness; struggled a long time to move forward, fists gripping stone and grass and muddy soil. Jack could tell a great war was going on within Kingman, and he wondered--not for the first time--if his traveling partner and companion might have a sort of brain fever.

Regardless, the man had saved his life more than once, and had willingly assisted Jack in his quest to find a cure for his amnesia--in fact, suggested it--swearing that the same black-hearted villain had wronged them both. Jack had asked him once what he would do with this lost soul should he ever find him. The look in Kingman's gray eyes had been enough to make Jack feel cold, all up and down his spine. *I will make sure he knows for what he is paying, then I shall collect. With my bare hands, if necessary.*

As Kingman crawled back into their makeshift shelter, Jack saw a bit of that look on the man's mud-spattered face even now. Jack took off his yellow scarf and handed it to Kingman. "Mayhap you'd like to clean yourself, such as you can."

Kingman took the cloth and stared into Jack's eyes. He was one of the few men Jack knew who was capable of the feat; most were unable to draw their gaze away from the acid-scarred web of red flesh that stretched from his left cheek past his jawline, ending in a set of swirling arcs on his neck. Kingman dabbed at his face a few times, then cleaned the cloth as best he could in a puddle that had formed in the shallow of a rock at the edge of their shelter. He handed it back to Dante.

"Whatever evil has occurred out there under the protection of this storm, it shall be avenged before the grass is dry, or I am was never Laird Roderick Kingman of Tuppeny." He began to methodically dry and reload his muskets.

Jack knotted the dingy yellow scarf about his neck. "Then we should get some rest, for the morrow will be a bloody day."

***

The squall, for all its ferocity, was short lived. By midmorning Kingman and Dante were trudging westward again, occasionally stopping to drink from a foam-whitened river with a course nearly parallel to their own. Soon they were standing in the smoldering ruin of a village.

Kingman's eyes surveyed the scene from beneath the stark ridge of his brow. Few of the huts were standing; wet ashes and blackened poles littered the muddy ground. "This village burned last night, before the storm had its way with what still stood."

"But where are the villagers?" Jack asked, using a pole to retrieve a bit of woven net from the tree where the storm had deposited it. "You don't have nets without net-makers."

"I do not know," said Kingman, the timbre of his voice betraying a terrible anger bubbling just below the surface. The two of them decided to search from one end of the village to the other, knowing that it would not require much time given the smallness of the place and the lack of any standing huts. It wasn't long before Jack heard a soft mewling from beneath a collapsed wall which had a great tree lying upon it.

He cried to Kingman and began levering the tree away from the wall. With much grunting and sweating, they were able to remove it. After the weight of the tree, the fallen hut wall was light as a feather pillow. Beneath it was a sight that brought tears of pity and anger to Kingman's eyes.

A child of five or so, or what had once been such, lay beneath, her skull caved in obscenely. Blood bubbled on her lips and she seemed distant, babbling a soft and fearful lullaby to herself. Kingman stepped close, allowing the shadow of his head to cross the girl's face. When it did, the child became hysterical; her arms flopped crazily, she rolled her black eyes around in their sockets.

"Kali-ya! Kali-ya!" She screamed over and over, blood spraying from her mouth.

Kingman leaned down, making a shushing sound as he did and eventually the girl's frenetic movements slowed.

"Kali-ya?" he asked.

"What did this?" Jack wondered aloud.

Kingman spoke to the girl in several different languages until finally finding one that she seemed to respond to. After a few frustrating moments, Jack asked what the girl was saying.

"I only understand scraps of it. Some of her words are similar to the Southern dialects, but other things she says make no sense whatsoever." Kingman put his hand on the girl's forehead, next to where the skull was so severely dented. She hissed and tried to withdraw but she was unable to move from where she lay on the ground. Kingman gritted his teeth together and stared for a long time at the child.

Jack reached into his pack and tore off a small piece of dried trunknose rat. After making sure his scarf was in place, so as not to scare her, Jack reached down and put the sugary meat into her mouth. The girl made an effort to chew, followed it with an effort to smile. Neither succeeded.

Kingman wiped at his cheek with one long finger as he watched. "This village was indeed home to the sons of the ancient Squensheherra. The child says"--he swallowed hard and continued with steel in his voice--"The child says a fiend came from above, aflame. It took the tribe for not giving enough. She said the giving place lies in yonder charred clearing."

Jack looked where Kingman was pointing. In the distance, he could see a black expanse of burnt field. Something protruded rudely from the devastation, some sort of writhing black mass. "What is it?" Jack asked.

"You go ahead and see," Kingman said softly. "I shall join you after a moment." He bent to offer the girl a drink from his skin flask and Jack, seeing the hurt in his companion's eyes, took one last look at the doubly wracked village and the only fragile soul who remained, then picked up his pack and did just that.

A few minutes later, as he came near enough to the thing in the clearing to see that it was a large wooden stump covered in crows, Jack flinched as a loud crack of musket fire pierced the air. The gunshot frightened the scavenger birds away; where they had been could now be seen a partially eaten woman bound hand and foot to the stump.

Kingman caught up a few minutes later as Dante swung his blade at the birds to keep them from perching upon the body. "See here," Jack said, "This woman had her heart ripped out." He pointed the end of his scimitar at a maggoty cavity.

Kingman looked, saying nothing.

"What creature would rip the heart from a living person and, finding it unsatisfactory, destroy a village?" Jack asked.

"I know not," Kingman said. "But I begin to wonder at the significance of that black organ beating away within its stone chest down below."

"As do I," Jack replied. "Now which way do we go?"

"I asked the child--I asked where there might be a city, an empty city, before--" Kingman took a deep breath. "Before I gave her peace. She pointed this way, said it was past the giving place."

Dante swung his scimitar at a crow brave enough to perch again on the corpse. It darted away, then approached again as if it thought Dante meant to play a game. "Perhaps we should start," he said.

A day's march brought them once again to the banks of a narrow river, on the other side of which stood a construction of terrible portent. A great wall faced them, nearly a league high and carved whole from some orange mineral. Hearing no noise or signs of occupation, the pair forded the river and made for the enormous jeweled gates that stood open in the center of the fortified wall.

"Something doesn't seem right," Jack said as they approached the walls of silent stone.

Kingman grunted. "Whatever lived here is gone now. The place would seem to be vacant"

Those words were proven wrong almost as soon as they were spoken. A gibbering rush of creatures, men with snapping dog's jaws and fresh red cavities on their chests, rose from covered pits before them, attacking as the pair passed beneath the gateway into an open square.

There were at least a dozen of the dogfaced creatures, some brandishing wicked looking spiked flails or poleaxes, others with blades and javelins. The snarling pack charged at Kingman and Dante as hungry wolves might, while the two men put themselves back to back.

Dante wielded the curved Kaffir blade one handed; in his other hand he held his long Ghentish dirk. Warm air blew his scarf as he waited for the mongrel attackers. At his back, Kingman held a musket in each hand. With the patience borne of long experience on the Tuppeny battlefields, he let the creatures advance within range before sending one shot into the open maw of a poleaxe-wielding dogman and another into the stomach of one about to hurl a javelin at Dante. The creatures started at the sound of the gunfire, but only for a moment. Kingman used that precious second to shove the empty weapons into his belt.

He had less than a breath to get his rapier up before the dogmen were upon them. At first the men fought in desperate silence, the clangor of steel and grunts of their exertion playing a grim tune of bloodshed.

Dante slew two with a great sweeping arc of his scimitar, then sunk the blade of his dirk into the thigh of another. A creature with a spiked ball and chain swung it high and fast, narrowly missing Dante, who danced away from Kingman as the battle progressed.

Kingman's side was blooded, the result of a glancing blow from a javelin. Nonetheless, his rapier sang gaily as he brought it to bear against one foe after another. "Die, you unholy brutes!" he thundered as he slit the throat of the last beast within reach.

He looked around for Dante. Seeing the man surrounded by the remaining creatures, he dashed to his companion's aid. Before he was in range, one of them was yowling on the ground with a gut wound, while the other two were warily circling the yellow-scarved swordsman. Kingman buried his rapier in one, then spun around and delivered the deathblow to the yammering dogman on the ground. Dante's scarf had come loose in the heat of the fight and now hung low about his neck. His eyes were cruelly lit as the last dogman turned to run. The Ghentish dagger sailed through the air and lodged itself in the creature's back. The dogman slumped to the ground, leaving the open square silent but for the sound of clapping hands.

The two men looked about, finally seeing a red robed figure on the balcony of a grand orange stone building. The figure clapped several more times, then hovered above them effortlessly.

"A splendid performance," said the floating man in a heavy Teo accent. "But not splendid enough to spare your lives." He wove arcane symbols with his hands and muttered words that dissipated in the air unheard by the men below.

Kingman felt the very earth beneath his feet growing warmer. Realizing the red-robed sorcerer's intent, he sprang away, pulling Dante with him. They were barely in motion before the ground around them was engulfed in a sphere of licking flames. Dante grabbed his dirk from the back of the dogbeast as they ran, sheathing it quickly as it was already almost hot enough to blister his hands.

Kingman turned to the floating man when he was out of the fiery circle. "What have you done to the Squensheherra?"

The sorcerer seemed taken aback. "You know of them? Do you come to steal their secrets perhaps?" He chuckled. "You are too late. You have just slain the last of the tribe, ridden by demons of their own choosing. The women and children gave their lives in a dark ceremony that their men might serve me."

"I'd wager they weren't as willing as you would have us think," Jack said, staring at the burning bodies within the magically summoned flames. He grabbed for his dirk again, despite its warmth.

"Hold, Jack." Kingman pointed the bloody tip of his rapier up at the floating sorcerer. "You, mage, what secrets of the Squensheherra have you stolen?"

"You would not begin to understand. But I will show you more than you wish if you trouble me further. Leave now, while I allow it."

With that, he flew up to the balcony again and withdrew.

Kingman took a look around. He gestured toward an opening at the base of the building. "Cautiously, now," he said.

Dante trailed behind his tall companion. Just inside the doorway, Kingman stopped to reload his muskets before they pressed on through the opulently carved and empty building. Up and around they went, their footfalls muffled in the dust of eons. More than once, either Jack or Kingman thought they heard something; a skitter behind them, something bustling in the walls. Their quick searches turned up nothing and before long, they found themselves in a sort of aerie. A great scaled bird--saddled, bridled, and stinking of heated iron--slept on a polished wooden perch. A ladder was propped haphazardly beside it.

"It seems our sorcerer has more than one way to fly," said Jack.

"Indeed," Kingman muttered. "He won't be far from this creature."

They made a circuit of the aerie, keeping well clear of the scaly bird. It opened one eye and stared at them for a moment, but made no move toward them. On the far side of the aerie they found a narrow staircase leading upward. The dust upon it was freshly disturbed. Kingman and Dante navigated the spiraling steps and eventually found themselves in a long, open chamber filled with books and burning incense. A series of markings which resembled those they had seen in the cave of the monolith had been drawn upon the floor.

A voice to their left drew the men's attention. "I knew you would not leave me in peace."

"To what end?" demanded Jack, turning toward the curtained dais where the sorcerer stood behind a black stone altar. "Why have you slain so many--an entire tribe!--What purpose can you claim?"

The sorcerer smirked. "I have studied the old ways for many years. More years than you would find easy to believe." As he spoke, his Teo accent became more and more pronounced. "I came to this island seeking magic that predates our civilizations. As did you, if I read the bones correctly."

The sorcerer did not wait for them to respond. Kingman's scowl was confirmation enough. "When I arrived, I found this vast city, vacant. And up there in the valley, a village of powerless fools who claimed to be descended from the ancient rulers of this very fortress.

Though I would easier believe them the sons of the Squensheherra's slaves." The word ended in a terrible hiss.

"Aye," Kingman said. "And what power have you found? The ability to turn savages into dog-headed beasts?"

The red robed man started, then grinned a crooked grin. "That. . . That was something I learned beneath the steppes of my homeland. But enough of this chatter." He leaned toward the brazier to his left, put something into it that made green smoke billow out. He began reciting an incantation that reverberated more loudly with every syllable.

As the sorcerer reached toward the second brazier, Kingman fired his musket at the man, but the range was too great and the ball flew wild. The smoke was now pouring from both braziers. The sorcerer leaned down to pick something up from behind the black stone altar. He stood with a basket that dripped redly onto the altar. The black stone seemed to drink up the redness as the drops fell.

Kingman and Dante stood frozen, staring at the bloody basket and the red sorcerer who held it.

"There is power in the heart," said the sorcerer. "Or so the Squensheherra believed. Blood magic and deeper pathways for channeling the Old Ones who move between the planes."

Jack spoke up then, but wanly, as if he were under the grip of a geas. "You mean you take their hearts to summon demons to this world?"

"That he does," Kingman said, forcefully, hoping to shake Dante from his near daze with his loudness.

The sorcerer cocked a finger at Kingman. "Not quite. The other demons were simply practice, something to do with the corpses of the villagers. With this basket of hearts, fresh carved from the women and children of yon village, I mean to summon and bind within me a great Old One, Brznthluz. Together we two will have power enough to make the kingdoms tremble at our feet!"

"You shall not." Kingman's fury built with each word. "You have slain children, destroyed the dying remnant of an entire race, taken the very *hearts* from innocents. I judge you evil, and I sentence you to death." With that he launched himself across the room, firing his second musket as he dashed toward the sorcerer. The second shot hit the red robed man squarely in the chest; pushed him back a step, no more.

Flames were already traveling from the sorcerer's fingertips to engulf the basket of hearts. His unintelligible chants rang from the rafters of the chamber. Kingman fell upon him, rapier drawn, but it was too late. The red robes stretched and ripped as the sorcerer grew steadily, almost doubling in size. Great bat wings unfurled from his back with a syrupy slurping sound.

One eye was still clearly the sorcerer's, but the other was inhuman and possessed of a carnal hate so fierce that it could only belong to something hellish.

Kingman's rapier flashed, but did little more than tear off the remaining robes from the demon-thing's body. When the red fabric fell away, it revealed a hole, deep and empty, that betrayed the sorcerer for yet another heartless thing.

It laughed, a guttural noise that brought Jack's charmed brain back from the faraway place it had been. He readied his scimitar and Ghentish dirk, advancing behind Kingman.

The thing swung one enormous arm and Kingman went sprawling across the chamber. His useless muskets clattered across the floor. He still held his rapier tightly as he sprang up.

Dante swung wildly at the demon-possessed sorcerer, but landed no blows. It howled its contempt at the small, scarred man as he closed yet again, silver blades dancing.

Seeing the futility of fighting such a creature with simple weapons, even Dante's blessed scimitar, Kingman shouted to Dante: "Away! We must away!"

Jack could not believe his ears. Kingman retreating from evil? He lunged one last time at the beast behind the altar, drawing a thin line across one of its thighs, then pounced back and ran after Kingman. As the two sprinted down the narrow stairs, they could hear the creature growling and spitting its frustration at not being able to fit in the stairway. By the time they had reached the aerie, they could no longer hear it.

Kingman gestured toward the scaly bird. "After you, sir. I do recall you being a slightly better rider than I." He stopped suddenly, stared into Dante's eyes.

Whatever he wanted to see in Dante's reaction was missing. "This is no horse, Rod," Dante said, dashing up the ladder. "But I hope to get a good gallop out of her nonetheless."

The bird was used to being ridden, and let the two men mount without resistance. Jack picked up the reins and snapped them. The bird took flight instantly. Within moments, they were soaring high above the orange rock walls and the rushing river. "Where are we retreating to?" Jack asked.

"Roderick Kingman does not retreat," Kingman said brusquely. "But he does choose where and how he will fight. Make for the beach."

The bird wheeled under Jack's urging and the great scaled wings were beating more rapidly than either of them had thought possible. Suddenly a bellowing came from above them. Kingman looked up.

The demon-filled sorcerer had continued growing. Now it took up a large area of the sky directly above them. It swooped down on the pair, knocking Kingman from the saddle. He grabbed the saddle strap with both hands, but was unable to pull himself back up.

Again the demon swooped, uneven fangs glistening, this time Jack dove the bird a scant moment before the creature's claws would have ripped through his entrails.

The dive did not help Kingman at all. Instead, it sent him reeling. Now one hand on the clawed foot of this iron smelling bird was all that kept him from rushing down to meet the jungle.

"Down! Down!" he yelled at Dante, who did his best to comply. He could see nothing of Kingman but the waving tips of his boots just over the edge of the bird's immense frame. They were flying inches from the treetops now. In the distance, Dante could see the cliff and beyond it, the sea.

Dante chanced a look behind him. The demon barreled toward them again, bat wings beating madly in the midday sun.

Kingman saw this and yelled at Dante. "Destroy the heart!" A moment later the demon was upon them. An instant after that, Kingman swung himself from the scaly bird's clawed foot and reached desperately for the demon while suspended in the empty sky.

He managed to get one vicelike arm around the creature's neck. With the other he released his rapier and began hacking at the demon's wings. The thing began to plummet. In the blink of an eye, they were beneath the green canopy of the trees. Kingman could no longer see Dante and his scaly mount.

Kingman leapt from the demon in time to avoid being crushed beneath its bulk. The thing seemed stunned by the landing, but otherwise unhurt. Kingman gripped his rapier securely and charged the creature, driving the blade deep into the base of its skull.

The demon lay still at first, face down in the rotting vegetation. Then it began trembling. It shook so hard that the very earth shook with it. The monster rose. It graced Kingman with a ragged, wicked grin. Laughter boomed from its ugly maw. Kingman did not wait.

Kingman knew he must buy time for Dante to get to the cave and destroy the heart. He prayed that his intuition about its origin was correct. He ran pell-mell for the cliff, full of vain hope that he could find some way to keep this terrible being Brznthluz from killing him.

As he ran, Kingman regretted not having picked up his muskets. Now, with his rapier lodged in the back of the creature's neck, Kingman was effectively unarmed. Unless he could get the blade back.

He looked over his shoulder. The hellspawn was still laughing, a mocking sound not at all dampened by the surrounding woods.

And it was coming for him.

***

Jack made for the cliff but was surprised to see when he got down to the beach that the entrance had been covered over by an avalanche in the tempest the night of their arrival. He could tell by the looks of it that there would be no speedy entrance. He remembered the green-filtered light that had shown in through the vegetation in the chamber with the monolith. That was the only other way in; if it too had not been covered by the storm's effects.

He clicked his tongue at the scaled bird and took to the air again, circling the cliff's edge. His eyes scrutinized every swaying leaf and flickering shadow in hopes of finding the entrance, or catching sight of his companion.

***

Kingman struggled to his feet as the demon-possessed sorcerer advanced upon him. Weaponless, bleeding from his ribs, and now with a sprained ankle from his fall, he stood his ground. Prayed again that Dante would be able to destroy the heart in time. As the wide-leafed trees began to smolder and burn behind the demon, Kingman knew he would not have long. He stood, facing the demon, taking one careful, limping step backward at a time. The demon seemed to relish having its prey crippled and slowed its pace to match Kingman's. One man-sized pace back by Kingman, one enormous step closer for the demon.

It made a gurgling noise at Kingman. One eye glinted madly; the other radiated odious, otherworldly evil. Kingman took another careful step backward, and found no ground beneath his boot.

***

Smoke rose from the forest. Jack knew from the way the trees were bending ahead of the flames that that was where he would find the demon; and Kingman as well, if his companion still lived. Jack scanned the greenery again from a lower altitude and still could find no sign of the hole that had illuminated that horrible scene embossed onto the black stone pillar.

He despaired at not being able to gain access to the secret cavern. "If we must end like this, fighting sorcery and devils, then let it be together, as brothers." He drew his scimitar and sent the bird racing toward the moving treetops.

***

Kingman woke with a start. Above him was a gaping hole in the earth, sunlight streaming through it like Heaven's grace. How had he fallen so far and survived? And how long had passed?

He heard a savage growl above him and realized with a start that he had not landed at the bottom, but on one of upper steps. His feet trailed below him onto the next crumbling tread.

Kingman crouched and struggled to regain his bearing. The top of the black pillar jutted madly before him. He clutched his side and began staggering down the crude stairs, dimly aware that they had probably not been used for centuries, or even aeons.

He had barely descended two of the steps when a chaos of scales and wings and steel came plummeting into the chamber. Dante and his mount had gotten somehow entangled with Brznthluz. The mount was on the bottom when the trio collided into the pointed tip of the pillar. Kingman heard a series of sickening snaps as the bird's spine and ribs gave way.

They were falling again, having bounced from the pillar, but their progress was slower now, with the demon's tattered bat wings pumping furiously. It was trying to take to the air with Dante. When Kingman realized this, he sprang from the step and plunged a dizzying distance to land upon the demon, narrowly missing Dante's whirling blade as he did. The combined weight of the two men drove the creature to the ground with a thud.

When the cavern floor stopped their descent, Dante bounced away, throwing his scimitar to Kingman. "The entrance was blocked," he said, by way of explanation, then darted around the corner into the darkness of the tunnel.

Kingman scowled at the demon, looked into the eye that he took to be the sorcerer's. "You surrendered your humanity and visited evil upon the innocent," he pronounced, the pain in his ankle and ribs all but forgotten as fiery vengeance-lust bloomed in his heart. "Now, foulness, surrender your life!"

With that Roderick Kingman went for the demon, ducking beneath its snapping, slavering jaws. He buried Jack's Kaffir scimitar in one oversized leg and left it quivering there. With a twist, he was upon the demon's back, both fists now hammers of rage as he pulled the rapier from the base of the demon's skull and plunged it back in, again and again.

Viscous droplets painted his face and the air around him when the rage-bloom finally began to fade. The creature no longer moved. Dante was there above him, saying something over and over, not quite in time with the plunging blade.

"I found it," he said. "I found it and cut it and it fell to ashes and dust. The demon-ridden mage is dead."

Hearing these words through the diminishing inner noise of his rage, Kingman drew a deep ragged breath and stepped back from the body, which had already begun to shrinking to a size closer to that of the Teo sorcerer.

"We're going to have a fine time digging our way out of here before Gintle_Rynthar returns." Dante said.

Kingman shook his head wearily. "Let us begin," he said. "I want to retrieve my muskets from that ill-fated city and bury what dead remain."

"Perhaps we can look for some scrap of the old lore with which to restore my memory," the scarred man added, wiping sweat and blood from his face with the yellow scarf. "Or at least something shiny we can sell in the next port."

Kingman nodded slowly, as if he were not quite sure what to make of Dante's words. "Aye," he said finally, sliding his rapier into the ring on his belt. "We should find our villain before I lose my taste for vengeance."

Roderick Kingman ignored his companion's quizzical expression. He limped toward the darkened tunnel instead, scowling and lost in thought. "We should start. These stones won't move themselves from our righteous path."

Hic Svnt Dracones
by Jay Wilburn

The grass ended in a sharp, dead line as if sliced in even perfection with a barber's blade. Gullan's mule stepped across the unnatural border onto the hardpan of the outer wastes. The sand did not blow between the tufts of grass and the growth did not reach over to the rocky barrens. The young wizard listening as the hooves of the horses behind him clopped against the cracked, brittle earth. He identified the armor and sheathed weapons of the escort party clinking with the movement of the animals, but he heard no conversation as they left the world of green magically protected from erosive evil beyond.

Gullan wanted to look back at the magic border of the kingdom again just out of professional curiosity, but he did not want the king's warriors to think he was afraid. So, he stared forward and sat up straight. He heard their rasps of the dry air through their lips over the breathing of the horses. He wondered if any of them were turning around to look back themselves.

Gullan smiled and blinked against the blowing sand. He pulled up the purple hood of his robes, but heat trapped around his head and the wind billowed inside hurting his ears and forcing him to hold the hood in place like a woman trying to keep her bonnet. Gullan had no issue with women, but he felt conscious about allowing the seasoned fighters to compare him in weakness on his first assignment as a royal guild member magic user. He knew minor spells to deal with the heat and the movement of the hood, but he thought it unwise to spend his energy before arriving at his destination. Gullan let go and allowed the hood to blow back down around his neck and shoulders in a cowl. He heard one of the men chuckle behind him and Gullan sighed.

The trail wound over encrusted dunes and down steep drops before forming a switchback up the next rise. Gullan expected to see the bones of fallen animals or the shallow graves of past warriors, but the landscape proved barren and empty.

The men whispered behind Gullan like a second wind scraping at the ground. He cut his eyes over without turning his head, but could not see them over the bunched material of his hood.

Gullan turned his eyes forward and spied the dark spit of stone stabbing up at the sky as they topped the next ridge. The tower stood like a needle in the wavering heat off the plateau that stretched out for unbroken miles in every direction.

He traced out to the horizon looking for the calcified fangs and ribs of the beasts this outpost was meant to hold off and slay, but saw nothing else rising from the landscape dominated by the singular structure.

The distances across the wild expanse were deceptive. The tower seemed to get no closer as they traveled along the rough trail toward it. Gullan dropped his eyes to the unruly mane of the mule as his head hurt from staring through the blazing light.

After a time, he lifted his eyes and the tower came into focus showing the details of the wind-blown stone up the shaded side with the sun setting in the distance beyond.

Gullan dismounted and coaxed at the mule's reins. The animal pulled back against the wizard's urging and caused him to stumble.

One of the men whistled and Gullan showed his teeth. He turned to speak back at what he thought to be an insult.

The broad, wood doors to the tower burst open at the center revealing benches and racks inside. A man in dark robes and a cloak lined with stars hobbled out with both arms raised bone-thin at his sides. His grey beard hung in a narrow braid from his chin past his belt to where Gullan assumed the elder wizard's bent knees lay below his robes.

The old man laughed. "Oh, thank the gods."

Gullan swallowed and opened his mouth to speak, but one of the warriors behind him cut the young wizard off.

"Are you Calfour?"

"Yes," the old wizard declared as he dropped his arm and hoisted a satchel up onto his shoulder.

"Calfour the enchanter of the Southern Hills?" the man said.

Gullan licked his lips and took a deep breath.

The old man nodded causing his beard to wag over his starry chest and belly. "One and the same. Are you inclined to tarry the night, Commander?"

"I'm inclined to drop these provisions, turn about, and ride hard for the enchanted edge, Master Calfour."

The men muttered in reaction to the commander's declaration.

Gullan looked from the armored men on their horses to the old wizard, "Just a moment. There is a transfer that needs to take place here."

Calfour waved his finger in a circle above his head. Gullan glanced up expecting to see magic emerge from the air, but he just saw dust scouring the stone of the tower from the natural wind.

The old wizard said, "Can you read the sign, young magic user?"

Gullan swallowed and looked about. He spotted block letters engraved into the stone above the open doors. He suspected they were heat etched by magic as opposed to carved: HIC SVNT DRACONES.

"Yes, sir."

"Do you know what that means?"

Gullan nodded. "Here there be dragons or this is the place of dragons."

Calfour clapped his bony hands. "Well, Hic Svnt, indeed. Enjoy your stay, boy. Keep us all safe. King and country are counting on you."

The wizard took the reins of the mule out of Gullan's hand. He turned the animal around and Gullan heard the packages and bundles of stores and supplies fall against the hard ground off the backs of the horses. He stared at the materials and thought that seemed like very little to tide him over for a year or longer.

Gullan grabbed Calfour by his cloak and halted his progress. "Wait, sir, this is my first assignment. You have to brief me on the process and show me the most effective spells against the creatures. Please. I was told you would prepare me once I arrived."

The commander cleared his throat. "Master Calfour, nightfall approaches and we must away."

The men grunted again.

Calfour nodded and waved his hand. "Go ahead, Commander. I will be right behind you – *right* behind you, I assure."

The men wheeled their horses about and galloped back along the trail away from the dying sun.

"I'm unprepared for this," Gullan said.

Calfour pulled his cloak away from Gullan's grasp. He mounted the mule's saddle and looked down on the young magic user.

"This is a throw-away post, child," Calfour said, "I ended up here not because of my dragon slaying power, but because I angered the guild masters by angering the royal cousins that oversaw the locks on the treasury. Every year they have dropped off supplies for another tour in this far-flung tower for a total of fifteen years. I have either finally been forgiven or forgotten. Either way, I'm retiring to a cottage on green ground and never crossing the political class again."

"I don't understand," Gullan said, "I just achieved guild member status."

Calfour shrugged. "I would guess they just ran out of assignments and you are a placeholder for one year. Do not bother the guild with correspondence or requests over the next year and when the next delivery of supplies arrives, they should come with your replacement. Consider yourself briefed, boy."

Gullan grabbed Calfour's leg with both his hands. "Please, Master, how do we stave off the monsters in the event of a dragon approaching the border? I have no training in this. If you have been here fifteen years and still live, share with me how. Help me protect the kingdom."

Calfour sighed. He looked after the horses retreating up the trail and back down at the young wizard.

"Listen, boy, the secret is that there is no secret."

"I don't understand."

"I've been out here fifteen straight years," Calfour waved his hand around him. "I have never in my life seen a dragon outside the pages of a zoology textbook or a mural of imagined, royal conquest."

"You've been lucky," Gullan shook his head. "What if I am not?"

Calfour sighed. "Lucky? That is comical, young man. By the way, if it ever comes up, do not imply that the murals of the royal cousins are fantasy stories to impress other men after you've had too much wine. They will stick you in a dragon watchtower outpost for years as an ironic punishment."

Gullan dropped his head and gritted his teeth as he stared at the elder wizard's boot. "What do I do, if I encounter a dragon threatening the kingdom, Master Calfour, sir?"

"Are you deaf, son?" Calfour growled. "There are no dragons. This is a wasted structure in a wasted land beyond the border of a kingdom that still clings to ancient superstitions. You are standing guard against imagined foes and sunburn."

"They would not build an outpost or waste an assignment for a lie," Gullan stammered.

"I'm not sure who this enlightened, noble 'they' are to whom you refer," Calfour said, "but the royal family would, the guild would, bishops and clerics would, and the superstitious poor would praise them all for doing it to keep their children safe from legends. It is a cheap lie to maintain and it has nothing except payoff."

"I don't understand how lies of this nature would have reward, sir."

"I cannot teach you everything about politics before my escort party has deserted me," Calfour said, "but the classes pay their taxes in return for no dragon attacks, people like me can be stored away and punished, people like you can look successful. With no dragons in the world, you will have staved off dragon attacks with a perfect record. Congratulations in advance, young magic user."

"Perhaps they are merely less populous due to our successes in the past," Gullan said. "Scarcity is not necessarily extinction or fantasy story."

Calfour rubbed his face with both hands and groaned. "There is magic and monster in the world for certain. But dragons are placeholders themselves. They were drawn on maps by lazy cartographers and explorers. They were copied over by apprentices for generations. One man draws a mountain in the wrong spot and it is redrawn for centuries until no one thinks to go see if it was ever really there. If you don't want anyone checking, you write HIC SVNT DRACONES to discourage them. If a brave soul does check, you simply suggest that in a land of dragons, mountains may be leveled from time to time and you may be next. Then, you build a tower against your mountain-eating legends on the very spot where the map says the mountain used to be to assuage the fears of the people who believed in the mountain and to buy their cheap love. That is how the lie pays well, son. Now release my leg. This old mountain is ready to move."

Gullan opened his hands and let them slide away.

The old wizard cleared his throat. "Is this not what you dreamed of as you trained to be a great wizard?"

Gullan shrugged. "My mother said I could not make a living drawing, but some guild members do."

Calfour laughed. "That is true. The elder illustrators of magic texts must die sometime. It is likely to be before you. Good luck, then, on all your quests. Anything else, my future illustrator and dragon slayer?"

Gullan shook his head, but looked up and said, "How do they keep the barren land from crossing the border into the green of the kingdom?"

Calfour winked. "Magic."

The old wizard kicked his heels into ribs of the mule and weaved forward between the boxes and bundles scattered around the cracked ground.

Gullan opened and closed his hands flexing his fingers.

The elder wizard called back without turning around in the saddle. "Cheer up. You have begun your first successful mission. It will blunt future failures."

"I would rather struggle with truth," Gullan said.

"Don't be so sure," Calfour said as the mule left the obstacle course of supplies and reengaged the dusty trail a few clips behind the other riders in the distance. "Also, pump the well on the bottom level of the tower twice a day whether you need it or not. It dries fast otherwise. If you have to prime it, it will take hours to bring the water back up again."

"Thank you," Gullan called.

Calfour's voice echoed and diminished from facing away and traveling farther across the flats. "The water is poisoned with alkalines we usually only use for curses and impotency potions. You'll need to boil it, filter it once through cloth and again through charcoal, and then use a purity blessing before you drink it. I always blessed it twice. You can never be too careful."

Gullan looked back through the double doors at the pump in the middle of the floor he had missed before. He looked back after the wizard and mule.

Gullan yelled. "You were going to ride off without telling me that?"

"You wanted to talk about dragons. It slipped my mind until now."

"What if you are wrong?" Gullan yelled. "What if you are wrong about dragons? What do I do if I need help then?"

Calfour's voice came back small through the wind. "Lock yourself inside, say goodbye, and drink the water unfiltered."

Gullan cursed under his breath and watched the warriors ride toward their long shadows.

He whispered. "You ride hard for such brave men and supposedly imaginary monsters."

He turned and looked toward the sun around the edge of the tower. Gullan lifted one bag of grain on his shoulder. He took a few steps as pain stabbed at his lower back. He allowed to bag to fall back to the ground short of the doorway.

Gullan held his back and sighed.

He stared at the retreating mule and scanned in a full circle around the empty wasteland. He thought about the colorful inks of dragons in his picture books as a child that he copied as he learned to draw. Gullan recalled the medical detail in his study texts as a guild candidate with detail as sharp as the kingdom border.

Gullan licked his lips. "I suppose I have nothing to save my energy for today. I might as well save my back."

He whispered the words in a hiss that echoed into and back from the ether in a tone that only came from evoking magic. The packages lifted up from the hardpan. Grain leaked from a torn corner of the bag that he had dropped. Gullan waved his palms forward and the supplies obeyed drifting through the double doors into the tower. As the pieces passed him, his robes billowed up from his body from the feedback of the levitation spell. A trail of grain drew a line from the barren ground onto the flagstones in the tower. Gullan flicked a finger to lower the bag to keep from losing anymore.

"I can't save the people, but I can spare some grain at least."

He followed the other airborne packages inside to see if any needed to be lifted into the lofts of the other levels of the tower. He looked up the spiral of the staircase corkscrewing up the wall toward the top of the tower through one wooden platform after another.

He knew the stairs of towers always spiraled with the wall to the right to foil right-handed swordsmen trying to invade up the stairs as defending swordsmen retreated. Gullan couldn't imagine any force wanting this tower.

He turned inside and took another look at the mule and its drawn shadow.

"Nothing to worry about while I am on watch."

He pulled the doors closed and dropped the latch.

***

Gullan was too far from the tower to get back in time.

He closed his sketch book and capped the ink bottles. He gathered his brushes into his fist.

He shook his head and whispered. "What are you doing? Run."

Gullan heard the roar sweep up from the valley. The wings moved more rapidly than he could follow with a piercing buzz. The shadow swept over the ground below and the wizard turned to run.

The tip of the structure came into view as he tried to cover the ground from his explorations.

Gullan wheezed for air. "I wasn't prepared for this."

He heard the buzz increase behind him as the creatures soared up into the air over the wide flats of the plateau.

Gullan turned and set down his drawing implements.

He stared up at the swarm of locusts spreading across the sky as they swept above him. "They aren't dragons. This is not my assignment."

Gullan looked out across the pulsing shadows over the dry ground. He wondered what they ate coming from even deeper in the barren wastes.

He swallowed. "Maybe this is why the land over the border is lifeless."

He turned and looked east past the tower knowing that the first farms were within walking distance of the magic border. There stood no wards to keep living creatures from crossing the line. This swarm would prove far more costly to the farmers than the fires of a dragon.

Gullan showed his teeth and peered up into the living darkness of the swarm. A few exoskeletons drifted down around him like snow as he watched.

He raised his hands above his head and splayed his fingers open. "I can do something."

His lips twitched as he spoke the words. They echoed off the unseen ether around him with magical force. He felt the majority of his energy exit his fingers as he completed the phrase. Gullan swept his hands north and watched the vanguard of the swarm wash to the side in a vast spiral.

Gullan dropped to his knees and gasped for breath as his heart thudded in his chest. He watched and waited. He knew he could not cast a spell across a hundred million insects. A grand magician older than Calfour might be able, but Gullan doubted it.

Gullan concentrated his power over the first few thousand and hoped.

The swarm followed the temporarily enchanted locusts and the entire population detoured sideways from their original path.

Gullan smiled, but gritted his teeth. "It won't last."

The creatures might continue on even after the influence of the spell left them, but he doubted it. Hunger and instinct were powerful spells too.

He lowered his head and cupped his hands. Gullan focused his remaining energy. He felt the thinness of his reserves, so he cupped his hands closer together. A spectrum of light gathered in the pocket of his hands like a tiny rainbow.

He whispered into the ball of light with an echo.

The light formed a tiny pigeon. Gullan opened his hands and the transparent bird blinked its eyes. The bird stretched its rainbow wings and waited.

Gullan set the bird on his shoulder and tore a page out of his sketchbook. He took the blue ink and dipped the brush. Gullan halted above the paper rested on the broken ground. A single cobalt drip fell on the blank page.

He looked up and watched the swarm detouring north. He thought it was possible they might continue north. Even if they didn't, locusts were not his assignment and warning might do little good. Calfour had warned against bothering the guild with correspondence.

Gullan sighed and told the locusts. "I have no stomach for politics. If trying to help people results in another year on barren ground, I will just practice my drawing for another year."

He bowed his head and wrote three sentences about the locust swarm from the west. He set down the brush and rolled up the note like a miniature scroll. He wrapped it around the conjured bird's leg. Gullan ripped the ends and slid them together to form a clasp.

"You know the way to the Magic Guild, little friend?"

The bird answered by twisting into the sky. The light from the sun obscured the bird's body as it fluttered toward the tower and beyond.

Gullan heard another thundering coming from the west. He looked up and saw the swarm thinning out as they veered away from Gullan.

He saw dust rising up from the edge of the plateau.

The beasts topped the edge and stumbled forward jostling one another as they approached Gullan's position. He stared until he could make out the stripes on the short fur and the needle teeth in the long snouts.

"Jackals," he whispered. "I will punch Calfour in the mouth when I return to the kingdom."

His breath caught in his throat. As the pack charged forward, he saw the glisten of blood in their hides. Bone showed through open wounds as they staggered in their desperate run.

"What is this? Locusts don't eat flesh. Do they? Why would the pack run the same direction as the swarm then?"

Gullan took a deep breath to still himself and muster his power. He echoed the words off the ether and threw his hands toward the south. The beasts were hideous, but Gullan did not want to send them after the locusts that may have devoured them.

A few of the creatures turned, but most charged on. Gullan saw the whites of their eyes and a few empty sockets too. Foam leaked out of the side of their black lips as they pumped their legs in a blind rage.

"This isn't good."

Gullan closed his fists and threw them out in front of him. He echoed a short, familiar phrase.

Flame boiled out of his knuckles and crackled above the ground in two, intense spouts. The fire washed over the jackals and sizzled their torn fur. As they screamed, Gullan closed his eyes.

The flame tapered and Gullan clutched his chest waiting for the burn to subside. A few of the beasts collapsed, but the others parted and passed the young wizard on both sides.

Dust billowed up around him and over him as the abused pack scrambled toward the tower. He tried to remember if he had closed the door. He hoped so.

Gullan stared in silence at the bodies smoldering on the ground in front of him. He thought there would soon be bones on the landscape like he had expected when he first arrived.

"Days of silence and now all this?"

The next noise was higher pitched.

Gullan stood and stared toward the west again.

Rats scurried up over the edge like a wave washing up from the horizon. He flexed his hands and felt the weak emptiness of having spent his energy on four spells in rapid succession. Their bodies twisted around one another in black mass with whipping pink tails. They pour forward swallowing the ground.

He shook his head. "I never even wanted to be a magic user."

Gullan snatched up his book and brushes and ran for the tower. The heartburn stabbed at his chest, but he pumped his arms and tried to keep from tripping inside his robes. Gullan wondered if the jackals' bodies might slow the rodents and buy him a few extra seconds.

"It wasn't the locusts that tore into the fleeing jackals."

He could not remember if he left the doors to the tower open, but now he hoped he had.

***

Sunlight glinted off the lens of the spyglass as Gullan leaned out the third level window of the tower. He could tell the cloud did not consist of locusts, but he could not identify the creatures yet.

The rats had passed by a week ago. Gullan had finally gotten the last of the stragglers out of his grain and had sent a second bird, but had heard nothing back from the guild.

He did not want to expend power before he knew what plague was visiting upon his outpost this time.

Gullan wondered from where the animals out of the west were originating. They gave all the signs of being natural beasts, but they fled across a land with no apparent capacity to support life and from even deeper in the wasteland. Gullan had grown up in the fields owned by the nobles of the kingdom and knew the processes of the natural world, the seasonal changes, and even the rare migrations of unusual animals. None of these fell into those categories of known things.

He lowered the glass and watched the patterns in the swirling mass of flying creatures. Gullan squinted and thought about the chimney swallows he had seen flying up and diving down in the openings in the barns on his father's indentured land.

"That's not a swarm. That is a flock. It is not dark enough to be bats."

He brought the glass back up and focused out to try to spy individuals within the flock. He saw the feathers and the shape of the bellies. He spotted the speckled pattern within the stripes and inhaled sharply.

"Not possible."

Gullan slammed the window shut and charged up the spiral of the stairs closing all the windows on the way up. He opened the trap door on the precipice of the tower and took one look to the west seeing the mass of birds rushing on him like a moving wall.

Gullan yanked the door closed and listening to them strike and scrape around the outside curve of the tower. A few thunked against the door above his head.

The noises around the tower faded and a few screeches remained.

Gullan pushed the trapdoor open gradually. He stood at the rampart and looked east as the impossible flock retreated. He looked down and lifted one of the bodies off the floor of the watchtower's roof. The bird's fragile neck was twisted at a deadly angle and one wing folded broken behind it.

He stroked his thumb along its belly looking at the feathers. He shook his head and squinted.

Gullan swallowed and whispered. "The Speckled Hashed Carrier? As I live and breathe."

He recalled plucking them in large piles for holiday meals when he was very young. By the time he was old enough to hunt alone, there was not a one to be found in the forests around the fields due to generations of heavy hunting. Once he was a young man, reports were they had even vanished from the shores of the Eastern Sea. Every time he ate quail, his belly missed the meat of the Speckled Hashed.

He set the body down on the battlement and stared east again. "No need to send warning of such a delicious plague."

Gullan shook his head. He remembered looking at the western edges of maps in his studies to see the artists' drawings of dragons. He wondered what else lay beyond the three word warnings over the wastelands where the maps ended. If there were natural fauna like locusts, jackals, and rats, there had to be flora and unpoisoned water. If the Speckled Hashes migrated, there must be another ocean and a hospitable shore on which to land. Hospitable shores surely had fishing villages of some creature resembling man or some other manner of tribes. Gullan figured there may be pirates or raiders preying on the shores as well. The forbidden west might contain all sorts of rare and supposedly extinct creatures.

"Something is driving them out of the west though."

Gullan turned and looked away from the sunrise. As he did, he suddenly wished he had brought the spyglass at the same time he was glad he had forgotten it.

Gullan swallowed and cupped his hands around his eyes to stare up at the motion in the sky.

What surprised him most was the stark white of the body. He expected green or red. Artists and illustrators had chosen a wide range of colors for the beasts in the text panels, but white was rare because of the lack of flare, Gullan supposed. He felt plenty impressed upon seeing the white dragon in that moment.

Against the blue sky, the scales and spikes shown with intense detail. The sharp tail whipped from side to side as the thick wings drummed low and deep against the air. The fans and flaps around its white skull made its head appear skeletal as it dropped its jaw showing jagged fangs. The black slits over its eyes were the only distinct breaks in its colorless form and they stared down at Gullan upon the tower as it undulated through the sky like a serpent upon the sea.

Gullan shook. "Calfour should be quartered in the guild courtyard."

Gullan ran pages of spells through his mind that consisted of little more than parlor tricks. He thought about a dozen curses that required plants in order to gather ingredients. He turned his eyes away from the beast and considered locking himself in the tower with the poison well.

Gullan lifted his hands and echoed the words he had used against the locusts. He swept his hands to the side and saw the monster falter in the air. For a moment, Gullan thought he might actually see the dragon turn and fly back the other way.

"No one will believe me."

The black slits of its eyes widened and the white dragon dove toward the tower. It folded its wings back against its body and the flesh behind its head widened like tumors.

Smoke leaked from its nostrils as its jaw unhinged. Flame erupted over its lips and preceded the dragon like a torrent.

Gullan dropped back through the trapdoor and slammed it closed. He heard the flame wash over the tower. He sweated in his robes from the intense heat and saw the air waver around him.

The noise subsided, but Gullan waited.

He reached up and cried out as he touched the heat of the door handle. He closed his fist against his chest and bit his lip.

Gullan threw his shoulder against the wood and knocked the door open. Black carbon coated every inch of the tower. Gullan stepped out and turned in a full circle. His boots scuffed the greasy ash back down to the dark grey of the stone that looked bright in comparison to the blackness left by dragon fires.

The young wizard spotted the creature pulsing up and down in the sky as it flew on eastward with no further interest in Gullan or his lonely tower.

Gullan threw out his fists and echoed the short phrase. A shallow burst of flame shot out from his knuckles over the edge of the tower, but came nowhere near the dragon heading toward the kingdom.

Gullan dropped his fists and clutched his chest from the burning pain. "I didn't even want to be a wizard. If my father had lived, I could be on a small square of a rich noble's farm now, waiting on you to come eat us and our livestock, you monster."

Gullan rolled his head and tried to think. In desperation, he spread his hands and closed his eyes. He reached out to the beast's terrible skull with his mind and whispered the words against the ether between them.

The connection struck Gullan like a waterfall. He screamed and fell to his back on the sticky soot without realizing he had dropped. The ancient mind of the dragon proved far too intense for Gullan's synapses to process. The languages of the creature's thoughts were alien to Gullan and the beast layered his mental processes around formulas and equations that exceeded anything Gullan could imagine.

Gullan pushed away and broke the spell. He was still screaming when he realized he stared up at the sky from his back.

Gullan sat up and spotted the dragon that flew on unaware that Gullan's small mind had touched him at all. He tried to remember any of it, but all Gullan could recall was "broken slumber," "evil kingdom," and "bed of gold."

Gullan shook his head as it throbbed. He wiped his hand under his nose and came back with blood.

He watched the white body silhouette into black as it approached the morning sun and the unsuspecting border of what Gullan assumed was the evil kingdom the ancient creature sought to make his bed of gold inside. He tried to recall everything he had read on the hoarding behavior of dragons and their long hibernation cycles.

He considered sleep spells and every bit of dark magic he had learned, but Gullan could think of nothing powerful enough to bring down the dragon and the creature drew farther away every moment.

"He did not even know I was there when I tried to infiltrate his mind."

Gullan considered for a moment.

"Maybe I can push an idea in instead of trying to take over the entire works."

Gullan wiped the last of the blood from under his nose and spoke the words again. This time he felt the connection, but did not try to be the master of the mind itself. He felt the connection through the ether, but it grew weaker with each flap of the dragon's wings.

Gullan licked his lips and tried to think of what to say.

He whispered across the invisible tether of magic he had created. "The tower is the entirety of the evil kingdom. Every human in the world lives inside and that is where they keep all their gold."

The magic tether snapped. Gullan opened his eyes and stared into the sun.

He sighed. "I'm sorry I failed you all."

But then he saw the white dragon arc back into the sky and race west toward the outpost.

Gullan smiled as he watched the powerful monster approach. His smile faded and he dropped back down inside the tower. The trapdoor stuck to the carbon for a moment, but he pulled it free and slammed the door closed.

Gullan ran down the stairs as the flames licked across the outside of the outpost heating the inside like a kiln.

One of the windows blew open on the level below him. Gullan held up as the fire poured through against the opposite wall charring the stone. The fire sputtered off and Gullan leapt over the sizzling steps beside the window.

The flame belched through the opening again behind him and Gullan screamed. Holes burnt through the back of his robes and the flesh of his back blistered. He tried to hold the wall beside him for balance, but the heat from the stone burned his hand. He staggered down the spiral.

The dragon struck the outside of the tower with its body and claws shaking the entire structure.

Gullan toppled and fell free down the center. He struck his chest on the edge of the next platform and barked out in pain. He dangled from his fingertips, heaving for air from his aching chest.

The dragon roared and flame enveloped the tower again. Another window exploded inward. Twisted tongues of fire licked at Gullan's knuckles.

He groaned and lost his grip. Gullan fell the last couple stories and landed hard on his feet. His knees buckled and he slammed to the floor knocking the wind out of him. One of his knees struck the pump pipe of the well with a load pong.

Gullan rolled to his back and tried to suck air back into his lungs and failed. He stared up through the tower above him. Flame sprayed in through one broken window and then another on the opposite side. The dragon roared and vibrated the floor under the wizard's battered body. He heard the sound circle the tower outside as the onslaught continued. The air distorted from the intense heat.

Black spots danced through Gullan's vision like living things.

His chest released and he drew in a painful gulp of hot air.

Gullan rolled to his stomach and clutched the handle of the well pump that still felt cool in contrast to the oven heat of the tower. He worked the pump arm over and over with one squeak after another. Water poured out across Gullan's back stinging his wounds. He continued pumping a steady flow of water soaking his robes and puddling under him in the curves of the flagstones. The water washed over his hair and dripped off his face as he breathed in the steam off the hot floor. Gullan continued pumping trying to keep the unfiltered water out of his eyes and mouth.

***

Gullan dropped the bandages away from his back and hands. The flesh felt tender, but the healing spells appeared to have worked.

Gullan sighed and picked up the scalpel again. He wrapped the wet blanket around his shoulders and over his head. He looked up through the splintered wood and broken platforms up through the chimney of the tower. Through the broken trapdoor, he could see a few of the stars.

He listened and heard the dragon rumbling in the back of his white throat just outside the broken, double doors behind him.

Gullan turned and looked at the piles of stone that covered the space left from the felled doors. He could see gaps large enough for him to crawl out or for the dragon to breathe through.

He knew the dragon never slept and would soon be spewing flame inside again. Gullan would run up the stairs to escape. As the dragon moved up to other openings, Gullan would run back down. He would watch and dodge more stone falling away inside the tower which he would pile by the door to deter the dragon's next attack.

He knew he should be sleeping to replenish his magic energy, but it wouldn't matter much since his food supply was scorched and he barely had time to treat enough water to keep himself alive.

Gullan turned back to the wall and carved the scalpel through the thick soot on the stone. He continued the curved lines of the scales of his rendition of the creature outside. He wondered if anyone would see it. Eventually, the dragon would break through to what Gullan had purposely convinced him was the kingdom he sought.

He moved the scalpel back to the head and added sharpness to the fans around the skull. The dark, negative image of his nemesis did not do justice to the grandeur of his stark white body. Gullan did not have his inks any longer to give a more realistic portrait.

"Looks like I won't outlive the guild illustrators after all, Calfour."

The tone of the dragon's rumble shifted outside. Gullan raised his head and listened to see if he needed to run up the spire again like a rat in a trap.

"Even the rats were smarter than me and escaped this beast."

The rumble dropped back down to the low sounds of rest.

Gullan sighed and went back to carving.

He sat back and admired his work. Gullan leaned in over the dragon and carved in block letters above the etching in the same style as the warning above the door outside: DRAGONS LIVE. PREPARE FOR THEM WHILE YOU STILL CAN.

He set the scalpel back on the floor with a click.

Gullan swallowed on his dry throat. "I truly wish you were here right now, Calfour."

The dragon's growl grew and light billowed outside brightening Gullan's work.

Gullan stood and looked up the stairs. He prepared to run, but did not move. He looked out at the flames above the stone blocking the door.

He remained still facing the monster and waiting.

Gullan had no children counting on his survival as his own father had.

"Except all the children of this kingdom. If this dragon breaks in and finds there is no gold, he will go looking for more."

Gullan looked up through the tower and considered his options.

"They will tell my mother and sisters it was my fault the dragon got past to attack the kingdom."

He closed his eyes and whispered the ethereal words hearing them echo doubly off the ether of the universe and the burnt stone that surrounded him.

The connection drove Gullan to his knees. Blood poured from his nose and ears. He pictured himself scrambling backward to keep from being swallowed in the dimensional complexity of the ancient mind so close to Gullan.

He felt the dark slits of the eyes staring at him through the physical air and along the tether in the ether.

Who are you to visit inside my mind, evil plague upon my kind? Tiny parasite that hath wrought destruction upon my ancestors? I shall sleep upon your precious gold painted with your blood.

Gullan clutched the sides of his own skull as the ancient languages screamed at him in other phrases he could not process.

Gullan whispered. "I am no one. I am the last man in the world and you have defeated me."

Then why do I still see you and feel you in my mind?

"I am a spirit and nothing more. You feel me upon the ether in your supreme victory. Now that I am gone, you have finally avenged all the death man has visited upon your kind. You live and we are no more. The gold of all the fallen kingdoms of man are within this tower. They are melted black into the walls by your fiery breath. Claw through the top. Crawl inside and claim the rest upon the gold which you have earned in your righteous vengeance."

The dragon roared and soared up above the tower.

The tether broken and Gullan slumped to the floor.

The tower shook with the impact and broken stone rained down around Gullan. He spit out rubble dust and rolled to his belly. He crawled out from under the blanket and scaled the stone piled over the door. A large chunk of stone landed on the discarded blanket and exploded.

Gullan tumbled out of the doorway and landed on his back staring up at the stars and the whipping tail of the massive, white dragon above the tower.

Stone fell around him outside. Gullan staggered to his feet and ran up the trail away from the tower.

He heard an explosion. Gullan stopped and turned to see the top of the tower missing. The walls split as the dragon forced his body down inside the tower. The dragon roared once more as Gullan stared at the white scales pressed against the openings of the small windows.

He heard the low rumble inside as the dragon became still.

Gullan bowed his head and turned toward the east. He walked toward the border of the kingdom during the night watching carefully to stay on the trail in the dark.

Gullan paused to rest and looked back at the ruins of the dark tower at a great distance. The white dragon remained hidden and sleeping inside as the young magic user had hoped.

Gullan whispered. "Slumber, ancient one. We have both earned it."

He turned and continued his trek back to the green kingdom. He intended to visit the Guild first and request Calfour's assistance with the king's warriors on the return quest to finish the dragon.

"You deserve to see this, old master."

He thought it only fitting after all of the elder wizard's years of keeping diligent watch.

It Takes a Mage
by Jennifer Crow

The sword appeared to consist of crystallized light. Almost transparent, flecked with golden motes, it would have been a proud addition to any king's armory. But at the moment, it protruded from the chest of a young guardsman, who lay with arms out flung and eyes glassy. Smears of blood and flesh marred the jewel-like beauty of the blade. It was not the sort of scene one expected to find in the antechamber of the great king's treasury.

Maga Ereth paced around the dead man, her gaze drifting from the corpse to the room in which it lay. Circular, like the squat tower of which it formed the basement level, it was constructed of thick limestone blocks, the individual pieces linked together by spell and will. Torches flamed at regular intervals in sconces of copper and horn, their smoke filling the air with a rich, resinous scent a little too strong for her taste.

She turned to the living guard that hesitated in the doorway. "And this is how you found him?"

"Yes, Maga." The senior guard's dark skin had a grayish cast, and Maga Ereth noted a tremor in his hands. "Not a thing touched since I found him."

"Good. Return to your post." The maga made a peremptory gesture, and the guard bowed out of her presence. Alone, she circled the body again, her noble visage set in a frown. Perhaps the guard thought her angry about this imposition, but in truth, she relished the chance to match wits with the mysterious killer. "Hold your secrets close, enemy, and I will cut your throat when I take them from you."

She knew better than to touch the sword, at least until she'd taken the proper precautions. As a maga, one of the most skilled artists of occult power, she carried streams of power within her, and therefore any reading she took carelessly from the blade might be tainted.

With a delicate touch she opened her satchel and spread the contents on a table beside the door. Jars of liquid, bone-white to midnight black, stood in a neat line, and before them rested the obsidian dagger she'd consecrated to her goddess, Ogana of the Deep Waters. Maga Ereth draped a stole over her shoulders, raw blue silk shot with silver threads and lined with thick, soft seal fur. It seemed heavier than usual, a sign that the killer she sought had wielded great power in the king's treasury.

"Ah. Let us unveil you." She took a sip of the bone-colored potion. A dry, ashy scent filled the room, sweeping away the foul odor of death as she shook a few drops at the head and foot of the dead man. Then, with a reddish fluid that dripped slowly like honey, she made a circle on the guard's chest, around the blade. She stood close enough that she could feel his spirit lingering, a smear of anger and fear at the edges of her senses.

With great care she touched the blade of her consecrated knife to the hilt of the mysterious sword, natural volcanic glass to magical glass. The murder weapon detonated, a blast that shook dust from the ceiling and thick walls. She'd thrown up a hand just in time to shield her eyes, but her dagger now bore a thin crack, and the magical sword had vanished as surely as if it had never existed.

"That shouldn't have happened," the maga muttered. The head guard poked his head in the door, but she waved him away. "I need quiet!"

He didn't respond, except to vanish again. Hopefully he hadn't noticed the result of her little mishap. Well, even that had given her information; the one who created the crystal sword wielded great power, both to create it and to leave a trap for anyone who might seek to use it after him. She considered who among her brother-mages might have created such a weapon, then used it both blatantly and badly.

Maga Ereth questioned herself. Was it the work of a mage, a male? She didn't know of a sister-mage who used such tools, but that meant little these days. She had spent so long on her island in the Sea of Tears, honing her craft and her grudges, and the world could spin into strangeness in a single generation, never mind three.

"Too long," she muttered. With a scowl, she tucked her obsidian dagger, now broken and mostly useless, into her belt to free her hands. "Let's try something a bit more . . . blunt."

Anyone with a bit of magic could use study, tools, and potions to refine and multiply their strengths. Some of the greatest mages and magas of the age were not particularly gifted, only stubborn and focused. But Maga Ereth combined the best of both, a raw well of power that she'd spent an age honing to a razor's edge. And if subtlety failed her, a dose of sheer brute force might knock open a window into her enemy's lair.

One of the bottles on the table held a thick, greenish liquid. When she opened it, the scent of the sea filled the air around her. She drank a quick gulp of the salty potion, grimacing at the taste, and waited for the goddess's power to sink into her marrow. Like the tide, her goddess pulled, and roared, and swallowed enemies whole.

When Maga Ereth opened her eyes, the dusty air of the antechamber had taken on a watery cast. Everything wavered, and the dead man had the look of someone who'd drowned in a storm—except, of course, for the blood stains on his chest, and the thin hole in his shirt and his flesh where the blade had slipped in and stolen his life.

"Beloved Ogana, show me a secret. Show me the hand that created the sword." The maga made a sign over the body, fingers curved and rising in waves. The air rippled, her will a stone cast into a still cove. Waves bent her vision, giving the scene before her a surreal cast. The goddess's eyes might not see as mortals' did, but she saw other things. A shadow moved across the antechamber, coming from the doors of the treasury. Something glinted; a sliver of light that Maga Ereth thought must be the sword.

But coming from *the treasury?* She shook her head, and stared at the shadow, willing it to come into focus. A faint sound, the brush of a foot on the stones, caught at her, and something flew past her head, so close that it sheered away one of her short dreadlocks.

She leapt to her feet, thrown out of the goddess's reverie. As she did, she lifted a hand, weaving the goddess's power about her as a shield.

"I said I wasn't to be interrupted!" she snapped, angry that she'd been caught off-guard. As she spun around, she saw that it was the king himself who'd come into the room.

"Have you found anything?" He held one of the guards' ceremonial sabers loosely, the tip scratching a line in the polished stone floor.

It was on the tip of her tongue to castigate him for showing off. But he was known for his temper even more than she was for hers, so she bowed, grimacing. "Not yet. Apologies, Your Majesty."

"No need." He made an offhand gesture that she thought must signal forgiveness. "I merely seek answers, as you do. Perhaps my method of hurrying you was ill-conceived."

She tried to gather the streams of the vision, but it had trickled away. "It's gone. I had almost seen the killer when you interrupted." She studied the king. His grandfather had been a man she was happy to call her friend and ruler, but his descendent was a mystery to her. He wore silk robes in rich jewel tones, tunic cinched with a wide, embroidered belt, his soft boots stitched with the same motif. But the knife at his belt had a simple design, and the leather wrapping the hilt was stained with sweat. "I drew the latent energies together, to focus them with the goddess's gaze. When you came in, those images dissipated."

To her surprise, he said, "It doesn't matter. I know who killed my guard."

"Really?" If that was the case, why had he brought her to the scene? Fear trickled down her spine. Did he mean to blame her for the murder?

"Of course. It was Kovalo. He's been promising vengeance for years now."

Kovalo. The maga turned that possibility over and over in her mind. "I thought he vanished after you ruined his tower? I have heard nothing of him since then."

"It must be him. Who else could do such at thing? *Would* do such a thing?" The king pointed at the body.

Instead of answering, Maga Ereth moved closer to the treasury door. "I saw him—the killer—"

"Then you know it was Kovalo!"

"I saw only his shadow. In truth, I could not say before the judges of the gods that it was a man, though I suspect it was. But he came from this direction—the treasury." She stopped before the gilded doors, with their ostentatious locks. "You are sure no one entered."

"I had my craftsmen install alarms. Magical ones, as well as mundane. I would wager my life that no person without authority crossed that threshold."

"And of those with authority?"

His dark eyes narrowed and his wide jaw clenched. At that moment, he reminded her of nothing so much as the crocodiles who sunned themselves on the river's banks, and who caught their prey with a formidable bite that let nothing go. "I am the only one with authority."

"Very well, then." She bowed again, and watched some of the tension drain out of him. "Would you be so kind as to let me see within the treasury?"

He swept past her and laid his palms on the doors. The maga felt something give way in the aether, and then the king took a heavy brass key from his pocket and inserted it in the left-hand lock, then the right one. The first turned clockwise, the other widdershins. As soon as the second lock gave, the doors swung silently open.

She'd expected a sort of treasure cave, gold and gems piled up like the loot of a robber chieftain, but the reality was both impressive and disappointing. Everything had its place, neatly labeled in someone's spidery hand. Closed casques stood shelved row by row, their contents listed. The walls held an array of weapons, often dated with the last owner's death.

"I had no idea," she said. Her hand hovered over the lid of a carved wooden box.

"Open it," the king said. She did, and within, on cushioned velvet, lay an emerald necklace. A light winked within the largest stone.

She gasped. "Is that—"

"Touch it and see."

When her fingers brushed the stone, it felt warm to her touch, like a living thing. She had the sense of something aware, a vast and abiding sorrow. "It's lonely."

"Well, I'm sure you of all people understand why I can't wear the Lady of Sorrows. It's safer here."

Safer for whom? She didn't speak the thought aloud, having learned long ago that more wisdom was gained from silence and patience.

"Bring me proof of Kovalo's destruction, and the Lady is yours."

Maga Ereth spun to face the king. "Your Majesty, that would be a gift beyond price."

"Not a gift. A payment for your service. An expression of my trust."

She closed the lid of the box. "I will look into the matter, but in my own way. And if I find it was not Kovalo's doing, you will accept my word."

"Of course." Despite his smile, his jaw was still clenched so tightly her own ached to look at it. She made a circuit of the treasury with the king on her heels, her attention fixed on anything out of place. Such as an empty place among the weapons on the wall.

As she paused, she asked, "What goes in this place?" She brushed the wall and sensed old blood and rage, so strong her nostrils flared as though she could smell it.

"I haven't found the right blade for that spot yet."

It was a lie. She couldn't decide if he knew she would recognize the falsehood. "I see." She resumed her tour. Weariness enveloped her, a backlash from the broken vision combined with the strain of trying to sort out what the king wanted from her.

Kovalo, she told herself. *He wants Kovalo dead, for whatever reason, and he doesn't feel he can do the job himself. Or he means to get rid of two mages with one stroke of the sword.* As she crossed the treasury threshold, returning to the antechamber, a whisper of power brushed over her skin. The king might have lied about some things, but she felt he'd told the truth about his treasury. No one could enter it without his permission and survive to tell the tale.

Maga Ereth paused only to retrieve her severed dreadlock from the floor. Deep in thought, she bid the king farewell and climbed the cool, dim stairway to the ground floor of the palace. The memory of the guard's broken body stayed with her, and she vowed to his spirit that she'd find his killer.

***

The rainy season was a distant memory, and the sun had long since baked the land of Yilkalor to a brick-like hardness. Maga Ereth no longer cloaked herself in cool shadows when she traveled; age chilled her, and she liked the way the heat drummed on the top of her skull and seeped deep into her. Mbaku, god of light and husband of her beloved Ogana, offered a blessing she'd come to appreciate more with each year.

The capital of Yilkalor fought a constant battle with both Mbaku's affections and the encroachment of the wilds—dust and sand from the northern deserts, and jungle from the south. Between them sprawled the city, at a sharp bend in the Kalor River, where its delta spread its marshy tentacles toward Ogana's welcoming bay.

The king's grandfather built a palace of golden stone on the bluff overlooking the Kalor. The rest of the city spilled down its slopes and spread raggedly at its feet, the walled compounds of the wealthy giving way to more modest baked-clay, and then wattle-and-daub hovels that crouched like abandoned souls at the edges of the swamp. As Maga Ereth made her way through those dregs of the city, thin-limbed children watched her and rib-sprung dogs barked at her heels. Insects swarmed around her, a buzzing cloud of flies that seemed to be at war over every bit of bare skin she revealed.

Growing weary of them, she took an iridescent blue bottle from a pouch at her waist and spread the potion inside on her face and arms.

A sudden silence drew around her like the folds of a cloak, and even the dogs whimpered and fell back. Relieved to find herself alone, she crossed a narrow rope bridge that swung over the lazy river. Beyond lay the dusty grazelands of the king's vast cattle herds. Beige clouds hung over the landscape, showing the animals had nearly exhausted the land and would soon need to move to other pastures.

They paid her no heed as she strode deeper into the dry lands, and the men and women who guarded the herds gave her little more attention. One lone woman, unarmed, could not have come to steal the precious cows, so she merited no notice.

When the maga came to a fork in the path, she turned to the east, which wended into the desert proper. Despite the protections she carried, and the favor of her goddess, the heat and the sun pounding on her skull gradually wore her down. She found herself hoping Kovalo hadn't abandoned Yilkalor after the king destroyed his tower, but at the very least, the mage's old haunts would likely give her a clue to his current location.

That night, after a little water to drink and a crust of bread from the king's table to eat, she wrapped herself in a light cloak and slept under the stars. Mbaku's first light wakened her, and as she sat up, she had the nagging sense that she'd dreamed something significant but forgotten it. Lost in thought, she trudged onward, and in the end she stumbled upon Kovalo's tower almost without noticing.

He had rebuilt it almost on the original foundation, and though the air around it shimmered with the spells he'd laid upon it, it still had the same slightly shambolic air. For a moment she cast aside her purpose in visiting, and smiled at the memories that rose as she stood in the shadow of Kovalo's tower.

It was only good manners to announce her presence. No doubt the king had expected her to drop a tsunami on her fellow mage's head without so much as a warning, but Maga Ereth had a suspicion that she might learn something interesting if she stopped to chat first.

"Ho the tower!" she shouted, using a smidgen of power to amplify her voice.

"I am busy, woman!" The voice was Kovalo's, but tinny, as if coming from a great distance. A trickle of sand slithered down the side of the tower, a trickle that soon turned to a veritable flood. "Go, or I will bury you and then prop your withered mummy at my kitchen table for company."

"I have news from Yilkalor." She put her hands on her hips, considering whether to blast the tower door off its hinges. Kovalo in an argumentative mood could take hours of persuading, and she wasn't feeling particularly patient.

"I hate that city, and you know it. You stink of the king's cows, by the way."

"As well mannered as ever, I see." She gestured, rattling the door on its hinges, and let a little sea water seep through the cracks. "Let me in, or I'll rust your locks and wait for you to beg me to free you."

"I would implore Mbaku to burn down the whole damned edifice first." But the door swung open, and Kovalo splashed through the puddles she'd made and beckoned her to enter. "I see I am to accomplish nothing more today until you have been appeased. Brazen bitch."

"Insolent bastard," she countered. There was no heat in either of their voices, the insults part of the rhythm of their odd acquaintanceship. The maga wondered if she dared call it a friendship. *Perhaps not, since I've been sent to kill him.* "What have you been up to? Why does the king of Yilkalor want you dead?"

"How should I know?" He stalked deeper into his tower, the ground floor of which had a herd of animal heads watching her from the walls. Despite their being dead, they tossed their horns or opened fanged maws in silent roars.

"Impressive," she said, pausing to stroke the velvet ears of a black-maned lion.

"A mere trick. We both know that. But it amuses me, and intimidates the ignorant." His workspace on the second floor was more crowded than ever, and musky with the scent of old experiments. "I beg you, do not waste my time. My studies are at a most critical juncture."

"Do those experiments include trespassing on the king of Yilkalor's treasury and murdering his guards?" The maga noted the shocked look on Kovalo's face. If he was feigning ignorance, she thought, he'd become much better at it than he used to be.

"I would not darken his door, not for every gem and coin he hoards. And as for murder, I thought you knew me better than that."

"It's been many years, Kovalo. Change comes to all of us."

He snorted. "Not that sort of change. Not to me." He began pacing around the workroom, much as she'd done on the murder scene, though his strides were longer. Anger creased his face, which she noted had only grown more handsome with age. At last he spun and confronted her, black eyes staring at her as if they could read her soul, breath harsh. She imagined him changing into a dragon, one of the great fire reptiles of the deepest desert, and fear sank deep in her belly like a chill from the ocean's heart.

"Well then. Let us say you speak truly. In that case, who else has the power to do such a thing?" She described the scene to him. He made her go over it again and again, dwelling in particular on the sword, and the way it had disintegrated when she touched it with her blessed dagger.

"Let me see your blade." He handled it gently, even though the crack had desecrated it. "Fine work. A pity you will have to make another."

She shrugged, unwilling to show how even this sparse praise affected her. No, she thought, she didn't believe he'd killed the guard, not even before she'd come to his tower. "You could not have changed that much," she said. At her confession, her raised a brow, but said nothing more. "But who else has the power? It was like a shaft of Mbaku's own light in the man's chest."

"Was it? From your description, it did not react as light and heat would when confronted with Ogana's gift."

She considered that. "There would have been steam," she said, taking the knife back from him and securing it again in her belt.

"Indeed." He ran a hand through the tight curls of his short-cropped hair. More gray flecked the black now. Maga Ereth remembered how it felt under her touch, and wondered how she could have forgotten the way ocean and sun, brought together with magical power, steamed and flushed the skin.

"Cold water shatters heated stone and metal." She tapped a finger on her lips. "An earth mage."

Kovalo gave her a patient smile, as if she were a slow student who'd finally come to the obvious conclusion.

"But I know of no earth mage . . ." She stopped and grabbed the other mage's arm. "Or do I? Whose herds have grown beyond all expectations? Whose city balances between desert and jungle? Who has knit the stones of his palace with spells?"

"Who wants you to dispose of me? Or more likely, who hoped we would dispose of each other?"

"That bastard." She shook her head. "How easily he played me. Do you know, he even offered me the Lady of Sorrows if I succeeded in killing you?"

To her surprise, Kovalo threw back his head and laughed. The rich, deep sound echoed like surf, and she found herself joining in even though she didn't know what he found so amusing.

"You have been out of the world too long, woman. I have the Lady. She has lived with me for a dozen years now." He crossed to a shelf at the back of the room, motioning for her to join him. With gentleness surprising in such a large man, he took a plain wooden box from the shelf and handed it to her. "Open it. Taste her story. You will not be fooled a second time."

It was true, the maga realized, as she lifted the lid of the box and took out the necklace that lay within. On the surface, it was less impressive than the one in the king's treasury, the stones only smoothed rather than faceted, the gold work heavy and rough. But the spirit of this one rose like a powerful dirge, enveloping her in a storm of grief. Sobbing openly, she returned the jewelry to its case and closed it. "God and goddess, Kovalo, I though the other felt like a living thing, but this is . . . wonderful." She dried damp cheeks with her sleeve. "The last maga who wore this . . . oh, the power she channeled!"

"Take it." When she tried to hand it back, he cupped his hands around hers and pressed it back into her grasp. "You will use it at the right moment. She wants the touch of a woman. She will never accept a man's hand. Not again, ever."

"True." Tears welled again in Maga Ereth's eyes, and her hands trembled as she secured the case. She had fled into the wilderness to escape the treachery of her emotions, and now they threatened to overwhelm her. "I'm not strong enough to wield her."

"You are exactly strong enough."

"Come back with me. I don't want to fight the king alone."

"No. I think this is a matter for the chosen of Ogana. Mbaku bids me stay here." His teeth gleamed in his dark face, as though he mocked her frustration. "When you are finished, you may come back and tell me of your great battle."

"I may," she said, unable to keep a sting of spite from her voice. "I may *not*."

He only laughed again, and the sound followed her as she marched down the stairs and out the door.

***

Though Maga Ereth had been gone for no more than three days, the atmosphere in the city of Yilkalor had changed. Clouds of smoke hung in the air, mingled with dust raised by tramping feet. The herds on the far side of the river had vanished, and the maga wondered if they'd been driven to their dry season pastures, or whether some more dire fate had befallen them.

A troop of the king's guards met her on the bridge, bronze helmets and spear heads gleaming in the late afternoon sunlight. "The king awaits you," their captain intoned.

"I have other matters with which I must deal this evening." She eluded the captain's grasp, but his comrades formed up along the bridge, blocking her. "You do not want to stand in my way."

The captain bowed, radiating fear. "We know you can kill us. We know you need only wave a hand to pass among us untouched. But the king awaits, and he will punish us if we fail to produce you."

She sighed. "And why is that my concern?"

"It is said that you are not like rulers, or even other mages. We've heard that Maga Ereth would never let another suffer in her place. We've heard you seek the murderer of our brother guard." He didn't flinch when she met his gaze.

"All right," she said. "Lead me to the palace." The squad fell in around her, clearing a path through the marketplace and up the wide road to the king's residence. She noted, though, that the streets were not as full as they usually were on a market day. Stalls stood empty, shops shuttered. Wine houses, often full to overflowing, held only a few sullen patrons who watched her pass in silence. "What's going on here?"

The guard captain shrugged his heavy shoulders. A bead of sweat slipped from beneath his helmet to trickle down the side of his neck. "Just a rough patch, maga. Nothing more." But he gave her a sidelong look that hinted at deeper concerns. She guessed he didn't want to discuss it in front of his command, so she held her patience as they trudged up the long slope to the palace. The vast building reminded her of a reptile squatting in the sun, towers like spines on its back, the gate like a gaping maw.

She shivered as she stepped into the shadowy passage that led to the main entrance. To her surprise, the king waited on the wide stairway, alone. A sweeping gesture of his hand, and the guards peeled away, returning to the city without a backward glance and leaving her with the king.

They regarded each other in silence for a long moment. At last the king said, "Tell me you have dealt with Kovalo."

"He was not the killer." She pressed a hand to her throat, reassured by the weight of the Lady of Sorrows. "But you knew that before you sent me."

He didn't bother responding to that. With a gesture and a word, he pulled a layer of stone blocks from the top of the wall and tossed them at her. Maga Ereth suspected he'd meant to do that whether or not she'd killed her fellow mage; prepared for the attack, she dodged. But he followed with a flurry of blocks, driving her into a corner. She drew moisture from the air all around and cast up a windstorm to throw them aside. It was, she noted, not the ideal ground on which to fight, for the king had earth and stone to call upon, but the sea was far away.

The king smiled, as if sensing her weakness. She called Ogana, and heard the ocean goddess's response only dimly, through the muting power of sand and rock.

"This is the house my grandfather built, and I have strengthened it beyond measure. No mage or maga may threaten me here."

The sea was far, she realized, but not the river, and not the deep cisterns of the palace, cisterns she'd built for the king's grandfather a lifetime ago. Fists clenched, she called. Called, and the waters answered with a rush and a roar. In response, the king threw a wall up, but his brute force couldn't match the finesse Maga Ereth had mastered in a hundred years and more of study.

Water wears down stone. In the natural order of things, such an effort might take centuries, even millennia, but the maga knew how to break those bonds quickly, with the Lady of Sorrows to aid her. Stone shattered to bits, pummeling the king even as the hungry river surged and swept him from his feet and down the steps of the palace.

"Your grandfather was a wise man," Maga Ereth told the king of Yilkalor. He washed up against her legs and clutched at them. She rested one sandal-clad foot on his chest, pushing his head under the rising waters. "He was a *great* man, and seeing your foolishness must grieve him as he watches from the sunlands."

Bubbles rose, at first in a rush, but slowing as Ogana took her vengeance.

The king's stupidity was a temporary problem, she thought, and one she could fix. When the bubble stopped at last, she lifted her foot and the king's body bobbed up, drifting toward the gate.

"You are a thorough woman." She turned and saw Kovalo sitting atop the gate, basking in the last light of the sun.

"He was a fool, and a killer. Like Ogana's tides, justice ebbs and flows, but sooner or later it reaches the shore." She sketched a salute at the sun-mage. "I think now I will return to my little island and wait for a wiser ruler to sit on the throne of Yilkalor."

Kovalo leapt down from the wall, landing as lightly as a sunbeam. "I hear the eldest daughter of the king has wisdom beyond her years. Perhaps I will nudge the council in her favor."

"Do what you will, you reckless fool. I've had enough of mortal politics for a time." She stalked toward the gate, but Kovalo dogged her heels.

"Who can blame you for caution? Or is it merely resentment?" A merry light gleamed in his eyes. "What does the Lady tell you about the future?"

"Nothing," she began, and then her hand rose again to her neck. A pleasant warmth lodged there, and a lump in her throat that might have been sadness. No, not sadness, but wisdom. "Or perhaps she tells me to stop by your tower more often."

"In good time." He pulled something from the satchel he carried. "I brought you a memento."

"The necklace was more than enough."

His smile deepened. In his outstretched hand lay the head of the black-maned lion, but shrunk to the size of an orange. "It is tied to both our magics. Let a little sea water fall on its ears, and it will return to its original size."

Maga Ereth touched the lion's soft ears. "And what shall I bring you in return? The hide of a sea serpent with which to upholster your furniture?"

"I am sure you will think of something. A maga as pretentious as you will have to present me a gift far more glamorous than mine."

"In your dreams," she shot back, but he'd already vanished, leaving only a glimmer of motes in the sunset. The lion gave a tiny roar, and she petted it with a fingertip before storing it in the pouch at her waist. She'd been too long away from the sea, and she longed to sit by a tidal pool and listen to the secrets whispered by the waves.

The Dragon Citadel
by Rie Sheridan Rose

It is said that sell-swords and magic are like fire and water. They cannot exist together in one place, much less one body. That is what is said. But what is said is not always the truth.

I can't pretend it is easy to hide behind my shield and armor. I am good with my sword—there is no one more skilled. But I am better with my magic…and it must be hidden from the world. To do so, I sailed halfway around the world to this foreign shore to try and keep my secret.

Even my cantrips must be cast unobtrusively. Though I volunteer to light the campfire at eventide, I am careful always to hide the spell behind flint and steel. I have managed to keep my secret from my travelling companions in the last five ventures…but this time…this time I fear will be my undoing.

I have never stayed with one company for more than one campaign. It has kept me safe. It has also kept me lonely.

However, my last foray proved different. I was the last signed. The party already had a powerful mage, so I hid easily. My only duties were related to my sword, and it was oft bloodied. But there was also Alin in the group…a ranger whose bow was as quick as his wit. His arrows might as well have pierced my heart.

When the campaign was over, and the loot was split, Alin asked me to continue on beside him. I couldn't say no, because my heart is his. But how can I hide my magic from him?

Tonight we share a room here in this roadside inn. Do I dare to share my secrets as well?

"What are you brooding over, Janquel?" Alin stands across the room, arms akimbo, grinning that cocksure grin of his. Copper fire falls about his shoulders, obscures one green eye. He is beautiful, and I love him.

"Nothing," I lie. "The cold."

"Let me build up the fire." He bends to the firebox, muscles rippling under the fabric of his shirt. I long to tear the fabric from his body; to run my hands over his supple flesh. Instead, I sigh, and busy myself about the food on the table. Simple fare—bread and mutton downed with a flagon of ale, but it will suffice.

Dusting his hands, he joins me at the table. "That looks good." Pulling out his chair, he throws a leg over and sinks down upon it.

It takes all my control not to fall upon him...I want him so badly. My hand shakes with need as I pull out my own seat and take my place across from him. A crust of bread is all I dare take as he fills his plate.

"Aren't you eating?"

"I'm not very hungry..."

With a shrug, Alin heaps more mutton upon the plate. "More for me."

I watch him eat. A bit of gravy plops upon his chin, and my fingers itch to swipe it off.

"I checked the notice board outside the tavern today. We have several choices for our next venture," he says, and gulps his ale. His throat works, and I shiver. "My first choice would be the party seeking Dragon's Citadel. There should be riches beyond belief if we find that legend."

"Whatever you think best, Alin," I murmur. I will deny this man nothing.

"With luck, there will be elves to slay along the way," he comments casually, eyes narrowing...and my blood runs cold.

Does he not know? Can he not tell by looking the heritage that runs through my veins? That *I* am elven?

I shrink back against the splintering planks, mind whirling as I try to think coherently. I am no match for him. I would lose a fight against his strength in any case...but I can't sit here like an animal and wait to be slaughtered! My magic surges within, ready to be used if it must be.

"From the time I was a small child, I was taught to fear the magic of elves," Alin continues. "They are an arrogant race, seeing humans as fit only to serve. My father died under the lash rather than tend their horses. My mother starved before my eyes when I could not earn enough for bread. I was six."

The words are hard, dripping emotion. I feel the raw tension behind them. Alin fights for a soldier's control, hands now knotted before him.

In the ensuing silence, I hear the heavy patter of rain upon the shingles overhead and contemplate the motives that urged Alin to request my companionship. Has he planned all along to destroy me?

"I have hated your people," the human continues at last. "Yes, Janquel—I know what you are. I sensed it the moment I saw you. Elves have brought me nothing but sorrow. But they were powerful. I could not fight them, with their magic and their wealth. So I grew sullen and feral, living on the streets like a rabid dog—snatching a bit of food where I could, and honing my resentment like a dagger.

"When I was thirteen, I was captured by the City Watch and taken before the magistrate. The Captain of the Guard spoke for me. He took me in and taught me bow and sword. He gave me the strength and tools to fight back and drew me into a secret squad of 'freedom fighters.' We started slowly.

"One by one, elves began to vanish. The magic cementing their control began to dissipate, and their rule to fail. We spared no one.

"There are no elves left in this land. Except for you."

I feel as if my heart has been ripped from my chest.

An entire race—my race—wiped from the face of the land? And this monster helped in that destruction? This monster…that I love?

"Then why have you spared me?" I croak, when I can at last draw breath to speak.

Alin looks at me coolly. "Because I want you to prove me wrong. I want you to show me that an elf can be trusted. I knew the moment I saw you what you were—but you did not behave as the elves I knew. I watched you close. I know you have magic, but you do not flaunt it."

"I have been in this country for months now. I have not sought to hide my blood. Why have I heard no whisper of this madness until now?"

"You deceive yourself if you think you have not tried to hide your heritage. Why else do you shield your magic? Your looks—though striking—are not exclusively elven in nature. No one who was not searching for the signs would see them."

Alin moves to stand beside the window, opening a shutter and gazing out at the rain. "You are safe with me, wizard." The barest smile brushes his lips and is gone as he glances over at me. "I will not harm you. Unless you force me to." He stares once more at the curtain of rain.

I am torn between fear and a need to comfort him. The ache to comfort wins out, and I step forward to lay a tentative hand upon his muscled forearm. I murmur, "I am sorry about your family. I too have hated individuals who brought such pain to those I loved—desired and sought revenge on folk who wronged me. But not all elves treat humans so. In my country, the elves hide in the shadows and wish only to be left alone."

A wistful expression crosses Alin's face. "I wish I had known your people under better circumstances. Perhaps I would have learned to understand instead of fear them. They were so grand and beautiful...like living ice sculptures. And their magic was wondrous. I still remember watching balls of light dancing at courtyard festivals when I was a very small child. Before I grew to hate everything they stood for."

"I am sorry for what was done to you."

He turns toward me. "It was not your fault. One thing I have learned—to my sorrow—is that judging a race by a representative sample is a fool's game." The sad little smile flits across his face once more.

I shiver in the draft from the open window, hugging my threadbare cloak to me.

"I wasn't thinking!" Alin draws the shutter closed and fastens the bar. "Come, sit beside the fire. Though summer is upon us, the nights are cold here beneath the mountain." He lifts his heavier cloak from its wall peg and spreads it across my shoulders. "Perhaps this will help a little."

I nod my thanks, hugging myself for warmth. The thick wool does help some, but the room is still damp and chill as the storm insinuates itself through chinks in the ill-made walls. My hunger—for food at least—has fled. With a sigh, I sink down upon the narrow cot, my back against the wall as I try to rest.

Alin moves to blow out the candle, and then I feel the bed shift as he sinks down upon the outer edge of the cot. The leather straps beneath the thin tick creak in protest at the extra burden.

As my eyes adjust to the darkness, I see his silhouette. He sits, elbows on knees, shoulders slumped, staring down at the floor.

He bears the weight of the world on those shoulders. It is a heavy load for any man.

***

I dream of soaring high above the earth in the guise of a bird, the wind ruffling my feathers. I am free, and I see the contours of home in the land beneath me. I bank into a turn, and a lone horseman canters across the plain below. The rider wears green and brown leathers, a bow slung across his shoulder. As I near, the horseman looks up, shading his eyes with one hand. It is Alin.

I prepare to land and shift form—and the ranger swiftly nocks an arrow, lifting the bow to his shoulder, and letting the shaft fly.

The bolt thuds home with a kiss of fire. As I tumble from the sky, I weep....

I jerk upright with a strangled cry. Alin sleeps beside him, one hand curled beneath his cheek like a child. He looks younger in his sleep and somehow vulnerable.

I massage phantom pain from my chest. What is to become of me? Why has Fate thrown me together with this stranger…?

Head buried in my hands, I groan.

Beside me, Alin stirs and wakens. "What is it?"

"Nothing." I manage a weak smile. "Bad dream."

He sits up on the edge of the bed. "Is there anything I can do to help?" he asks softly.

"I'll be fine."

He moves to the window and opens the shutters. "The storm is over."

I wonder if he is correct.

He turns toward me, his face grave. "Why did you come here? Why do you hide your powers?"

"Magic is feared in my land. As I say, the elves of my kingdom hide in the shadows. I have concealed it all my life. If your people knew that I had magic as well as the power of my sword, how would they react? Wielding strength and magic in the same hands, would I be safe here?"

"I will help you to hide in plain sight. It is the only way I can begin to redeem myself."

"You have nothing to prove to me."

Alin looked up at last. "I must prove it to myself."

He feels responsible for it all, I realize. As if he single-handedly caused the genocide. This is his price for aid. He seeks redemption.

Is it mine to give?

"It was not your responsibility, Alin. You acted as you were told."

"But I killed innocents—women, children…for no other reason than their heritage. That blood is on my hands, and can never be washed away. I can never forget. It haunts my dreams. I am dead inside." Horrors skates in the depths of Alin's eyes, but he faces me squarely.

How can I heal such hurt? This is a grown man. I cannot hug away his pain as if he were a child.

Alin shivers, as if shaking off the pain, and slings his gear over his shoulder. "Come. If we start now, we should be able to make camp at the ruins of the Dragon's Citadel by nightfall."

"What about the party that seeks to adventure there?"

"We will leave some for them…perhaps." Alin's grin flashes, bright as the stars, and it is hard to believe he was ever despondent.

I followed him without a word, out of the inn and up the gentle slope of the mountain to its crest. The path Alin has chosen winds down the slope on the opposite side of the summit from that we climbed.

Walking downhill through the tall trees is actually quite pleasant. It reminds me of my childhood haunts, and I feel my heart lighten.

Gradually, I coax my companion out of his depression. "That's better, lad," I say with a smile as Alin laughs over a bit of foolishness.

"I'm no child," he replies. "Why do you call me so? 'Tis like we're of an age, you and I. Though you may well outlive me, we start the same path, elf."

I doubt this is true. I am well over a hundred, and he looks to be no more than thirty, but I let him hold the lie. "I'm sorry. I mean nothing by it," I murmur, hearing bitterness in his tone. I lay a hand on Alin's shoulder. "I'm not much good with words. I've always let my magic or my sword speak for me. I'm sorry. Can we not still be friends?"

Alin shrugs away from me. His shoulders are tight, and the hands at his side are balled into fists. "You would be friends with a mere human? I am flattered."

I feel my cheeks go hot. Not even a veneer of subtlety cloaks the sarcasm. "I said I was sorry."

"It doesn't always help." Alin moves away from me.

I follow, the beginnings of a headache tapping at my temples. Damn. Now I've offended him, and it will make for cold companionship. Must I always turn away those I care for? Will it ever be my turn to share my life with an equal, a partner?

The wistful query was offered up to anyone who would listen.

***

Despite Alin's prediction, we do not reach the ruins before the sun sets. The nagging tapping in my head has become a blacksmith's blows. I cannot concentrate for the throbbing, and it is hard to keep to the ranger's pace. I begin to lag behind.

Finally, Alin calls a halt. "We'll get no further in the dark."

I nod and sink down upon a rock with a sigh. I massage my temples, trying to drive away the pain. It is spreading. My joints are on fire.

The mountainside is cold, and growing colder. A light mist begins to fall, and soon my clothing—more suitable for sunlit meadows and new growth forests than mountainsides—is soaked through. I shiver, huddled beneath my inadequate cloak while Alin tries in vain to light a fire.

"Let me," I say, no longer needing to hide the magic from this one, at least. I speak the spell, and the fire dances into life, hissing displeasure as the mist tries to befriend it.

It does me no good. I am shaking and cannot control it.

"We must get you warm," Alin scolds, throwing his cape across my shoulders.

"I'll…be…fine," I protest. "You…will need your…cloak." I try to give it back, but Alin catches my hands.

"Stop. You are still weak, Janquel. If you're not careful, you'll be ill. I can't carry you any great distance. It serves us both to keep you well."

"I d-don't understand. Elves…usually don't feel…the cold." The shudders wracking me are worsening. And so is the rain.

Alin kneels before me, placing the back of his hand against my forehead. "You're burning up." He pulls the heavy cloak tighter about my shoulders. "I must find us some shelter from the rain."

I nod miserably, resting my forehead against bent knees. I hear Alin moving about the clearing.

Soon he returns to my side. "I've found a small cavern nearby. It'll keep the rain off our heads. Come, can you stand?"

"I think so." With difficulty, I stagger to my feet and, leaning heavily on Alin's shoulder, manage to reach the cave.

Alin has spread our blankets in a pallet in the corner of the small cave, and now he helps me to lie down upon them. I huddle beneath Alin's cloak and try to stop shaking.

"Lie still," whispers the human. He lies down beside me, drawing the cloak over us both. "It will be warmer this way."

I sigh an acknowledgement, turning toward the wall of the cave. I feel Alin's warmth against my back. A feeling of peace washes over me, and the ache in my head lessens. The wracking shudders gradually die away, and I sleep.

***

When I awake sometime later, the rain is gone, and moonlight fills the clearing outside our cave. It limns the side of Alin's face as he sleeps, and I find myself studying the human's features. It is a strong face, handsome and proud.

As I gaze down on the ranger, Alin's eyes flutter open, and he smiles sleepily.

"How is your head?"

"Better."

"Are you still cold?"

I shake my head. "Not anymore."

"Good." Alin rises to one elbow. "I'm glad you're feeling better."

"I have you to thank for it."

"I was glad to help."

Suddenly, I feel trapped inside the confines of the cave. It is too close within the rocky chamber. Alin is too close. The urge to touch him…

As if sensing my confusion, Alin raises a hand to lightly touch my cheek.

I tentatively press that hand against my cheek. I have dreamed of his touch, and did not do it justice. My heart is thumping in my breast, beating out a cautionary tattoo.

Alin sits up amid the blankets, eyes searching my face in the moonlight.

I hold my breath. My heart pounds even harder.

Alin bites his lip in the moonlight then seems to come to a decision. "I told you I was a guardsman and a soldier. I started as a cadet as a mere lad, and a not uncomely one." He shifts, staring out into the moonlit clearing.

He begins to speak, catches himself, sighs and begins again. "There are other things that the captain of the guard taught me, Janquel," he whispers. He glances over his shoulder with a crooked smile. "Shall I teach you?"

I consider what he is offering. Is he offering that which I have desired from the moment I saw him? Does he mean what he is saying, or is this merely another attempt to atone? Does he feel obligated to subjugate himself to me because I am an elf or does he truly care? How can I know if this is real...?

"I-I'm sorry," Alin murmurs, turning fully away from me. "I thought you...I misunderstood." His voice is heavy.

I reach out to touch his shoulder. Taking a deep breath, I shake my head. "No, you didn't."

Alin draws me into a rough embrace.

My heart swells nigh to breaking.

***

When I next awake, I am alone in the cave. A surge of panic runs through me.

Sunlight pours past the cave mouth, and I sit up. The events of the night before seem no more substantial than a dream, and, for a moment, I find myself wondering if they were mere phantoms brought about by the fever.

I push aside Alin's cloak and step out of the cavern. My companion is nowhere to be seen, and I feel a moment's cold panic.

Then a cheerful hail comes from somewhere up the slope.

"Ho, sleepyhead! I thought you would stay abed till noon." Alin comes bounding down the rocky path towards me.

I feel my heart rise into my throat. "You should have woken me."

Skidding to a stop beside me, Alin laughs. "You needed the rest."

He raises a hand to my cheek. "It feels as if your fever has broken." His hand lingers for an instant, and I lean into that touch, then he steps back.

"I found some berries, and a few early nuts. It isn't much, but the best I can do."

After a hurried meal, punctuated by much laughter, I help Alin pack our belongings, and we continue towards the Dragon ruins. There is a sense of camaraderie between us that lifts my soul; a quiet joy that leaves me awed by its strength.

But as we move on through the forest, unease begins to cloud my contentment. One look at Alin's grave expression tells me that I am not the only one to feel it.

The way becomes more difficult. Tangles of undergrowth begin to encroach on their path, and I recognize the protection spells that guard the paths of home. "There is elven magic at work here," I murmur. "I can feel the power."

Alin's hand strays to the bow slung across his back. "This is a haunted place."

"Aye."

"Will it know me?" he whispers, a ragged edge to the words.

I sympathize with his fears. Elves and dragons have long been allies. If there are any of either left in this desolate place, they may well know his aura. But I will speak for him if necessary. I will not lose what was so recently found.

"All will be well. I'll not let anything happen to you."

"Would you have a choice?"

The question shakes me to my soul. What if he is called to account and I can't stop it? It would destroy me.

I almost walk into the wall before I see it, stopping myself just in time. I stare up at it as Alin moves to my side.

The wall rises in one seamless expanse of stone that soars up from the floor of the glade to tower twice my height over our heads. It appears to be made from a solid block of a greenish rock polished like a gem and shot through with veins of gold.

I reach out and touch it. It is warm, and a vibration thrums through it, as if it lives. The wall curves away from us to either side. I can see no break anywhere along it.

"There must be a way in," I murmur.

"The elves had magic—perhaps they could fly above it."

"If the elves of your land were anything like my people, not all the race had magic. Some have other gifts. I find it doubtful all could fly in any case. Shall we seek a door?"

"I'm afraid," Alin admits, unable to meet my eye.

"There is no shame in that," I answer softly. I reach out a hand. "Come. Together?"

Alin clasps my outstretched hand. "Together."

***

It takes a good half an hour of hard travel before we finally find a break in the curve of the wall. Even then, it's less a portal than a whim of fate. Some long past storm split one of the great trees asunder, and the fallen trunk provides us a precarious bridge to the top of the enclosure.

Taking great care where I set my feet, I climb to the top and peer down into the compound. What I see inside stops my breath in my throat, and I clamber out onto the broad surface of the wall to get a better look.

"What is it?" calls Alin anxiously.

"Come and look." I cannot keep the awe from my voice. "It— it's beautiful."

Inside the wall's protective embrace, time has stood still. The city below the wall is a blending of draconic and elven architecture. It might even now be sleeping before going about its daily business. Impossibly graceful towers and spires rise to the treetops, their green-gold stone blending seamlessly with the living growth.

Clustered at the bases of the towers are the low-slung, wide-doored dwellings favored by dragons when they deign to live with two-legs.

The courtyard is patterned with a mosaic of interwoven knots and sigils that lead the eye in dizzying circles. And yet, the pattern does lead somewhere—to a sumptuous palace of smoldering gold at the north face of the courtyard.

I sense Alin beside me on the wall and reach to steady him. "Careful. It is a long drop."

"You're right," he whispers, "it is beautiful."

Some distance around the perimeter from us, a sturdy vine grows out of the forest floor, reaching through the tiles of the court to hug the inside of the wall. I point it out to my companion.

"Look, we can get inside there." I start across the broad path of the wall.

"Janquel, wait!"

I turn back to Alin. He has not moved.

"What is it?"

"I cannot go down there."

"It'll be all right. I promise you."

"How can you promise that? I can feel the power of this place rising to choke me. I have spilled too much blood."

"Nothing will harm you, Alin. I'll be with you. But we came all this way to seek out the Dragon's Citadel. It would be a shame to retreat without at least a look. The party who posted that notice will be only days behind us. Don't you want to see the treasure? After coming all this way?"

Alin swallows hard. "I will come, if you wish it."

I clasp his elbow, and then lead the way to the latticed vine. I scramble down it as if it is a ladder. Alin follows more slowly.

Standing on the mosaic of the court, I look around me in awe. The open doorway of the golden building beckons nearby, and I start toward it. The tap of my boot heels ring across the paving stones.

The golden building appears to be some form of meeting hall. It is designed for both elves and dragons. The doorway yawns upon a large round chamber. A slab table rises out of the floor, as if carved from the same block of stone. The table is low to the ground.

"They would have sat upon cushions to hold their councils," I explain softly, circling the table. "Dragons do not use chairs, and so it would have been considered rude for the elves to do so."

Alin trails behind me, fingering his bowstring.

Set into the curve of the wall is a walk-in fireplace wide enough for us to stand together arms outspread and still not touch fingertips.

"Who dares to disturb my council chamber?" comes a musical voice from the room beyond.

I spin on my heel and almost overbalance into the fire pit below the hearth. Alin catches my wrist and steadied me.

There is a feminine laugh from the shadows, and a figure steps into the open. She is elven in feature; her hair a pale cornsilk river cascading about her hips. But there is something alien about her that warns she is not what she seems.

A golden circlet sits upon her brow, supporting a single emerald. Her dress is a blue-green silk that shifted in the sunlight like dancing seawater—or dragon scales.

I have heard of such. Were-beasts, half-elven and half...other. She could be our undoing. Especially if she has heard tale of Alin's deeds. Which, apparently, she has.

"So, Alin Kin-slayer. I wouldn't have thought you stupid enough to seek your own destruction so readily...but perhaps you did not know that the Dragon Citadel was still occupied. Few do. Parties of adventurers come at least once a year hoping for riches and finding me instead."

Her features began to blur and elongate. She grew to three times her height, and wings of green-tipped gold sprang out of her shoulder blades. She was a small dragon by most standards, but still a foe worthy of the name.

I drew my sword with a ring of steel, and Alin put arrow to bowstring. We would not go easily. And we would fight together, now and always.

Alin let fly his first arrow. It flew wide of the mark, nicking the dragon's wing in passing.

It riled her more than hurt. She roared, and breathed a cloud of noxious fumes our way.

"She's a bane-dragon," I called to Alin. "Don't breathe her poison!"

He nodded grimly and began to circle around her, hoping to draw her attention. It worked.

Foolishly, she began to turn with him, keeping her eye on the one she considered more dangerous. It was a mistake.

Soon, her exposed back was to me. The spot between her wings was vulnerable—as all adventurers knew—and not five paces before me.

I sprinted forward, sword held ready. My blade struck true—and shattered into a dozen pieces. Apparently, what adventurers knew and the truth were distant cousins at best.

She whirled, teeth bared in a snarl. I expected her to slay me without mercy. My hand instinctively sketched a ward. The most powerful I knew.

She lunged forward, but the ward held. I was sure that her magic could best my own...or at the very least she would turn on Alin, who was beyond the range of my protection.

Instead, she shifted back to her original form. "I will make you a deal, elf," she growled. "I could use magic like yours. I will let you live—and your pretty pet too—but only if you remain here in my fortress as my defenders...and companions."

I glanced down at the broken hilt in my hand. "I will be poor defense."

"Your magic will be enough, but you may avail yourself of weapons from the armory; choose a dwelling from the elven towers. Let us rebuild what has been destroyed."

***

And that is how we come to be sitting here, my children. Now, off to bed with you.

I reach out a hand to Alin as we watch the younglings scatter. No one knows anymore which of them are his and which mine. No one cares. And as long as our dragon is content, she lets the two of us be. Here, we have found a home where we both can be free.

As Retribution Falls, so too Truth
by Jason M Waltz

Direk spun, pulling the short sword from his belt and sending it end-over-end across the room. In his right hand the sword named *Retribution* punched past the attacking knight's guard and through his dented visor. Direk jerked *Retribution* free while he watched his thrown weapon tumble through the air.

Its heavy hilt struck the descending steel edge of the pendulum blade sprung free by his entrance. The impact sent the trap wobbling above his crouch. The short sword bounced away, and the weighty blade tore along the far wall. He heard the curses and stumbling footfalls of the remaining guards that fled before it.

Their confident stances and blatant smirks behind their knight sergeant had given Direk more than enough warning. That and the whispers of danger his shadows had breathed to him. He smiled, grim and hard, at the *thunk* and scream that sounded behind him. A sharp *twang* jerked his attention upward to the flapping end of one of the heavy pendulum ropes. His eyes found the remaining two ropes attached to the blade now bucking about the room, striking stone and furniture and flesh at will. Already their rotted strands parted.

Direk fell to the floor and rolled back toward the stairwell. A corner of the dangling blade snapped above him and slammed into the wall a knife's edge away. Shards of stone attacked his face and he jerked away.

Retribution wrenched free of his grip with a clash of cymbals. His hand stung and the floor grew slick with his blood. Yet the severed contact with *Retribution* hurt worse.

He rolled into the doorway, expecting a strike from the giant blade and not the booted feet he met. He kicked off the wall and drove a shoulder into the feet, knocking their unseen owner into the stairwell, and pulled his legs into the aperture.

Another *twang* sounded within the room, followed by crashes and shouts. Clouds of powdered rock made Direk cough. A helmet bounced into his leg and spun against him, revealing half a man's brutalized face.

Booted feet pounded up the stairs and he reached for *Retribution*. Too late he remembered its loss. He shoved himself upright and lurched into the chamber, trying to scan both the ceiling for the dangerous pendulum and the floor for his dangerous blade. Shadows called his attention upward.

The last rope snapped. He dove into the room.

The falling blade smashed through the doorway and lodged in the stairwell. The walls trembled and added dust from the rafters to the clouded air.

Direk ignored the shouts from the stairs and wiped the grime from his eyes. He had to find *Retribution*. He pulled himself through the debris in search of his sword. Weird movement in the settling dust drew his attention.

Swirling eddies twisted and jerked away from a spot of black, revealing the ebon gleam of his deadly blade. Not a speck of dirt or stone lay upon it; a support timber from the edged trap laid cleanly split in two halves on either side. Relief washed over Direk as he stretched for the sword.

Another hand appeared through the dust. The knight sergeant rose from a pile of fallen stone. Direk leaned forward, but his grasping fingers came to a halt short of the hilt. He snarled and stretched to no avail. The other man reached for the sword.

"Don't touch that hilt!" Direk's sharp command boomed in the destruction's aftermath. He struggled, an exposed nail from the fallen timber spiked through his jerkin. The sudden rending of the cloth sent him sprawling. His injured hand buckled and slipped, and he rapped his jaw against the floor.

"I am going to kill you with that sword, Lord of Vengeance. With your very own sword."

The sergeant grunted, and rocks tumbled aside. He rose to unsteady feet and grinned through a mask of blood. His fingers—

"That's *Retribution*, you fool!" barked Direk.

—closed upon the hilt.

The man blanched, yet despite his haste to release it, he could not.

The knight sergeant's body went rigid. His jaw snapped shut and blood welled between his lips. Terror rose in his eyes as his body stretched upright. Immense unseen forces pulled him to his feet, then his toes, and then into the air. Blue lightning arced through the room. His tendons and veins bulged beneath his skin.

The joints of his body dislocated with loud *pops* a moment before the strain rent him asunder. The splatter of shredded meat and organs striking across the room outlasted his agonized scream.

Silence followed.

Direk knew it would not last. Duke Culciff's men would regroup and be upon him soon. With his subterfuge at entry wasted and time no longer his ally, he could not allow further delay. He could not allow the duke to flee.

He stood to find his short sword, the familiar weight of *Retribution* settling on his hip. He found the sword embedded in the thick wood of a wall beam. He reached for it and saw the ugly wound that sliced through the back of his hand and wrist. Flashes of white bone glinted in the blood-caked mess, and his fingers refused to uncurl over the hilt.

Direk sighed. He had not wanted to summon any of Vengeance's essence so soon. Not at all if he could avoid it. Even now, if speed were not required, he would ignore the power he could feel eager to be released.

He took his role as the left hand of the king very seriously. He even enjoyed exacting the king's vengeance, for he believed in its necessity. Yet he considered it a point of honor to fulfill each assignment as a man rather than as the embodiment of Vengeance's power. If he did not owe it to his quarry, he owed it to himself.

He could not ignore the abilities his rank as Lord of the King's Vengeance granted him though. Direct access to Vengeance and all its resources was formidable, quite possibly the most intoxicating power in the realm. He answered to only two entities: his friend

King Wincuff, from whom he took his assignments, and the god Vengeance, itself the bastard offspring of the gods Otuus and Ez-Wrayal, from whom he took his power.

A single mental tug upon the percolating power released black tendrils of shadow from the dark corners of the room. They whisked across his hand, filling the gap in his flesh and taking away all sign of the injury.

To another eye his hand would appear whole. Never so to Direk. He would always see the difference.

Another piece of him gone; replaced by unhuman matter. Mortal substance replaced by…*What? Immortal? If I, or most of what makes me a man, am replaced by Vengeance, will I gain immortality? More likely I will simply exist no more, my humanity gone, my body nothing more than a host.*

Direk clenched his whole hand around the hilt and pushed the thought away. He tugged the blade from the wood, a full half of its length sliding free with ease, and spun. Foes waited, and he was eager to face them and lose himself in battle. He laughed at their expressions and strode to meet them.

"Come on, curs! Challenge the King's Vengeance will you?"

His harsh voice sliced through the last remnants of duty or belief or loyalty keeping the four remaining soldiers between him and their lord. All broke and ran, dropping weapons and armor alike, concerned with naught but their own lives.

Direk snorted, amused and angered at their flight. He sensed the pull of Vengeance, its desire to exact itself upon the cowards. Viciously he reined it in and ignored the burn of pain that rushed through his body at the denial.

"Culciff!" Direk vented his frustration in a yell that rattled the walls. "You cannot hide, Culciff. No matter it be here or anywhere, King Wincuff will have his vengeance." He stepped into the inner stairwell and descended.

A barrage of crossbow bolts slammed into the walls around him. Direk did not duck. He freed Vengeance to flow before him and walked straight into the withering fire. The bolts did different things as they struck the blocking shadows: some fell to the floor, others turned sharply away, some even disintegrated or simply vanished. Direk did not pause at the hastily erected barricade of furniture the bowmen hid behind; he simply unsheathed *Retribution* and scythed the blade before him.

The sword sloughed through wood, adornment, armor and flesh alike. Men screamed and shadows laughed. Direk remained impassive through it all.

Another swipe of the inhuman *Retribution* sent the rest of the impedance clattering to the stone floor. No one rose to stop him. All lay dead at his feet.

The last torch at the far end of the hall snuffed out. Subtle sounds declared men moved into position within the shrouding darkness.

He barked a laugh. "Do you truly seek to fight me in the dark?" None answered. "Let it not be said the King's Vengeance blindly consumes all. It is your lord's death that is sought this day. Sought and taken. Stand aside, attempt not to thwart the king's rightful claim, and Vengeance will spare each and every one of you. This I, Direk, Lord of Vengeance, swear."

Mutters greeted his pledge, followed by the shuffling of many feet and curses. His shadow-enhanced eyesight pierced through the blackness, and Direk smiled thinly at the departing men. Half of the force arrayed before him fled. Still a score of men remained...and something else. Something strong hid among them.

Direk did not wait. "So be it," he said and sent his shadows after the soldiers. He hoped their futile efforts to survive the brutal specters would distract whatever bided its time. One breath; two breaths. At his third inhale, Direk entered the hall. He walked steadily down its center and took no heed of the carnage occurring to his right and left. He watched for only one thing: the source of power lurking in the fortress hallway.

The attack came from behind, almost surprising him. A last second twinge traveled across his senses, the strange sensation enough to send him into a second spinning defense.

Retribution flowed to his fore, anxious to strike. Direk's eyes snapped onto a hulking figure silhouetted between him and the remaining torches in the tower stairwell. He tensed, prepared for assault. Instead of lunging toward him though, the unknown foe swung its arms wide, spreading its cloak across the hall.

Searing light burst from the blazing weapon exposed by the open robe. *Retribution* hummed in rage, its immediate hatred like the gnashing of teeth in Direk's mind. He recognized the sensation as a compounded version of the twinge—*cringe?*—that had warned him of the attack. Despite the sudden brilliance, he also recognized the unmistakable aura of Justice about the weapon his assailant wielded.

"This is not your fight. I am here on king's business," Direk declared. He swung an arm before his eyes and rapidly blinked away the spinning sparkles that would have blinded a normal man. The extraordinary sensory augmentation powered by Vengeance's shadows kept him far from disabled.

Though diminished by the weapon's glare, the hall possessed more than enough nooks and alcoves to harbor shadows. It but needed one to ensure Vengeance's presence. Direk's sight returned. With it came recognition of the long-lost weapon.

"You dare to carry *Truth*?" he queried.

The voice that answered was that of Tiadore Sentchkal, Duke Culciff's Master of Sword, once King's Swordmaster. Direk had sparred often with the man in years past and knew his prowess. Armed with *Truth*, Tiadore was a formidable opponent.

"I've carried truth all my life, Lord Direk. Who better, then, to carry its embodiment?"

Indeed, he spoke true, as well Direk knew. The man's forthrightness was renowned; it was believed he had never uttered a lie.

"I have no desire to kill you, Direk. I but wish to spare my lord, the Duke."

"King Wincuff has declared his vengeance, Master Sentchkal. We both know there is no alternative here."

The older man nodded. "Then I shall kill you, and Wincuff if I must, for Duke Culciff has not deserved such decree."

Truth flashed forward even as the swordsman spoke, nearly taking Direk's sword hand. The Lord of Vengeance leaped back, surprised by the speed of the strike and more that his hand remained intact. He grasped for the short sword in his belt and found nothing.

Direk cast a quick glance to his hip and stumbled in astonishment. Blood flowed from his opened side, and his second sword was gone. He stared at the pink of sundered flesh where his belt and trousers had been sliced open.

Fear coursed through him. Tiadore's strike had not missed. Direk had assumed the target had been the hand holding *Retribution*. He retreated, stumbling over his fallen blade as he circled away from the advancing man. Vengeance roared in Direk's mind and demanded he allow it to retaliate.

Truth darted back and forth, weaving a devilish path of precise strikes that would have diced Direk's body had they connected. Only Direk's submission to *Retribution*'s own supernatural prowess kept that from happening. He blinked in shock, then spat the sudden bile risen in his throat.

"You will not have it so easy, Sentchkal. I would have spared you."

Direk drove forward with all the strength of his legs. He evaded *Truth*'s shorter reach and plowed his shoulder into Tiadore's chest. Momentum forced the man into the wall. Direk pressed against him and pounded his fist into the swordmaster's belly. Once, twice— each blow searched for his groin.

The unrelenting flow of blood down his leg frightened Direk. He knew his best chance lay in ending the fight quickly. That or turning more of himself over to the essence of the always-willing Vengeance. His stomach churned at the thought even as his feet slipped in his own blood. His third punch slid off Tiadore's ribs into the wall.

The swordmaster kicked Direk's sliding feet out from beneath him and pushed away from the wall. He landed a punch of his own to the back of Direk's neck. Direk's arm numbed, and it could not bear his weight nor stop his fall.

He hit the stone and rolled. He kept on rolling, feeling the repeated strikes of *Truth* slamming into the floor just behind him. He cried out when his wounded hip scraped across rough debris.

Direk bit his tongue in shame. The burst of pain and blood in his mouth roused him from his fear. He made a choice then, immediate survival more important than all else: he relented to the clamoring voice of Vengeance.

Hot anger swept through Direk, erasing pain and fear and even reason. Then cold rage poured through his body, staunching his loss of blood and slowing time almost to a standstill.

He watched Tiadore's sword move with infinite slowness toward him. He saw drops of sweat grow and lengthen on the man's set face.

His own sword arm moved barely faster. *Retribution* swept up from beneath *Truth* and twisted inside Tiadore's reach. The tip of the longer sword stretched for the swordmaster's gut.

Truth thrust down. Tiadore's rigid knuckles slammed into Direk's grip and knocked *Retribution* aslant.

The black sword slid into the man's side, passing smoothly through chainmail and leather vest, linen shirt and muscled flesh. The white sword impaled Direk's forearm and lodged in his bone. The twin strikes bent the combatants into each other and brought them face to face.

Direk's eyes widened; Tiadore winked. Direk roared in pain and spat into Tiadore's clenched teeth. He wrenched *Retribution* free of the man's side, sneering at the grimace and cry that escaped Tiadore's lips. Then he slammed his head into the man's mouth and tried to pull away.

In his rage Direk had forgotten Tiadore's grip on the sword embedded in his bone.

The swordmaster staggered backward, pulling Direk with him and grinning wildly through mangled lips.

"Counter," he gasped. "They counter each other."

For a moment Direk was confused. Then realization dawned.

Truth and *Retribution* acted as counters to each other. The powers of Justice and Vengeance waged on equal terms here. Even though Tiadore bore *Truth* as a weapon of Justice, he was not the king's agent here—not authorized to thwart the demanded Vengeance.

Though supernatural powers swirled about them, this battle would be settled by man, not magic.

Desperation matched realization, and Direk reared back, fighting Tiadore's hold. He savagely rocked his arm free of *Truth's* point while slamming the hilt of *Retribution* into Tiadore's side. The man yelled in pain and used *Truth* to slap away a second blow. His mouth snapped at Direk's escaping hand, and his teeth clamped around Direk's thumb.

Direk howled, rage and fear and even sorrow unleashed in his cry. Tears welled in his eyes and he trembled with accumulated injuries. Then the adrenaline of survival flooded his body.

Direk raised a knee into Tiadore's body. He did not aim. He sought to inflict massive damage and free his hand. He slammed his heel upon the other man's insole and brought that same knee up again. Even as it connected with Tiadore's abdomen, Direk felt the man's teeth grind through his flesh and tendon.

He screamed.

Through tear-filled eyes Direk saw Tiadore's exposed right ear and bit back. He snapped his teeth without hesitation, and flung his head back, ripping the swordmaster's ear from his head. Tiadore's answering scream finally allowed Direk to pull his thumb free.

Direk could not bring *Retribution* to bear. He thrust his injured hand into Tiadore's face and scratched for the man's eyes. Tiadore grunted and twisted his head from side to side until he managed to wrap Direk's arm against his body and pull him close in a massive hug.

Neither man had time for tactics, nor room for reason or even thought. All that mattered to both was surviving and escaping. Direk dropped *Retribution* and reached for Tiadore's throat.

He caught it on his second try.

He dug his fingers into the flesh and squeezed. Tiadore dropped his arm from around Direk's midsection and pounded at his body. The swordmaster tried to find Direk's groin. Instead he found Direk's injured hand. Immediately he bent the severed thumb back, snapping the bone.

Tiadore's follow-up punch to Direk's throat choked off the Lord of Vengeance's agonized shout. Direk's fingers convulsed on Tiadore's throat, and he sunk his fingernails behind the man's esophagus.

He pulled with every ounce of strength remaining him.

Blood splashed over Direk's hand, and the swordmaster sagged against him. Direk lay gasping upon the floor. Every fiber of his being cried in agony. Sensations rolled through him, each one overwhelming the last until his very nerves recoiled: the coldness of the stone floor seeped into his flesh; the hot fire of his ruined thumb speared into his brain; the hilt of a sword dug into his back; his lungs fought for air. Unconsciousness threatened to swallow him.

Sharp pain emanated from his hip and forced him to move. He recalled his initial wound and tried to roll away from it. Tiadore's weight pinned him in place.

Fatigue crashed upon Direk, followed by a terrible feeling of waste. He pried his fingers open and let drop the sodden mess that had once been a man's throat. He groaned and pushed the dead man aside.

Behind all of it roiled Vengeance, its exuberance at victory painful in Direk's heart. To survive this battle he would have to accept even more of Vengeance's essence. To live, he would have to become even less of a man.

Direk wept and rolled to his knees.

Tiadore—if not a friend—had been a peer, a respected comrade in arms. It had not been Direk's intention to kill the man. As far as Direk knew, Swordmaster Sentchkal had not betrayed the king's trust. It seemed that all of Direk's plans had gone astray this day.

He ignored the tendrils of Vengeance swirling about him and pushed himself wearily to his feet. He would finish this fight under his own power.

The blood loss was too great. Determination failed him, and he slumped sideways into the wall. His shoulder found the floor.

Bitterness welled within Direk, and he spat gobs of blood and bile upon the stone. He heard nothing beyond the drip of liquids and the rattle of dislodged rubble.

Direk sighed and realized that choice had predetermined this decision. He ignored the gleeful sensation that pulsed through him and accepted what must be—what he had known all along had to be.

Direk opened his mouth and allowed the essence of Vengeance to snake into him.

The darkness flowed in and filled him with rapture. In the back of his mind, in the depth of his soul, and in his very core, Direk screamed in panic. He barely heard the distant and muffled sound. The tears coursing down his face vanished. So did the pain, and the euphoria of healing, and then all feeling.

Direk, personification and Lord of Vengeance, rose to his feet.

Black armor flowed across his body. It encased him in steel, while shadows billowed about him and cloaked him in ebon. He clenched the fist of one hand as his other tightened upon the hilt of *Retribution*.

He did not look about. He did not look down. He did not see the desolation surrounding him. He did not witness the flicker of *Truth*'s departure. He strode deeper into the castle.

Direk had a duke to find. The king had demanded vengeance.

Kamilda of Ys
by DJ Tyrer

In the days when the world was young and the twin suns burned bright in the sky, Ys was the greatest city in the world and ruled an empire greater than any would follow. But, disaster struck Ys with the loss of the White Ship carrying King Kastain, who drowned in the treacherous waters of the Demhic Ocean, leaving his only daughter to rule the city in his stead.

***

Queen Kamilda of Ys watched her court with golden eyes sharp as those of a hawk. Any monarch of Ys had to be vigilant, but a Queen, especially such a young one, all the more so. Everywhere were plots as factions vied for power, even as the courtiers danced and sported. Even the least threatening and mendacious of plots, those seeking to provide her with a consort, threatened to deprive her of her power. Which was not an outcome that Kamilda was willing to countenance. The worst plots sought to slay or enslave her and place another on or behind the throne. The beautiful, golden-haired queen was resolved to resist all such challenges.

Behind many of these plots, whether to espouse her or to dispose of her, was her aquiline cousin, Duke Alar of Aldon. Should Kamilda die, he would succeed to the throne and he had made multiple attempts to court her. Such was the ubiquity of the Duke's power and plotting, Kamilda's spy chief, Atlas Crookback, had an entire coterie of spies dedicated to monitoring him and his followers.

"Your brother watches me like a hawk," the Queen said without a trace of irony in her voice, leaning forward to speak privately to her cousin, the Countess Kassilla.

"He desires that which you sit upon," Kassilla replied with the hint of a smile upon her lips.

Where Kamilda was golden-haired and yellow-eyed with a radiant beauty like that of the suns, her cousin was wanly skinned with silvery hair and pale grey eyes that were reminiscent of the moons that orbited the world. Whilst the Queen tended towards seriousness of mind, even dourness, due to her early receipt of power and responsibility, the Countess had a more sardonic attitude towards life.

"Your brother skirts dangerously close to treason."

"My brother is an expert at walking the narrowest of political tightropes."

Kassilla kissed her cousin's hand and took her leave of the Phoenix Throne, moving delicately through the courtly throng to her brother's side.

"As you are like unto the moon," her brother told her, "the Queen is like unto the sun and I would remind you of what happens to a moth that flies too close to the flame..."

"Is that a threat, dear brother?"

"Merely good advice, my sister. Kamilda is not fit to rule our empire and, as the nearest and fittest male heir of her father, I intend to replace her."

"You speak treason, brother."

"I speak truth! There is no treason in doing what is best for our city. I am destined to rule: I am merely the tool of destiny. She shall fall and I shall rise. And, you, my darling sister, shall be my consort: do not seek comfort in the frail embrace of a woman; she cannot satisfy you, nor can she protect you if you would betray me."

"Opposing you is no betrayal if I act in accord with my oaths and my hearts. I serve our Queen – do not betray her or else I shall oppose you."

"Then, we are at an impasse..."

"Indeed."

***

For Kamilda, there was little respite from the onerous duties of state. Even sitting in the gorgeous courtyards with their roses grown magically from silver, gold and crystal, she was constantly at the beck and call of her ministers. At times, the Queen felt more like a servant than a monarch.

To escape for a few hours, she would join her cousin, Kassilla, for a ride into the foothills that ringed the central mountains of their island home. There, beyond the idyllic pastures, there were caves in which shepherds sheltered from the rain and wind. Long before her accession, Kamilda had trysted there with a handsome youth, a shepherd boy named Astor, although she had found the experience unsatisfactory.

There, in the hills, she and Kassilla would picnic in meadows within steep-sided gorges, then retreat into a concealed cave where they could be alone, unseen and unjudged. For a few hours, snatched here and there, the two women could be themselves, unfettered by the strictures of the court, free to love and be loved.

But, no matter how glorious the time they spent together was, those few hours soon drew to an end.

"Come," said the Queen, rising from her cousin's embrace, "we must be getting back before I am missed."

They headed out from the cave and mounted their horses, pointing them in the direction of the coastal plain and the city of Ys.

But, their return journey was not to be unmolested.

It was Kamilda who sensed it first. "Something is coming."

"What?" asked her cousin, turning in her saddle. Then, she sensed it, too. "Demons!"

They barely had time to react before a half-dozen things that looked a little like men and a little like bats and a little like insects and a little like half-decayed corpses with ragged, leathery wings appeared around them. Their horses reared and panicked, and they barely remained in their saddles.

Kamilda had begun to chant a prayer of protection to the Elder Gods that warded Ys. In her haste, she was unable to invest it with much power, but it would hold them back for a short while.

Kassilla uttered an incantation and thrust out her hand at one of the demons, a flash of green light arcing from her hand to it and causing it to recoil with a howl of pain.

Kamilda, now, reached for the pendant she wore upon a chain around her neck and which bore the triskelid symbol of Ys. Saying the ancient words, she called forth the demon that was bound within it, a writhing monstrosity with a myriad of tentacles that entered into battle with the demons. It seemed the more powerful, but even with so many limbs was unable to battle all the demons at once.

The problem was that the summoning of demons and the casting of rituals was a slow and tedious work not suited to battle. As Queen, Kamilda was obliged to wear certain protective items, but she had only worn the bare minimum today and doubted they would last for long. The defensive and offensive spells that she could cast would be too weak to be effective.

Kassilla, however, wary of her brother's threats, had not come devoid of protection. She tore three acorn-like charms from her bracelet and threw them to the floor, each transforming into a silvery figure, like a statue of a warrior armed with a spear. The three of them levelled their weapons and advanced upon the demons, stabbing at them with mechanical precision, destroying first one then another of the monstrosities before they were overcome by their vicious claws.

Kamilda's demon had destroyed three, before it vanished into a puddle of yellowish ooze upon the ground. That left just one, and it came at them with an alien vigour despite the titanic struggle it had been through. Kamilda's words were failing and the spells she threw at it were more like pinpricks than mortal wounds.

Kassilla took from her belt a certain knife that she had enchanted and began to slash at the clawed limbs and snarling half-face as the demon lunged wildly at them, each blow causing a livid cut to open in the demon's greyish skin until, finally, it reared with a roar of pain, allowing her to plunge the blade into its chest. Whether it had a heart like mortal creature, she could not know, but the blow was successful for it let out a piercing ululation then seemed to split open with a release of yellowish light, then collapse into a formless mound with the appearance of rotten meat.

"It was Alar," she told Kamilda as she wiped the blade clean on a tuft of grass. "It was my brother who sent these demons against you – against us."

"Are you certain?"

"He as good as warned me – and, I could sense his ties to his creatures. Doubtless he knew I would be riding with you and that we would leave your guards behind. What he didn't consider was that I would bring additional protection with me following his threats."

"We must return to the city immediately, before he can send more against us," and, with that, they spurred their horses and rode thence as swiftly as they could.

***

Despite their strong suspicions and Kassilla's affirmation that she had sensed her brother's ties to the demons, they lacked the evidence to prove that he had plotted against his Queen. By the time the court sorcerers were able to attend the location of the attack, the putrid remains of the slain demons had long since evaporated and what spiritual traces there were had faded to nothing, leaving them clueless; there were too many in Ys skilled in the ways of demon summoning to lay the blame at his feet without strong evidence.

Atlas Crookback set even more men onto watching the Duke of Aldon, but Alar's followers were too loyal – or, too terrified – to betray him and he was skillfully circumspect in his activities, ensuring that the spymaster could ascertain nought but the vaguest hints as to his activities and nothing to implicate him in any crimes, not even when someone attempt to poison Kamilda's wine at a banquet, leading to the death of Lord Toros and his wife.

***

"I fear our beloved Queen is just no longer capable of holding together the Empire that her father left her," opined Count Ithil of Thales as the news of the latest revolt on the fringes of the empire of Ys was unveiled by the Duke of Aldon to his guests.

"She has dispatched Admiral Kadian with a grand fleet to re-impose order," Kassilla commented, keen to protect her cousin's honour. Had she dared, she could have told them that her brother was suspected of being behind the revolts besmirching Kamilda's status.

"Thankfully, she has a man to rely upon," Alar said, turning her words of defence into a slur.

The Counts of Kalvados and Erlet then entered into a spirited debate as to whether the recalcitrant subjects ought to be brought back under the rule of Ys or be obliterated through the use of one of the Great Rituals that had brought them their empire in the first place. Alar was certainly on Erlet's side in the debate, advocating the use of mighty magic to enforce their rule.

"What we need," he told his assembled guests, "is someone strong enough to do what must be done to maintain our rule over the world."

"And, that someone would be you?" his sister asked, archly.

"I would be the logical choice, despite my natural inclination to remain a loyal servant of our Queen."

"Well said!" the Count of Erlet commented, echoed by the Count of Thales.

"Thank you," the Duke murmured, obsequiously.

***

With her vision focused upon the far corners of her empire, Kamilda paid little heed to what her cousin was plotting closer to her throne. Until, as chaos seemed to engulf everywhere her rule ran, he finally made his play to overthrow her.

Dissatisfied with the Queen's seeming inability to maintain order, many within the army and navy had been suborned by Duke Alar and rose in support of him to her dismay when he made his move.

The uprising began with an enormous inferno, a tornado of flame, erupting in the barracks of the Queen's Guard, removing at a stroke many of her most loyal soldiers. Within moments, hordes of demons manifested throughout the palace, slaying key figures and causing chaos to distract the Queen and her advisors from what was happening. Although Kamilda and Kassilla, who was with her, were kept safe by the presence of the sorcerers, wards and bound demons put in place since the attempt on her life, the fighting elsewhere took many lives, including that of Atlas Crookback, in the opening minutes. With so many killed so quickly and so many loyal warriors overseas attempting to enforce her rule, Kamilda found herself immediately beleaguered as so many of her troops either declared for Alar or stayed conveniently unavailable as the Duke marched upon the palace with his personal guard and sorcerers and flanked by hordes of gibbering demons.

"We are under attack!" Naotalba, the chief of her sorcerers, shrieked as he ordered forth his acolytes do battle. "Release all the bound demons and elementals that we have! Begin the summoning of as many as you can manage. Call upon the Old Ones. Carry out the protective rites." He turned to his Queen. "I do not believe we can hold them back for long, your Majesty. So many of your soldiers and sorcerers are overseas fighting and so few of those we have here have heeded the call. We will be overwhelmed, unless you undertake one of the Grand Invocations."

There were several of these rituals that could only be performed by the ruler of Ys, most of which were so devastating that their use was totally impractical for their current situation. Her best options were the Rite of Invoked Destruction, The Calling of the Unlamented Dead or The Invocation of the Dragon. With her chief sorcerer preoccupied with the slitting of slaves' throats as part of a ritual summoning of Ravager demons, Kamilda turned to Kassilla and presented her with the question of which.

The building shook as something terrible smashed into it. Whether a powerful curse or the fist of some mighty demon, they had no idea this deep within its walls.

"That cannot be good," Kassilla commented, before answering her cousin's query. "The Rite of Invoked Destruction is indiscriminate and will kill our own people as easily as my brother's; depending upon how many men he has uncommitted to this battle and how many demons he has yet to unleash, it could leave us worse off than we are now.

"The Calling of the Unlamented Dead would certainly be the quickest option, but you know full well that the souls it summons have a tendency to turn upon the Summoner, again potentially harming us more than him.

"Although the most difficult of the three –" She was forced to pause a moment and release a searing dart of purple energy at a Writhing Wailer that had burst through the wards to menace the Queen. The wound was enough to give the nearest sorcerers to unleash their own spells or direct demons toward it, destroying it.

"Although the most difficult of the three," she began again, "The Invocation of the Dragon is our best chance: the Dragon God has always enfolded Ys within his protective wings and it is through His power that our empire has waxed great. Call upon Him now in our hour of need and I am certain He will answer. Do it, cousin, do it..."

"I shall," Kamilda nodded.

She crossed to Naotalba and told him to summon as many priests and sorcerers as could be spared. "And, we shall require a good pyre and two-dozen Sacred Virgins."

He gave a curt nod and began issuing orders. A number of priests and sorcerers arrived promptly and began the ritual preparations and a short while later, a terrified gaggle of Sacred Virgins were ushered in from the Third Precinct of the Imperial Temple. The pyre was built and lit; blazing crucibles were placed at the points of a pentacle; the chant began.

Kamilda stripped off her golden robes of state and allowed Kassilla to sponge her clean so that she would be pure for the ritual to come. Their actions were mirrored by the Sacred Virgins washing one another for the same purpose: now that they had an aim, they no longer sobbed with fear, but moved with a purpose.

Once she had been cleansed, the High Priest in his golden robes and pallid mask of bone stepped forth to anoint her before Kassilla clothed her in a simple shift of pure-white linen as befitted a supplicant of a God.

Finally ready, Kamilda began the ritual, calling out to the great god of Ys to come to her aid, to save the city from treachery. Ranks of sorcerers and ashen-faced guardsmen supplemented by demons and fiery elementals stood guard about them as the sounds of conflict grew ever closer. Slowly, one by one, Naotalba led forth the Virgins and tossed them onto the pyre with all the casualness of a practised sorcerer. The smell of burning flesh filled the hall and the screams echoing from the flames merged with the chant into an overwhelming cacophony.

The attackers had reached the many doors of the hall and were desperately fighting to break through and assault the Queen. Doubtless, Alar was well aware of the ritual that Kamilda was performing and hoped to disrupt it; it looked as if he might succeed. Not necessary to the ritual, Kassilla had joined the defence, wielding her dagger and curses against the demons sent by her brother with much success.

Seeing that the defenders were nearly overwhelmed, Kassilla drew back and approached near to her cousin: she desired to tell her to hurry, but knew doing so might disrupt the ritual at a vital moment.

"Oh, please hurry," she whispered to herself. Glancing over her shoulder, she could see demons, something like mantises and something like apes, overwhelming the few remaining guardsmen and ripping weary sorcerers limb-from-limb. It seemed that they were doomed.

Suddenly, the flames of the pyre and crucibles leapt high and Kamilda screamed to heaven. The roof of the palace split asunder and masonry fell to the floor, crushing friend and foe alike. The now-visible sky grew black as if from the oily black smoke of the pyre and something solid seemed to form out of it.

An enormous figure that was a little like a dragon and a little like a squid and a little like a man in its vague outline loomed above the palace as the forces of Duke Alar finally burst into the hall.

But, had they expected the summoned eidolon of their God to save them, they were to be disappointed, for a thunderous voice spoke and said, "Too late!"

"Too late!" echoed Kamilda in despair.

"Too late! Too late!" cried Kassilla as Naotalba collapsed dead to the floor from his exertion and the shock.

A demon surged forward only to be seized by one smoky claw of the Dragon God and crushed into nothingness. The other claw reached down and plucked Kamilda and Kassilla away, leaving Alar to rage impotently at their disappearance; for, though he had won, he could not rest easy in his victory, knowing they yet lived.

***

"Do we yet live?" Kassilla asked her cousin. They appeared to be lying in a mountain meadow at the heart of the island.

"I believe so," Kamilda said, helping her to her feet and hugging her in relief. "Our god lifted us to safety at the last moment."

"Better that he had destroyed my brother."

"Better that we live, rather than die."

"Yes... still..."

"Too late", he said. "Ys is a nation of the strong, and Alar had won this toss."

"Indeed," said a voice from behind them. They turned to see a youthful shepherd walking towards them across the meadow.

"Astor, is that you?" Kamilda asked, surprised.

"I am he you knew as Astor, yes," he smiled, "but, I am also he who brought you here..."

"You mean...?" she gasped, confused.

"Yes, I am the god upon whom you called."

"But..."

"You have always been dear to my heart, Kamilda, since before you were born, and I have watched over you always. Had you only called upon me sooner, I could have smashed Alar with ease..."

"Is... is it possible for me yet to defeat Alar?" she asked him. "Surely, Admiral Kadian and my generals will rally to my cause...?"

"It is too late. Alar has proven himself strong and they shall rally to him and accept him as King, now that you are gone."

"But," asked Kassilla, "what do we do now?"

"You have two choices," the youth-cum-god told her. "You may go together to some remote pastoral idyll and dwell together for a long and happy life, leaving Alar as King of Ys."

"Or?" prompted Kassilla.

"Or, you may call upon me to perform the Rite of the Inundating Waters to overwhelm the city, the entire island, and the usurper that sits upon its throne. Once before, I sent such waters over the Earth and only the pleas of a young shepherd boy – he whose form I wear – kept me from destroying the entire world, filling only the abyss that became the Demhic Ocean."

Kamilda looked at her cousin, yearning for a life of bliss with her, the life that they had always been denied due to her rank.

"Avenge yourself upon my brother, my beloved," Kassilla urged her."Do not allow him to profit from such treachery."

"Such a course shall doom you both," Astor cautioned.

"Regardless," Kassilla said, "I could not bear to live knowing that Alar goes unpunished."

"But, our love..."

"Your kisses will be as ashes on my lips as long as he lives..."

"Then, we shall overthrow the land with the sea."

"So be it," Astor said with lowered gaze. "The rite demands a sacrifice, a flow of blood to call the flow of water..."

"I understand," Kassilla murmured, drawing her knife once more and slashing it across her throat to release a torrent of blood.

"No!" screamed Kamilda, seizing her cousin as she collapsed to the ground.

"Yes!" cried Astor and held up his arms as if to call the sea forth over the island.

Kamilda was oblivious to the roar as the sea rose up in a cloud-foamed wave and fell upon the land, submerging the island beneath it. She knelt over her dying cousin, watching as her eyes glazed and her face grew pale like a colourless, waxy mask.

"This is not what I wished!" she cried.

"Too late," Astor said. "Ys is drowned."

***

Kamilda's eyes fluttered open at the kiss of misty spray upon her face. Sitting up, she looked around, confused. She appeared to be lying on the beach of a small island, a couple of acres in size. With a shock, she realised that the broken remains of great walls and toppled arches protruded from the sand and from the surrounding sea like a multitude of broken teeth. Amongst them, she noticed elements familiar from her palace and realisation dawned. Yet, these were not the ruins of Ys newly-tumbled by the sea, but masonry long-weathered and worn by winds and tides, half-buried by sand and strewn with weed.

"This is what you willed," she heard Astor's voice, and she turned to see him standing nearby on the beach.

"This is Ys?" she asked, knowing the answer.

"Yes. Long drowned and faded from memory into myth."

"But..."

"This is the course you chose, Kamilda. You cast aside your chance for a life of love in order to have a moment's vengeance. Alar was destroyed and all the people of Ys with him; but you lost your love and, now, you are trapped here for the remainder of your days... I am sorry..."

Those final words seemed to echo away on the breeze as the youth vanished in the blink of an eye, a vaguely-draconic cloud forming in the sky and drifting lazily to the horizon. Now, she was alone with her thoughts, her memories, and her regrets...

The Aggrieved
by David L. Craddock

-1-

Viktor had been the one who discovered the cave. He and his two best friends had spent their boyhoods sitting in its mouth, Abbuv was afraid to go back further, and so were Viktor and Keltin, though they wouldn't admit it, cooking fish over campfires, telling ghost stories that made Abbuv squeal, and sharing the deep secrets of youth: the girls they wanted to ask to the spring dance, aspirations of becoming bards and traveling the world telling grand tales in exchange for soft beds and hot meals.

They had not visited the cave in months. They were sixteen, now, men in the eyes of the elders of Strawbridge, and men were expected to learn a trade and start families. It was Viktor who had occasion to call them back. He led Keltin and Abbuv on the walk three miles outside of Strawbridge and into the mouth of the cave, where he shared the deepest and darkest secret of his young life.

"I'm going to kill my father, and I need your help."

They reacted about as he expected. Abbuv's plain face remained blank as his slow mind turned Viktor's words over but failed to grasp them, like a waterwheel with leaky fins. Slowly, realization dawned. His slanted eyes widened in alarm.

"Kill him?" Abbuv said. His tongue poked out from between his lips, muffling his words as if he'd spoken around a mouthful of food. *Kill 'im?*

Keltin had been fingering the silver trimming sewed along the collar of his cloak between thumb and forefinger and admiring the way the setting sunlight glinted against it. Abruptly his fingers stopped, and his head swiveled slowly toward Viktor.

"You're not serious," he said. It was not a question. Keltin was a novice, raised to the cloak and collar just that afternoon, and novices were supposed to take even the most shocking of surprises in stride.

He almost succeeded. Keltin kept his face smooth, but he pinched his collar hard enough to turn the tips of his fingers white.

"I am," Viktor said, and was surprised at how steady his voice sounded. Inwardly, he was terrified. "I have to. If I don't kill him, he's going to kill me."

"That won't happen," Keltin said. His tone was sympathetic but confident. "The magister's keeping an eye on him." He nodded as if that settled the matter.

Anger washed away Viktor's fright. He hardly noticed. Anger had been his constant companion for weeks, as familiar as a sunrise.

"My father's not afraid of the magister," he said. "More likely, the magister's afraid of him."

Keltin frowned but did not dispute the claim. Abbuv looked back and forth between them.

"Why you want to kill him, Viktor?" he asked. It sounded like *Why ooh wanna kill 'im, Vikor?*

Abbuv's genuine confusion cooled Viktor's temper.

"Because he killed my mother."

Keltin began to sputter. "That's not... we don't know... the investigation is--"

"I was there, Keltin. I saw him do it."

-2-

Viktor's tone was soft, but his words cut through Keltin's protests like a knife.

"You were there?" Keltin whispered.

"Yes."

Keltin's angular face became full of sympathy, and Viktor felt tension drain out of his shoulders. All traces of Keltin the Novice were gone. Keltin the Friend had arrived at last.

Keltin sat on one of the three large rocks they had arranged around a fire pit he had carved with his Talent years ago. Holding an open palm over the pit, where burnt twigs and ashes lay, he spoke two words and jerked his hand away as a flame soared up, licking the ceiling before settling into contented crackling. Shadows danced along the cave walls. Abbuv watched them with an expression of awe.

"Tell us what happened," Keltin said.

Viktor sank onto his rock and shrugged, resting his arms on his knees.

"He was drunk, as usual, and she did nothing wrong, as usual. Burned the meat. That was her crime. She offered to cook him up another piece, and he just..." He closed his eyes but the horrors of his mother's final moments played out against his eyelids.

Viktor jerked when he felt Abbuv's calloused hand settle on his shoulder. Abbuv's plain face was crinkled in concern. Viktor gave him a small smile and patted his hand.

Absently, Keltin touched his novice collar. "You should go to the magister. You should," he pressed when Viktor shook his head. "Tell him what you saw. You're a respected member of our community, Viktor." His voice softened. "Your mother was, too. If you swear that you say is the truth, he can protect you. The village guard--"

"They won't help," Viktor snapped and looked away. *Tripped,* he heard his father say. The smugness of his father's tone saturated the memory, dripping from it like a rag soaked with blood. *She just tripped.*

Keltin straightened. "I'll vouch for you. The magister trusts me as much as he trusts his own blood."

Viktor swallowed a sound of irritation. Keltin the Novice had returned. Neither man noticed the deep flush of shame that had crept over Abbuv's face at Keltin's words.

"Everyone in the village knows we're friends," Viktor said.

"Just like they know Ralad is a drunk," Keltin said. "If we tell the magister, he can send the guards to--"

"They're not the knights of Solomnia, Keltin. They're a militia. They're more comfortable spearing bales of hay than they are sticking a sword in a man's belly." *Especially a man who could probably jab them hard enough with one finger to break a few ribs.*

"And you, Viktor? Could you stick a sword in a man's belly? In the man who fathered you?"

"There was little fathering involved."

Keltin raised his hands in assent. "I'm only thinking of you, my friend. What if you're caught? You would be the one tried before the magister, and your friendship with 'buv won't carry you far. The magister is a wise and impartial man, and--"

Viktor fought to keep his tone even. "I appreciate what you're saying, Keltin. Truly. But if you want to help me, then think this through. I saw my father... I saw *Ralad* kill my mother, and he knows I saw. He'll know I was the one who gave him over."

Keltin hesitated. "Are you saying you don't want to report your father because you're afraid? Because the magister can protect you," he finished in a rush.

Viktor clenched his fists so hard his nails cut into his palms. Once again he felt Abbuv's big hand alight on his shoulder, light as a feather. This time, his friend's touch, and the innocence in his eyes, brought no comfort.

"I want to do this myself. I have to. For my mother."

Liar, a voice at the back of his mind whispered. He shoved it away.

Despite the heat from the flames, Keltin drew his cloak around him.

"I won't kill a man. Not even a man like Ralad."

"You don't have to kill him." Viktor looked between Keltin and Abbuv, who had settled back and adopted his blank stare. He no longer felt fear. Only the urgency of self-preservation. "I'll do it. I just need some help."

Keltin tried to speak up but Viktor overrode him.

"I hold no illusions about my strength compared to Ralad's. There's no way I could take him in a fight, even if I got him drunk first. Not that he'd need much help from me." His gaze settled on Keltin. "I just need an edge."

"Such as?" Keltin replied after a moment.

Viktor licked his lips and leaned toward Abbuv. "Abbuv, the swords my father keeps around the forge are too large for me. I'm not strong enough, you understand? So I wonder if you might be able to stea-- to borrow one. Could you do that?"

Abbuv squinted and glanced at Keltin. Keltin was frowning at Viktor.

"What is it you need from me?" Keltin asked.

Viktor gestured at the flames. He forced himself to look respectful, even a little awed. "You're the sorcerer-in-training, Keltin. What do you recommend?"

As he'd hoped, Keltin puffed up slightly. "I'd say some sort of poison. Nothing man-made, because that could be traced back to you. It would need to be magical in nature." He started as if coming out of a trance. "Not that I'm agreeing to--"

"Of course not. I'm only asking you to consider what I'm asking." Out of habit, he glanced out of the cave. The fiery gold of twilight was fading to darkness. His curfew was drawing near. An icy vein of fear wormed its way down his chest and into his belly. He ran a shaking hand over his mouth.

"You are my closest friends. I have no one else. Please."

Abbuv, apparently bored with the conversation, hummed a tune and drew in the dirt with his fingers. Keltin studied Viktor for a long time. He rose and looked at the mouth of the cave. A light breeze stirred the leaves and moaned through the cave opening.

"We should get back. I have lessons in the morning."

Keltin waved a hand and started toward the exit. Abruptly the fire winked out. A few tendrils curled up from the ashes, crooking and beckoning like ethereal fingers. Viktor followed him out. Behind them, Abbuv scrambled up from his rock and hurried after them, a whine rising in his throat. At the sound, Keltin paused and put an arm around Abbuv's shoulder. Abbuv was trembling.

"Sorry, 'buv. I forgot." He held one hand palm-up and whispered a word. A glowing white ball hovered above his fingertips, illuminating the windy road and patches of trees on either side.

"Better?" Keltin asked. Beneath his arm, Abbuv grew still. He stood straighter and nodded gruffly.

"This way," Abbuv said, and set off like an intrepid adventurer, marching with his chest thrust out. The ball of light trailed above his head, tinkling softly.

Chuckling, Keltin took a step forward. He paused when he felt Viktor's hand on his arm.

"Think about it," Viktor said. "That's all I ask."

Then he set off without waiting for a reply.

-3-

Viktor awoke before dawn the next morning, tiptoed out to the kitchen where he nibbled on bread and cheese, and crept out of the house. Not that he had needed to move as quietly as a shadow, he reflected as he hurried along Strawbridge's narrow dirt streets. His father's snores were louder than the explosions produced from Keltin's magical experiments.

He reached his mother's pottery shop a few minutes later, a cramped building bunched in between the butcher's shop and the cobbler's hut. *His* shop, now. The countertop, peaked roof, and shelves where she--they--kept their supplies were pockmarked and rickety. *Shabby,* his father said. *Loved.* His mother's descriptor.

Viktor shrugged out of his coat and shivered as he looped a leather jerkin over his head. The shop was open to the elements, like most of the establishments around Strawbridge. He wouldn't be cold for long. Rubbing his hands, he took down two jugs of water, grunted into the quiet at their weight, and poured them into a mixing bowl.

Strawbridge woke up around him as he dropped a wad of clay on the countertop and contemplated it. A bowl, he decided. He dipped his hands into the water and began to wedge the clay, smacking and twisting it to squelch any air bubbles to prevent them from becoming embedded in the finished piece like small stones. When the clump was ready, he dropped it in the center of his stone wheel and gave the wheel a spin. Pulling up a stool, he wet his hands again and pounced on the clay, cupping his hands around it before it could unravel. Slowly, he ran his fingers up its length, coaxing it into an upside-down cone.

Glancing out to the street, he drew a trickle of Talent, letting it coat his hands like water. He smiled as he continued to shape the clay, which now resembled a fat and lazy mountain. Keltin had his spell books and a massive store of Talent. Viktor had the deftness of his spindly fingers and a sliver of Talent. Not enough for him to reach novice rank, and even if he possessed more, his father could not afford for him to study under the magister with the other Talented. Not that Ralad would even if he had the money.

Viktor didn't care. He had enough Talent to create things, things equal parts beautiful and practical, and that was enough.

He lost himself in the rhythmic smoothing motions as he pinched a hole in the top of the clay and widened it slowly outward. A light caught his eye. The sun peeked out shyly from behind Strawbridge's two-story inn, the second largest building in the village after the magister's estate. Horses trotted along the roads, pulling carts loaded with supplies bound for neighboring towns. Maybe even Solomnia, he thought. Strawbridge was big as villages went, but the capitol's sprawl of paved roads, marble bridges, gleaming turrets, and mansions reduced it to a speck, and a dirty one at that.

Viktor had never set foot in Solomnia, but he would. He, Keltin, and 'buv would go together one day. They would load up a wagon with food and blankets and trundle up every paved road, seeing firsthand the sights villagers who had visited the capitol spoke of in tones of self-importance while their less-privileged peers set them up with drinks in exchange for tales of life beyond Strawbridge.

Dimly, amid the stomp of hooves and the buzz of conversation filling the streets, he heard the sound of a hammer ringing against steel. His smile wilted, then bloomed in full force. Ralad was on the other side of Strawbridge. Not far, but far enough for the moment.

Whistling, he dried his hands and carried his bowl over to the kiln, blissfully unaware that he and his friends would be dead in four days.

-4-

The next time Viktor looked up, his father was there. The tang of soot and booze had tickled his nose for several minutes, but he had blocked them out, absorbed as he was in his craft. Then the smell sank in and his heart started racing the way it always did when he felt his father's eyes on him. Watching. Weighing. Discarding. As if Viktor were a fish deemed too small to keep.

He straightened, brushing his hands on his apron.

"Hello." He would not call the man *Father*.

Ralad's face twisted in a crooked smile. "Vikky," he said, biting into the word. His smile stretched when he saw the rosy blush spreading across his son's face. Viktor looked over and noticed Abbuv standing a short distance away. His shoulders were hunched, as if he wished he could wedge himself between the pottery stand and cobbler shop and hide.

"Brought your friend by to walk you home," Ralad went on. "Dummy's good for nothin' around the shop, but he's man enough to walk my daughter home." He guffawed.

"Don't talk about him like that," Viktor replied instinctively. He wished he hadn't. Ralad's smile fell away. In a flash he reached over the countertop and closed sausage-sized fingers around Viktor's slender wrist. Ralad squeezed and Viktor cried out, his voice shrill. A few passersby glanced over, saw the blacksmith, and hurried on. Viktor could see their thoughts play out against their averted faces: *It's a man's business how he chose to discipline his family. Best not to get involved.*

"Or what?" Ralad asked in a low voice. He squeezed again and boomed laughter when his son cried out again. Behind him, Abbuv cried his name over and over.

Eventually Ralad tired of the game and threw Viktor's hand away. Viktor floundered back, arms flailing, and staggered against his finished bowl. It spun off the table and crashed to the floor. Gray fragments scattered every which way.

"Be home before dark," Ralad barked, and stomped off.

Viktor could feel more eyes on him. Abbuv inched closer.

"Ooh okay, Vikor?" he asked, sniffling. "Ooh okay?"

Viktor nodded but didn't look up. He didn't want his friend to see him cry. He began gathering up the ruined bowl with shaking hands. His wrist was turning purple. No, just darkening. He'd already worn a faded bruise around his wrist like a bracelet. His father had just remade it.

And he had done nothing. Just like he had done nothing to save his mother. He hated himself for it, and for how his cowardice made him feel.

That's what this is really about, isn't it? the voice asked as he threw away the fragments, hung up his apron, and walked beside Abbuv toward home.

Yes. If he was being honest, this was about more than his mother. Ralad had made him feel utterly helpless, and not just on that night. It wasn't her fault. He knew that. It wasn't his, either. It was Ralad's.

And Viktor would see him dead for it.

-5-

They walked in silence, Abbuv letting Viktor walk a few steps ahead as the sun sank into the horizon. Viktor did not notice. Anger and humiliation burned through his veins. In his mind, he killed his father over and over. His imagination became a bottomless toolbox that gave Viktor the implements he needed to spill Ralad's blood in countless ways.

He fantasized about approaching Ralad from behind while the hog sat at the dinner table shoveling slop into his maw. Viktor grabbed a fistful of greasy hair, yanked back, and ran a knife across his throat. Blood poured down his broad chest in a freshet. Ralad tumbled from his chair and thrashed on the floor, clawing at his torn throat and drowning in his own blood.

In the next fantasy, Viktor was big enough to hold a sword twice his height in one hand, which he hid behind him. He wrapped one hand around his father's thick neck and pulled him close, as if to hug him. With his free hand, Viktor rammed the blade into Ralad's gut. The tip burst through the other side, covered in blood and entrails like wet towels over a line, and--

"Look," Abbuv said, pointing ahead. "Keltin. Keltin!"

Viktor blinked, tearing himself away from the blood-soaked stage where his fantasies played out. He looked to where his friend pointed. Between two huts, light flickered from behind a screen of trees a short distance off the road. Abbuv was running forward, his short, powerful arms swinging at his sides.

"Wait, 'buv," he called, hustling after his friend.

He found Keltin wrapped up in one of Abbuv's bear hugs and struggling to breathe. The sight made him laugh, and his laughter pushed back the dark cloud hovering over him.

"He's going to need those ribs, 'buv," Viktor said, placing a hand on Abbuv's arm.

Abbuv released his grip and stepped back. His grin folded his mouth into a slit and crinkled his eyes, and Viktor laughed harder. Abbuv's grins weren't his most flattering expression, but they were open and heartfelt.

"I thought I might catch you on your way home," Keltin said, rubbing gingerly at his chest with one hand and resting the other on Abbuv's shoulder. "What I have to tell you probably shouldn't be spoken in too public a place."

The dark cloud drifted back in.

"You've decided?" Viktor said quietly.

Keltin nodded. "I'm sorry, Viktor, but I won't help you. At least, not the way you want."

When Viktor remained silent, Keltin continued.

"I want to talk to the magister, and I want you to come with me. Tell him what you saw."

"It would be my word against Ralad's," Viktor said.

"And your word might hold more weight. Almost everyone in town has seen your mother's bruises." Viktor could see Keltin's face go red. "And yours."

Viktor drew his lips into a thin line. Keltin just wasn't getting it. For as smart as he was, he couldn't see the chain of reactions his suggestion would set off. *No, that's not entirely true.* Keltin just assumed people followed the rules. He based that assumption on another assumption: that deep down, people were rational and good and just.

That was how Keltin had grown up. In a big house, raised by fine parents who had paid a small fortune so their Talented son could study under a magister because it meant a better life for Keltin. Even better than the life he had been born into, if that were possible.

"Ralad hurt me today," Viktor said. "'buv saw it. A few people did. They slowed when they heard the commotion, and they hurried on by even faster. Ralad didn't care. He's getting bolder. Or drunker. Or both. Any one of those people who saw what happened tonight could report him, but they won't."

Keltin was staring at him in horror. "They might," he said finally, but he sounded feeble.

"Suppose they do. What then? My father pays a fine, maybe spends a few nights in jail. Then he's out again. And if *I* turn him in? If he learned that I was responsible for his incarceration, he would kill me, Keltin."

Abbuv made a sound of fright. Keltin was quiet for a long time.

"I'm sorry," Keltin said. "I can't help you."

Viktor's mouth tightened. "You mean you won't."

Keltin looked away.

"Fine," Viktor said. "We'll do this without you." He turned to Abbuv. "'buv, I need you to--"

Keltin moved to stand in front of Abbuv. "He's not going to help you, either."

"That's not your decision," Viktor said. He took a step toward Keltin, meaning to shove him out of the way. Keltin raised a hand, palm out. Viktor's eyes widened.

"You wouldn't."

"Leave him alone and I won't have to."

Viktor ground his teeth and stole a glance over Keltin's shoulder. Abbuv was staring at him with wide, bright eyes. His mouth hung open.

Abbuv's fright was like a bucket of ice-cold water dumped over his head. Viktor stepped back.

"Fine. I'll do it myself."

Viktor turned and walked into the trees, letting the darkness swallow him up. When he emerged on the road, he glanced back to make sure his friends couldn't see him. Then he ran.

-6-

Viktor was locked in a duel against phantom swordsmen with a stem of wheat when Viktor met him on the road the next morning. Abbuv whirled and jabbed at his chest.

"Got you!" Then he laughed and threw an arm around Viktor's shoulder.

Viktor felt a grin slide into place. Abbuv's mind only had room for joy, and his attitude was like rays of sunshine blasting through rainclouds. He had likely forgotten all about their tense confrontation on the way home last night. He had probably forgotten that Viktor wanted to kill his father, and for a time, Viktor forgot, too. Abbuv jabbered on about the swords he would get to see made at the forge that day. Viktor realized he envied his friend's simple, colorful view of the world and the people who walked it. Ralad treated him horribly, too, but the notion of killing a tormenter was as alien to Abbuv as walking was to a fish.

They parted ways at the green that split Strawbridge in two, and Abbuv took his sunshine with him. Viktor opened the pottery and tried to recreate the bowl Ralad had ruined. As the sky filled up with clouds, his thoughts grew blacker. He thought of Keltin and his friend's selfish refusal to grant the only favor Viktor had ever asked of him. His eyes landed on a shard leftover from yesterday's scuffle-- *A thrashing that's what it was and you didn't do anything you're so weak*--and he entertained visions of Ralad returning today and grabbing him again. Hurting him again.

Viktor hoped he tried. If he did, this time would be different. Viktor would fall to his knees, squealing, letting Ralad think he was breaking his son's spirit along with his arm. Then Viktor would close his fist around the shard and jam it into Ralad's eyes.

Something cold and wet crept along his pant leg. He shivered and jumped up. The rim of the bowl had bowed over like a pouty lip. Cursing, he tried to massage it back into shape, but it was no use. The bowl had regressed to a soggy gray lump.

Disgusted, Viktor scooped the clay into a bin, washed up, and closed the pottery. He stood with his hands on his hips, watching the other vendors set out their wares while townsfolk ambled up and down the road. Three women clustered around a pie stand across from his little stand and breathed in freshly baked apple, grape, and peach pies. Viktor thought they smelled like ashes.

He took two steps on the road toward home, intending to ransack the cupboards and live in the cave until he figured out where he should go next, when the ring of hammer on steel caught his ear. It sounded different today. Faster. The hearty swing of a man who had *not* passed out underneath the kitchen table after downing three jugs of booze.

Viktor changed direction, quickening his step. He rounded a corner and stopped. The forge was in sight, but he didn't want Ralad to see him. He eased back a few steps underneath the overhang of The Gull's Cry tavern and marveled at what he saw.

Ralad stood behind Abbuv, who wore a stained apron. Abbuv's face shone with sweat in the red-orange glare of the furnace. He swung a hammer in smooth, measured beats, pounding a slab of steel. Minutes later, he set the hammer down and glanced at Ralad. Ralad stood absolutely still, saying nothing. Viktor thought his father's face looked pink. That was just the heat from the fire, probably.

"What do I do now?" Abbuv asked. *What'oo I do now?*

Ralad snorted. "You too stupid to have paid attention all these months?"

Viktor felt a desire to charge into the forge and shove his father's head into the flames. He didn't. Abbuv was plenty capable of handling himself.

Coward.

"Well, dummy?" Ralad said. "Hurry up or that steel comes out of your pay."

Abbuv's whole face scrunched up. Then he brightened. With gloved hands he picked up tongs, directed the two metal teeth to bite down on the steel, and carried it over to a tall cylinder filled with oil. The steel sighed, exhaling steam as Abbuv lowered it into its bath. Abbuv watched the bucket closely. His tongue stuck out, and his lips twitched. Viktor realized he was counting. Fifteen seconds later, Abbuv pulled the slab out and stuck it into the furnace.

Another slow count passed. Abbuv pulled the slab from the fire, placed it back on the anvil, and took up his hammer. *Wham. Wham. Wham.*

Viktor smiled with pride. *Way to go, 'buv.*

Looking around, he realized he wasn't the only one cheering Abbuv on. A growing throng of townsfolk crowded around the forge, chattering. Ralad's face darkened but he remained as still and silent as a statue with his big arms folded across his chest.

Rain began to drizzle down. Viktor ventured out from shelter and into the mist. He hung toward the back of the throng and stood on his tiptoes. He couldn't see much, but he could hear Abbuv's steady pounding and the measured puff of the bellows breathing on the coals.

The crowd continued to swell. Their low murmur rose to an excited drone. Viktor eased around to the far edge of the crowd and peered over. Abbuv held a pair of tongs over the oil, preparing to pull out a blade--a real blade!--and carry it over to the furnace.

"You sure about that, dummy?"

Every head swiveled toward Ralad. The babble faded.

Abbuv paused, his face crinkled in confusion. All but the hilt was still submerged in oil.

"Ready for the furnace," he said, although Viktor detected a trace of doubt.

Ralad snorted. "What do I know? Only been a smith my whole life. Do what you want. *You're* the brains around here." He smiled nastily. His yellow teeth glowed dully in the firelight.

All eyes were fastened on Ralad's. All eyes except Viktor's. He tore his gaze away from Ralad and frowned at Abbuv's blade, still clutched precariously in the tongs. With a start, he realized that Ralad was watching the blade, too. The blacksmith's grin broadened.

Viktor felt the familiar anger leak in. He didn't know much about forging swords, but he did know that the balance between tempering and quenching was delicate. And Ralad was distracting his friend on purpose.

"Your blade, Abbuv," Viktor shouted from behind several sets of shoulders.

Abbuv blinked and looked down. His eyes and mouth widened in horror. He yanked the steel free, splashing a few dribbles of oil onto Ralad's apron. Ralad roared as if his arm had been cut off. No one paid him any mind. They watched as Abbuv rushed over to the furnace and shoved the steel in. After a quick count, he carried it over to the anvil, pale and trembling. He raised his hammer, hesitated, and brought it down.

The blade shattered like glass.

Ralad stomped over and tore the tongs from Abbuv's hand.

"Now you've done it, you dumb ox. See what you did, eh? I give you an expensive block of steel to work and this is how you repay me? And repay me you will, dummy. Last time I trust a man-child too stupid to tie his own--"

Abbuv, tears pouring from red, blotchy eyes, had been standing with hunched shoulders and bowed head. Now he gave a great cry and shoved Ralad with his short, stubby arms. Short, stubby, and powerful. Ralad stumbled back, caught his heel on the anvil, and went sprawling to the dirt.

The crowd gasped. Viktor couldn't join in. His throat had swelled shut.

Grunting and wheezing, Ralad hauled himself to his feet and thrust a quivering finger at Abbuv.

"You're finished here, you get me, dummy? You're done. Go home and tell your pa I ain't keepin' you on. Go home and tell him you lost another job 'cause you were too stupid to do as you're told."

Abbuv wilted.

"Stop yelling at him," someone said.

Ralad whirled and faced down the crowd. They shrank back.

"Who spoke up?" Ralad yelled. Spittle flew from his lips. His eyes bulged so large Viktor thought they might leap from their sockets. "Huh? Be a man and say it now I'm lookin' at'cha."

Silently, the crowd dispersed. Viktor slipped back underneath the overhang of the tavern and watched.

"Get out," Ralad screamed at Abbuv. "Don't ever show your face 'round here again."

Slowly, his breath coming in hitching sobs, Abbuv shuffled out of the forge and set out on the road home.

-7-

Viktor trailed after Abbuv until they were out of sight of the forge.

"'buv," he called, loping up behind him.

Abbuv did not turn.

Viktor caught up and put his arm around Abbuv. "I'm sorry, 'buv. You did great. The whole town saw. You did grea--"

Abbuv wailed and threw his arms around him. Viktor patted him, trying not to breathe too deeply. Abbuv was his friend, but he also reeked of sweat and smoke.

Abbuv said something against Viktor's shoulders. It was hard to make out, but Viktor thought he caught "ruined my sword."

An idea came to him.

-8-

Abbuv took a last shuddering breath outside his father's house. His father said grown men didn't cry. They used their minds. He went in and saw his mother sitting in the parlor, holding a glass and staring out one of the big windows. Abbuv smiled and went to sit down beside her.

"You'll get the furniture dirty," she said without looking up.

Abbuv straightened hastily.

"Sorry," he said.

Mother took a sip of her drink. Abbuv told her all about his day at work. Most of it. He decided to leave out the part where his master yelled at him never to back.

Mother didn't say anything. She raised her empty glass to her lips and held it there, staring out the window. Abbuv picked up the glass bottle half-filled with the drink Mother liked and held it out to her. She wrinkled her nose but held out her glass.

"Go bathe."

Abbuv bathed slowly. He was starting to feel scared. It was almost time to talk to his father. To tell him that he had lost his job. His father wouldn't hit Abbuv the way Viktor's father hit him, but he didn't have to.

Resentment flickered inside him. Then it was gone, like a spark on wet wood.

Viktor. Viktor's plan!

Abbuv's face split in a grin.

He dressed and went to the library and stopped outside the door of his father's study. He could hear voices, loud but still muffled. He thought he recognized... yes! Keltin! His other best friend was here, studying. Keltin was always studying. That was why Abbuv's father liked him.

Another spark of resentment. Then: *Viktor's plan!*

Narrowing his eyes, he looked left, then he looked right. Viktor had said to be sneaky. There was no one in sight, so he trailed along one wall covered in bookshelves, pretending to be very interested while making his way to one of the bookshelves on the far wall. The one that held bigger books bound in old leather and covered in big words and symbols. Magic books.

Abbuv chuckled at his sneakiness. His mother was still sitting in the parlor, his father and Keltin were still closed away talking. No one suspected anything.

He jumped when the study door opened. Keltin and his father came out.

"...that last one," his father was saying. "Report back to me if you run into trouble."

Keltin was nodding and had a serious look on his face. Keltin always looked serious when he and Abbuv's father were talking about the Talent.

Then Keltin noticed Abbuv.

"Hey, 'buv!"

Forgetting all about his sneakiness, Abbuv beamed and prepared to give Keltin a big hug. Then his father noticed him.

"You are home early."

It was not a proper question, so Abbuv didn't think he needed to give a proper answer. He just nodded.

"Why are you home?" the magister asked, impatient now.

Abbuv looked down at the floor. He put an arm around his stomach. He was scared again.

His father took the gesture for an answer.

"You should be resting if you feel ill. Why are you in my library?"

Abbuv wet his lips. "I'm looking for a book."

His father's eyebrows lifted. "The words in these books are too complicated for you, Abbuv." He paused. "Too *big*. They are too *big*."

Abbuv wracked his brain for a response. "They smell good," he blurted out. Abbuv had to keep from cackling. He was being so sneaky.

The magister looked confused, then annoyed.

"Very well. Just be careful with them. They are not toys."

"I know."

"And they are not to leave this room."

Abbuv thought it best to just nod at that.

"Have you seen your mother? Tell her to make you a tonic."

"She's looking out the window."

The magister's face tightened.

Abbuv decided to change the subject. "I made a sword today."

His father didn't hear him. He had already turned back to his conversation with Keltin, who was torn between looking concerned for Abbuv and listening to the magister.

Slowly, Abbuv turned back to the shelf, bent down, and inhaled. He hadn't lied about liking how books smelled. He began to feel annoyed. How long did his father and Keltin plan to talk? He wanted them to leave so he could get back to *Viktor's plan*.

After a while, his father patted Keltin on the shoulder.

"Excellent work today, my boy. I'll see you at dawn tomorrow."

"Yes, magister. Thank you, magister."

The magister strode from the room without a backward glance. Abbuv watched him go. He noticed Keltin watching him and put on a big smile.

"I'm sorry you're feeling unwell, 'buv. Your father is right. You should lie down."

Abbuv nodded. "I will. Just looking at books first."

Keltin stretched. "Listen, since you're home early, I thought maybe we could go to the cave. Viktor, too. I think it would do us all some good."

The notion excited Abbuv. He was about to say it sounded like a great idea when he remembered what he would be doing later that evening.

"I'm sick," he said.

"Right. You should lie down, first. But maybe later." Keltin winked. "I'll just tell your father the fresh air would do you good."

Abbuv stayed quiet. His father would listen to Keltin, and he didn't want that.

"No," he said. "Not tonight. I don't feel well. Bye, Keltin."

Keltin blinked. "Oh. All right, then. Maybe tomorrow. Feel better, 'buv."

Abbuv nodded and smiled. He would feel much better by tomorrow morning.

He watched Keltin cross the room. At the doorway, Keltin turned back. Abbuv waved. Keltin waved back and disappeared around the corner.

Abbuv went to the shelf that held some of his father's magical books. He slid one out, looked at it, put it back, and checked over his shoulder. He heard his father shouting at his mother, but he closed his mind off to it. He was just about to give up and try to sneak into his father's study when he found a book bound in leather the color of blood. The spine was ribbed, and the letters on the front were big and black. There were strange pictures on it, little men with horns dancing around a fire. Abbuv's heart began to gallop.

Checking over his shoulder, he slipped the book beneath his shirt--Viktor was just *borrowing* the book; this was not stealing--and snuck out of the house. Once his father's big house was behind him, he took off at a gallop, whooping joyously on his way back to the forge.

He was so sneaky.

-9-

Viktor didn't have a plan. Not really.

He was nestled in the alley beside his father's forge, watching as the tradesmen closed up and trundled home. Dusk faded, and darkness fell over Strawbridge. He peaked out. Still no sign of Abbuv. That was fine. That gave him time to flesh out his glimmer of an idea into what he had described to Abbuv as a *plan*.

And it wasn't a bad idea, either. Right now, Abbuv was rooting around his father's library for a spell book. A "scary-looking" spell book, as Viktor had described it, since Abbuv wouldn't be able to make out most of the words on their covers. A book that Viktor hoped would contain an enchantment he could use to imbue a sword with fast-acting death.

All he was missing was just such an enchantment, and a sword to hold it. Abbuv would supply that part. He would wait for Abbuv here, and then they would break into Ralad's forge, and Abbuv would steal a sword. Probably a short sword; Viktor wouldn't be able to hold anything larger, much less draw enough Talent to imbue it.

He would praise Abbuv's resourcefulness, and then convince Abbuv to let him borrow it. That was the tricky part. Abbuv wouldn't want to part with a sword. He would probably want to sleep with it under his pillow, to show it off to...

Viktor grinned. It was a vulpine expression that would have made Abbuv cower.

You can't take it home, 'buv. What would your father say? No, best to leave it with me. And once I'm done with it, once I've cut out Ralad's black heart and made him eat it, you can--

A single pair of footsteps pounding over the dirt roads reached his ears. They were coming toward the forge. Viktor tensed, not knowing who it was yet still *knowing*. Ralad had rooted out his intentions and was coming for him. He would kill his only son right here in this alleyway, and then tell the militiamen who stumbled across the body that Viktor had *just tripped*, had somehow fallen hard enough to end up disemboweled and headless with his insides painted all over the walls and ground.

Viktor shrank back into the shadows until his back hit stone. He wished he could fold himself and slip between the cracks.

The footsteps slowed near the forge, stopped.

"Viktor?" *Vikor?*

He expelled a quiet breath and stepped out into the road. Abbuv was standing there, holding out a red, leather-bound book, and beaming as if he'd caught the big fish all the grandpas said had lived in the lake outside Strawbridge for a thousand years.

Keltin was with him.

"What are you--?" Viktor began.

Keltin raised a finger to his lips and nodded toward the alley. Without waiting, he ducked into the darkness. Abbuv hesitated until a small white orb, fainter than the one Keltin had created back at the cave, pushed back the shadows, then practically skipped in. Fuming, Viktor trudged behind him.

"Before you get angry at 'buv, I followed him," Keltin said to Viktor. "I was finishing up lessons with the magister when we found 'buv in the library looking..." His lip rose in a half-smile. "Sneaky."

"*Very* sneaky," Abbuv corrected.

"So I followed him and made him tell me what was going on. He told me what Ralad did to him this morning, and how the whole town saw it. And then he showed me this"--he took the book gently from Abbuv--"and I decided to step in." He tapped the book's cover. "Do you have any idea how dangerous this is, Viktor?"

"I'm not trying to put Ralad to sleep, Keltin. *Dangerous* was precisely what I wanted."

"I mean no offense, but your Talent is not great enough to perform any spell you'll find in this tome."

"I don't need a fireworks display," Viktor snapped. "I just want him dead."

"Was that your plan? Have Abbuv steal a weapon and you curse it using this?" He shook the book.

Abbuv frowned. Then his eyes widened and he gasped, looking at Viktor. Viktor couldn't bring himself to meet Abbuv's eyes.

"See what you've done?" he snapped at Keltin. "This is just like you. Always interfering, butting in where you're not wanted. Why don't you just--"

"I'll help you."

Viktor's mouth dangled open. "You will?"

Keltin nodded slowly. "I've been thinking about what you said last night. About Ralad hurting you where people could see. Then there's what he did to 'buv today, and... and your mother."

He took a deep breath. " I have to know, Viktor. Tell me exactly what you saw. I know it's painful, but if I'm going to help you--and you *do* need my help--I need to be sure."

There was a long silence.

"He told the guards she tripped." Viktor's mouth twisted as the memories invaded his mind. He had been coming out of his room when he'd heard his father's drunken complaints. He'd heard the meaty smack of his father's bear-sized paws on his mother's face and frozen in the doorway, watching her spin and crack her head against the mantle and drop to the floor, motionless. And Viktor had stood there, feet nailed to the floor.

"The guards came running when he called for them. *He* called them, Keltin. Don't you see? He knew how it would look, and he didn't care. 'She just tripped.' That's all he said. No fancy story. No remorse for the wife he claimed to have lost in a tragic accident. Not that it mattered. They knew what happened. And they didn't refute it. They were afraid of him."

Just like you *were afraid of him*, the voice whispered, and the rest of that night came rushing back.

From where he'd hid behind his bedroom door, Viktor had watched as the guards looked at Strawbridge's blacksmith, his arms as wide as their torsos, then at each other. They had removed the body without question. When the door closed, Ralad had lumbered across the room, swaying from drink, and shoved through Viktor's door. Viktor had stumbled back until his back hit the wall. Ralad came right up to him and leaned down.

"Your mother's dead, Vikky." The spirits slurred his words. His breath stank of booze and meat and triumph. "She fell down and hit her head." He enfolded one of Viktor's twig arms in his hand. "I guess you saw that."

To his eternal shame, Viktor had looked away. His father had stood in the doorway a few minutes longer, looming over him like a mountain. Viktor had trembled in the mountain's shadow.

Ralad left, slamming the door behind him. Viktor had stood there in the dark. Then he became aware of the warmth spreading down his leg. He had crawled into bed and cried silently, hating his father. Hating himself.

-10-

The three friends stood there, each staring at the ground. Tears cut lines through the dirt on Abbuv's cheeks. Finally, Keltin spoke.

"I'll help you on one condition."

Viktor waited.

"We keep 'buv out of this. "

"No," Abbuv said, and glared at them.

"Yes, Abbuv," Keltin said. "You don't want any part in what we're going to do."

Viktor was stunned into silence. Abbuv usually listened to Keltin. He respected him as an elder of sorts, even though the friends were all the same age. Viktor thought it was because of how Keltin carried himself: serious, authoritative, with an answer to any problem at the ready He reminded Abbuv of his father, except Keltin wasn't ashamed of Abbuv's slow mind. When Keltin said something, Abbuv went along with it, even if Viktor wanted to do the opposite.

To Viktor's and Keltin's utter astonishment, Abbuv shook his head again.

"No. Ralad hurt Viktor." Abbuv's big, hairy fists trembled. "He called me names. He made me feel bad. I want to help Viktor. I *will* help Viktor." Keltin looked helplessly at him, then sighed.

"I don't like it, but I guess I can't stop you."

Abbuv only nodded, as if Keltin were the slow one and had only just arrived at a conclusion Abbuv had figured out hours ago.

Viktor looked between their friends. They had shared a tight bond since they were toddlers tumbling over the Strawbridge green. Now a new bond connected them. It coiled between them like a black snake, draping over their wrists and binding each to the other. Viktor wished he felt regret for involving them. He didn't. He felt only bloodlust.

"What do we do first?" Viktor asked.

Keltin chewed his lip. "You said you wanted an edge."

"I can't go toe to toe with him."

"I think I have something for you. Something that will put both our minds at ease." Keltin looked at the book again and shuddered. "A curse, but not nearly as volatile as these."

"What is it?"

"A spell called the aggrieved. It's cast on a weapon. The weapon seeks out a target to avenge one who was wronged at the target's hands. Once the weapon avenges the victim, the spell dissipates."

Viktor narrowed his eyes, thinking. "How does it seek its mark?"

Keltin shrugged. He looked uncomfortable. Viktor felt a twinge of doubt. Keltin's smugness annoyed him, but he had to admit that he, like Abbuv, felt more confident when Keltin felt confident.

"Like any other weapon, I suppose," Keltin said. "Someone must wield it."

Viktor made a sound of exasperation. "If it was that easy, I'd just go home and grab a knife."

Keltin lifted a finger. "The aggrieved accounts for that. You see, it..." His brow furrowed. "The spell book reads, *Vengeance flies as straight as an arrow, and the aggrieved always strikes true*. I take that to mean it cannot be stopped once the spell has been cast."

Keltin fell silent again, studying the ground. His lips moved as if reciting a passage. Viktor shifted from foot to foot.

"Let's get started, then."

"Not tonight. There's no time. I need you to gather ingredients for me. And it has to be you, Viktor. Abbuv and I can only contribute two elements for this spell. My contribution is its casting. Abbuv's contribution is a weapon forged with intent."

"Intent?"

"A new weapon, one unsullied by any other purpose," Keltin explained. He laughed softly. It held no mirth. "We need you after all, 'buv."

Abbuv stood straighter.

"All right," Viktor said. "What do you need from me?"

"Two ingredients, and they'll both be hard to come by."

"Name them."

Keltin ran a hand through his hair.

"The first is the blood of the victim. Your mother."

Viktor felt ice form in his veins. "How am I supposed to get that?"

"The ingredient isn't literal. You'll need something *of* her, though." Keltin swallowed. "A bit of flesh, or..."

Viktor felt his stomach lurch. "You mean I have to dig her up?"

Keltin's tone hardened. "If you can't do this--"

Viktor met Keltin's gaze. "What else?"

"This next one *is* literal, I'm afraid. If you can't go through with it, I'll understand."

"Out with it."

Keltin studied him for a moment. Then he spoke.

-11-

Viktor arrived home after dark. Ralad was waiting for him at the kitchen table. Three empty bottles of booze lay on their sides. Fluid leaked from their necks, pooling in small puddles along the table.

"Where you been, Vikky?"

Avoiding Ralad's eyes, Viktor hung his cloak by the door and circled around the table to the small fireplace. A kettle of stew boiled over a small flame, filling the modest home with the scent of meat and vegetables.

"Just closing up the shop. I stayed late to talk to some customers. They wanted--"

"You're lyin'," Ralad said, his voice just above a whisper. "I stopped by the shop on my way home. You wasn't there. Asked the butcher and the cobbler if they seen you. They said you closed up early. Early this mornin'. So I'll ask again: where you been, Vikky?"

Viktor could feel Ralad's eyes boring into his back. He turned around.

"I didn't feel well."

"So you was out picking flowers until after dark? That it?"

"No. I went out walking. I thought the fresh air might clear my head."

"They run out of fresh air at the pottery?"

"The butcher's bloody meat tends to spoil the air a bit."

Ralad snorted and flapped a hand at him. "Get me my dinner."

Viktor rummaged through the cupboards and produced two porcelain bowls--his mother had made them both; they were the finest items the family owned--and a clay ladle. Mother had made that, too. His thoughts strayed, as they had since leaving his clandestine meeting with Keltin and 'buv, back to the task Keltin had set him and the sheer impossibility of it. *More impossible than digging up Mother's corpse?* He shuddered. *Yes,* he decided. *Mother can't fight back.*

As if to provide the motivation he needed, Ralad spoke again.

"Butcher's shop don't smell that bad to me. You got your mother's weak stomach, boy. She was weak, and so are you."

Ralad's words, and the contempt behind them, thawed his dread. Viktor gave himself no time to think. He turned, raised the bowl of soup above Ralad's head with both hands, and brought it crashing down with all his might. There was a sharp crack as the bowl broke into three big fragments. Soup splattered against the tabletop, the wall, and clotted in Ralad's greasy hair. The blacksmith grunted and slumped forward, as if in prayer to the gods.

Calmly, Viktor examined the jagged shard in his hand. He could end it right here. He could stab Ralad with the shard, poke holes in him until he drained out all over the floor. *Death by dishware.* Dishware his mother had made. It was perfect, really.

Ralad groaned and began to stir.

Panicked, Viktor slashed the shard across the back of Ralad's neck. A line of red opened up and drooled down into Ralad's collar. The big man howled. Viktor spared a glance at the point of his shard. It was flecked with red.

Blood of the mark.

Ducking Ralad's flailing arms, Viktor dashed toward the front door and fled, his father's shouts following him into the night. He would return home only once more.

-12-

Viktor wandered the wilderness, alternating between staring blankly ahead and at the shard in his hand as if wondering how it had come to be there. The horizon began to lighten, and Viktor realized he'd been circling the cave, never wandering too far from it. He headed toward it and saw a tongue of firelight flicker from the mouth. Keltin and Abbuv sat on their rocks, cooking breakfast and talking quietly.

At Viktor's approach, Abbuv leaped to his feet and enveloped him in a bear hug. Keltin waited until Abbuv had released him to come forward.

"Did you get it?"

Wordlessly, Viktor nodded.

"Want breakfast, Viktor?" Abbuv asked from around a mouthful of eggs.

Viktor smiled, but shook his head.

"You know what comes next," Keltin said.

Viktor's throat seized up. He nodded, turned, and left.

-13-

He took his time releasing the animals from the barn that stood about a half-mile outside the cemetery. Then he gathered what little Talent he had and ran his hand along bales of hay arranged in one corner. A Talented of Keltin's strength could have ignited them from afar. Viktor had to make do with scant resources, as always.

Smoke rose from the bales in a lazy curl. Viktor hurried out and made his way around the cemetery, watching the lone girl adorned in the cloak and collar meander up and down rows of gravestones. She was in the affluent section of the cemetery, where mausoleums and crypts decorated with fresh flowers and presided over by marble statues stood with their backs to the lumpy headstones that made up the poorer section. When she mounted the steps to the largest crypt, Viktor slipped behind a mausoleum and peered out, watching her.

The novice brushed away a few leaves from the top of a marble gargoyle, sniffed the air, and looked up. Thick plumes of smoke rose up from the barn. Flames capered around the rear wall, feasting. Boredom slid off her face. For several moments she was as still as the marble gargoyle, its mouth open in a fearsome roar, hers agape in fright and indecision. Then she dashed toward the growing roar of fire and the frightened bleats of farmyard residents.

Tightening his hold on the shovel, Viktor moved in a crouch to the last row of headstones and faced his mother. Her headstone seemed suited to her: plain, small, unassuming. Not beautiful, not ugly. Just sort of *there*. Like him.

Weak, Ralad's voice whispered in the back of his mind.

Stop thinking and just do it.

He gathered his Talent and put his hand to the cold, hard earth. The dirt began to warm and soften. Perspiration broke out over his face. Frustration threaded through his anxiety. Keltin would have made this look easy. Keltin made everything look easy.

By the time the ground was soft enough to break, his clothes were drenched. Cool air plastered them to his skin. Viktor rose, shivering, and planted his shovel. Its head slid into the earth like a fork sinking into moist cake. He threw dirt to one side and dug again. His arms were shaking. Several minutes later, he set the shovel aside and heated the ground again. Cramps seized his stomach. Voices rose up from the barn. They were high-pitched, sad and frightened. A woman was sobbing. Smoke drifted up and out in a thick plume.

You shouldn't have done that.

The sound of his mother's voice cut through his concentration. He picked up his shovel and returned to digging, faster than before. The top of her coffin--a plain wooden box--appeared. Viktor slipped down into the hole, oblivious to the dirt streaking his pants, boots, and shirt. He was not oblivious to the worms wriggling through the walls, the ground, and over his mother's box. It was thin. The scent of earth and bad meat pounced on him. He gagged and clapped his hands over his face and fell back against the dirt wall. He tried to turn away but couldn't. The gap between earth and box was thin.

He reached toward the lid with one hand.

Is this how I raised you, Viktor? She didn't sound accusatory. Only sad and dispirited, the way she had sounded in life.

He jerked his hand back and moaned.

A bit of flesh. That was all Keltin needed. He had his belt knife. Just open the lid, feel around with the knife--it was a small box--and then go back to the cave. Back to his friends and away from the accusing look he would see in her blank eyes as they sank deeper into her sockets.

Is this how I raised you?

Weak. Ralad's voice. *Coward.*

Viktor slumped over his mother's box and wept.

-14-

"Did you... get what we need?" Keltin asked when Viktor came walking slowly into the cave.

Viktor nodded and sat on his rock. Keltin lifted his hand, then let it drop.

"You hold onto it. I'll let you know when I need it."

Keltin left soon after, off to his lesson's with the magister. Abbuv and Viktor stayed in the cave. They didn't say much. Abbuv walked around the cave, drawing on the walls with stones and glancing into the dark throat that led into the cave's belly. Viktor stared into the fire, trying not to think about the revelation he'd had on his way back to the cave. His mad scheme was now his one and only option. There was no going back.

Keltin returned late that afternoon. His face was ashen, and his eyes were jittery.

"I told the magister I wasn't feeling well," he said, sitting down and dumping his books and a large sack beside him. "And that's the truth."

Viktor gestured at the sack. "Is that it?"

"Yes. Everything's ready."

Abbuv joined them. They spent their last evening together talking in snatches, speaking a few words and retreating to private thoughts. By sundown, all talk had died out. At full dark, Keltin gathered his things, and paused.

"Are you absolutely sure about this, Viktor?"

Viktor rose slowly. "Are you backing out?"

Keltin hesitated. He shook his head.

"Practicing this art could cost me everything. But you're my friend. You need my help, and you've got it."

Viktor turned to Abbuv. Abbuv nodded, his expression grave.

"Let's go," Viktor said.

-15-

They split up and made their way to the alleyway near the forge. Viktor worried that Ralad might see them, but he overheard some of the other tradesmen say that the blacksmith had not gone into work that day. *Maybe I killed him*, Viktor thought. He banished the thought. He had never been that lucky.

When the street was deserted, Keltin ushered them inside.

"Get set up, 'buv," Keltin said. "I'll cast the screen."

Abbuv went to the anvil and placed Keltin's sack atop it. Reverently, he drew back the cloth to reveal a slab of steel. He stroked it as if it were a small, furry pet, and turned his attention to the furnace and bellows.

Viktor inspected the forge, noting contradictions for the first time. Tools were arranged neatly on shelves and around the furnace. The counters were pitted and stained, but clear and tidy. There was no trace of the drink; no scent of ale hanging in the air, no discarded bottles or steins. Viktor wondered why Ralad's pride in his work and forge had never carried over to his family and home. With a twinge of regret, he pushed the thought aside. It was too late to mend that fence.

He watched as Keltin walked the perimeter of the forge, muttering under his breath and waving one hand. When he finished, Keltin went to stand beside Viktor.

"What did you do?" Viktor asked.

Keltin gestured beyond the forge. At first, Viktor saw nothing-- then his eyes widened. A fog was creeping in. It swallowed rows of tiny homes and rolled over stalls, stands, and shops. The fog slowed as it neared the forge, pulling up short of the walls.

Behind them, Ralad's furnace roared. The bellows exhaled like a winded giant. Viktor flinched, then caught Keltin's smile.

"Don't worry," Keltin said. "No one..." He leaned back against the door and stifled a yawn. "No one can hear or see us."

"Are you alright?" Viktor asked.

"I didn't sleep well last night," Keltin said, covering another yawn. He pushed away from the door and went over to where Abbuv was tapping away at the block of steel. He began to speak in slow, drawn-out phrases, waving his hands over the block.

Viktor let his eyes drift to Abbuv's work, but he wasn't *watching*. Not really. His anger had washed over him again, soaking through to his bones. This was Ralad's fault. His mother's death, forcing Viktor to drag his friends into his battle. Ralad was responsible for all of it.

Sometime later, Viktor heard Keltin tapping his foot against the floor. He looked up to see the novice looking at him and gesturing toward a wooden cylinder. Abbuv reached over and dipped a poker with a glowing tip into it. Oil bubbled out and slobbered down the sides. Keltin's tone had grown louder, harsher. His face was twisted, and he spat more than spoke the incantation. Viktor noticed that the forge had grown uncomfortably warm, as if they were in a small, windowless room at the height of summer.

Or trapped in a burning barn.

Viktor hustled over to the anvil, digging the bloody shard out of his pocket. Using pincers, Abbuv dipped his glowing blade into the oil. At the same instant, Viktor dropped the shard into the oil. Viktor squinted as the forge grew hotter still.

Then he remembered his next and final contribution.

Positioning his back to Keltin, he fished another item from his pocket and dropped it into the oil. He braced himself, expecting the cylinder to explode and drench them in scalding oil, or for the sword to erupt in a shower of shards that slashed them to ribbons.

Nothing happened. Viktor relaxed. He looked up and got caught in Abbuv's stare. *Did he see?*

Before either man could speak, an eerie red light oozed out from the cylinder and spread outward, bathing the forge in a low, red glow. Oil bubbled up and splashed out. Keltin cut off the incantation and raised his hands to his face as a hot wind rose from the cylinder. Viktor tried to cry out but the wind stole his breath. The heat plastered his clothes to his body. Sweat stung his eyes.

"--it," Keltin was saying between gasps for breath. "Take the aggrieved."

-16-

Squinting, Viktor turned back to the anvil. Abbuv stood over it, holding his sword in a gloved hand. The other hung at his side. He gaped at the sword as if mesmerized, unfazed by the rising heat. Abbuv noticed Viktor and offered him the sword.

Viktor considered for only a moment. Shielding his face against the heat with one arm, he reached out blindly, found the hilt, and closed his fist around it. All at once, the forge grew cool. Viktor opened his eyes. The first thing he saw was the sword. It was beautiful. The blade, a short sword, gleamed in the firelight from the furnace and extended to a fine point. No chips or scratches marred its length. Viktor tightened his hold and smiled as his fingers slipped between the ribs of the hilt for a surer, more confident grip.

He looked up at Abbuv in wonder. Abbuv was more than a budding swordsmith. He was an artisan, and his first creation had all the trappings of a masterwork.

Then the aggrieved took him.

A thread of heat wormed its way through his hand, up his arm, and into his brain. He opened his mouth to cry out as some unseen force wrested volition from him.

--Be silent. The voice was low and sibilant, but soothing, firm yet gentle.

Viktor closed his mouth.

"Are you all right?" Keltin asked.

It was all Viktor could do to keep from striking Keltin down right there. He realized he hated Keltin. Hated him for pretending to be Viktor's friend when he probably joked about Viktor's paltry Talent and poor family behind Viktor's back.

--Not him, the aggrieved whispered. *Not yet. The mark. Feed me the mark.*

Like the wind throwing rain around, the aggrieved redirected Viktor's wrath. Ralad. Ralad had ruined his life. Ralad would pay.

"I'm fine," Viktor said with difficulty, not trusting himself to meet Keltin's eyes. Instead he looked at Abbuv and managed a smile. Abbuv, who had looked worried, grinned back.

"I have to go," Viktor said, looking out over Strawbridge. The fog was receding, as if shrinking away from him. Gray light touched the horizon. Had they really been here all night?

"Where?" Keltin said.

"Home," Viktor said. "To Ralad." He knew Ralad would be there. Probably dumping booze down his throat. But he also *knew*, because the aggrieved *knew*. Viktor was looking right at him-- through the stands, stores, and houses of Strawbridge, and through the wall of the home where he'd grown up.

Without another word, he turned from his friends and strode out the door.

-17-

Ralad lurched up from the table when Viktor barged in. Growling, he deliberated between threatening his son or thrashing him without delay. He took a closer look at Viktor and his mouth snapped shut. Maybe the boy really was sick. Viktor's eyes were bloodshot. His skin was pale as snow. Even his lips were drained of color. He stood hunched, like a cowed dog. Or a dog ready to pounce.

Ralad tried to speak again and had to swallow past a lump in his throat. That made him angry. Then he took another look at his son. Viktor had one arm behind his back.

"What you have there, boy?"

Slowly, Viktor withdrew the aggrieved from behind his back.

Ralad raised his brow. "And what do you mean to do with that?"

But Ralad knew. He planted his feet and waited.

--Feed me.

Viktor leaped forward, riding a wave of rage.

-18-

Keltin and Abbuv shuffled into the cave and sank onto their rocks. Abbuv yawned while Keltin got a fire going.

"Get some sleep, 'buv," he said thickly. It took all his energy just to sit upright.

Abbuv perked up. He pointed to his bedroll.

"We're on a camping trip?" he asked.

"Mm-hmm. We sure are." *Only without the fish and ghost stories, because we're living one. It's real, and we're writing it. Right now.*

Abbuv spread his bedroll by the fire and snuggled down deep. Keltin poked at the fire, trying not to think about what Viktor was doing right now but unable to think about much else. He had cast the spell, and that bonded him to it. He could feel it the same way Viktor had felt Ralad. The mark.

Keltin was connected to the mark, too. Ralad was still alive. He was angry, and frightened. No, that was like calling the magister a *competent* sorcerer. Ralad was terrified. Part of Keltin was glad about that. Ralad deserved to die in the throes of stark, raving terror for what he had done to his family. Part of him hated that he, Keltin, had consented to set these events in motion.

"'buv?" he said.

Abbuv opened his eyes and blinked sleepily. "Huh?"

"How are you feeling about all this? About what we did last night?"

Abbuv was quiet for a long time.

"Sad."

Keltin nodded. "I feel sad, too. Do you think Ralad deserves to die?"

Keltin regretted the question instantly. Such ponderings were too vast for Abbuv. Such ponderings were too vast for *him*.

Abbuv propped up on an elbow.

"Ralad is a bad man."

Keltin thought about that. It wasn't exactly an answer, but it left no room for dispute. He opened his mouth to ask what Abbuv thought they should do next. His friend was staring into the flames, looking melancholy. Keltin decided to change the subject.

"You made a beautiful sword, 'buv," he said cheerily.

Abbuv brightened. "I love it. Viktor helped."

Viktor's contributions dimmed Keltin's attempt at brightness.

"I guess you saw what Viktor added to the oil," he said.

Abbuv nodded. "He put in a shard with his dad's blood on it."

Keltin felt his heart begin to beat faster. *Blood of the mark. That would do it.* He didn't want to ask the next question, but morbid curiosity tugged on him.

"Did you see what else he put in?"

Abbuv frowned. "Can't remember."

Keltin sighed, partly in relief. Abbuv certainly didn't deserve to be haunted by the memory of his best friend depositing one of his dead mother's fingers or a scrap of her cheek like it was some special ingredient in a stew. Neither did he.

"Oh!" Abbuv said, startling Keltin. "I remember, now! It was a rock."

-19-

Decades of hard labor in the forge had shaped Ralad into a man as hard as the iron and steel he beat and bent to his will. Many patrons of The Gull's Cry had put that hardness to the test by imbibing in one cup too many and confusing alcohol-fueled stupidity for boldness. Ralad welcomed that. He enjoyed caving in faces with fists bigger than his biggest hammer, and the feeling of bones crumbling beneath his fingers. Like drinking, brawling was a release, an escape from the reality that he had sacrificed his dream of becoming the king's personal smith just because he'd let one drink too many convince him to charm the flabby pottery wench who had wandered into The Gull's Cry for a cup of hot cider one cold winter night.

Tonight, his son, the scrawny, bookish consequence of his moment of weakness, had decided he was brave. Like father, like son, Ralad supposed. Ralad had made the same mistake once, and his pa had broken him for it. It hadn't been the first time, but it had been the last. Now, Vikky would get what he deserved. What he'd had coming for him for years, just like his mother. Ralad would have to--

Viktor sprang at him like a snake with a single, gleaming tooth. Ralad took an instant, unwillingly, to admire the craftsmanship of the weapon. It was a smith's instinct. For all his failings as a husband and a father, he was damn good at his job, and he knew quality when he saw it. Then he roared and threw himself to one side. Booze made him clumsy. He crashed against the wall, rocking a shelf filled with the pottery wench's doodads that tipped over to the floor. Snarling, he spun around unsteadily--and for the first time since leaving his pa's house forever, Ralad was afraid.

Viktor was coming for him. He clutched his short sword like a dagger. His stride was quick and sure. Ralad could feel the heat of his son's loathing, as if his eyes fired flaming arrows.

Ralad bellowed again and was aghast when Viktor's lips curled upward. Viktor--*Vikky*--had heard a tremor of fear in that cry. Ralad roared louder, as if to drown his cowardice. He balled his hands together as in prayer, and then brought them crashing down where Viktor stood.

He might as well have tried to pummel smoke. Viktor stepped aside almost casually. Ralad pitched forward, off-balance, and Viktor darted back in and caught him on the end of his blade.

Ralad tried to scream as the blade slipped smoothly into his belly. He managed a yelp that trailed off in a long wheeze. The steel burned like a bar of iron fresh from the furnace, white-hot and ready to be shaped. He could feel it burning as it slid deeper into him, a monster that chewed through flesh and guts at a touch.

There was a sharp tug, and the burning intensified. Ralad looked down. There was a gash in his belly. It was smoking, and long, red vines poked out of it, pink and glistening like worms after a rain. He tried to shove the worms back in. They poked out between his fingers.

A hand on his shoulder guided him to his knees. He looked up at Viktor through a blur of tears. *Cryin. I'm cryin.* He wondered why. There wasn't much pain, now. Just a low, dull throbbing in his middle.

Viktor knelt before him and cocked his head, as if unsure what he was looking at. Then he drew his sword along Ralad's throat. Once again, instinct compelled Ralad to admire the craftsmanship of the weapon. He barely felt anything. The edge of the blade was fine. He felt his chest grow wet and warm, then his middle, his arms, his hands. He looked down. Blood covered him like an apron.

Blood. My blood.

Viktor pressed harder and began to saw back and forth, and that Ralad *did* feel. He tried to scream but managed only a thick, gurgling cry as the blade parted flesh and tendons as easily as it would have parted water.

-20-

--Behold your prize.

Viktor looked down. In his right hand he held the aggrieved. In his left, he held Ralad's head. He raised it and looked Ralad in the eye for the first time in years. The blacksmith's eyes were wide. They blinked once, and his jaw shifted, as if were searching for a word. Viktor watched as Ralad's eyes slowly glazed over. The face became waxen. Blood dripped from the severed neck like booze from the empty bottles on the table.

An overwhelming sense of loss filled him. Viktor threw the head aside and slid down the wall. He was shuddering uncontrollably. The anger was gone, now. He felt utterly spent, and more than a little ill. His grip on the sword slackened.

All at once the aggrieved flared up. Keltin screamed as the blade went from warm to blistering. Raged flooded his senses and cut through his scream.

--He was never your father. He planted his seed in your mother out of drunken lust.

Yes, Viktor thought, his fingers tightening on the hilt. Ralad had never loved them. He had hated them. They had been a drain on him--the pottery maker who had swooned over the handsome blacksmith and his rippling muscles, and the son who had always been small and physically inferior.

--Keltin. Keltin finds you inferior.

A black rage rolled over Viktor like the fog that had settled over Strawbridge.

Keltin. Smug, superior Keltin, with his father's money and his father's name.

--Keltin holds us in his hand.

Viktor understood immediately. Keltin had cast the spell, held the aggrieved and Viktor like a dog on a leash. Could Keltin sever it?

No. He was missing a vital component. But he was a threat, and had to be stopped.

Viktor stood absolutely still, listening to the aggrieved's counsel.

-21-

Keltin felt Ralad's death. It chimed in the back of his mind like a tiny bell swallowed by the rush of a waterfall.

"What did you say, 'buv?" he asked. His throat was dry, and his words came out as a croak.

"A rock. Viktor added a rock to my sword."

Keltin's mind raced. "Tell me exactly what you saw."

"Well..." Abbuv scrunched his face. "First, Viktor put in a piece of a broken bowl. It was bloody."

"And?" Keltin leaned forward. "What next? Be absolutely sure."

Abbuv sat up, frowning. "Then the rock. Just those things."

Keltin bolted to his feet, looking around frantically. The cave felt like it was closing in. *A rock. Not a piece of his mother. Not the blood of the victim.*

"Keltin?" Abbuv stood up and tugged on his sleeve. "What's wrong?"

Holding up a hand, Keltin closed his eyes. His connection to the mark had been severed. Ralad was dead. The aggrieved had killed the mark, satisfying one end of the spell. But it had no victim. Only a boundless appetite for vengeance.

He took a deep breath. His connection to the aggrieved made him feel warm, like a fever. A fever that was growing hotter.

His eyes shot open.

"Abbuv. Hide. Now."

-22-

The aggrieved's whisper slid through Viktor's mind like dry leaves skittering across dry roads. Shops, homes, and the walls of Strawbridge flew by him. Then he was among the rolling hills and trees, and those flew by in a blur, too. His lungs felt like they were about to burst. He begged for a moment to rest. The aggrieved didn't hear him. Didn't hear, or didn't listen. It stoked the fire blazing out of control in his gut, throwing on memories that fed his rage like dry kindling.

Keltin strutting around in his novice robe fingering his silver collar.

Keltin bragging about being chummy with the magister.

Keltin getting his tuition paid for by his father, who shrugged off the cost of his son's education as if it were a loaf of bread.

Keltin withholding help from Viktor, forcing Viktor to go along with *his* plan.

--He hides from us.

Viktor stopped. He stood upright, but his chest heaved and burned. His face was flushed. His stomach roiled. He wanted to vomit, to lie down and sleep, to forget the way the blood had spurted and seeped from the stump of his father's neck. The aggrieved wouldn't let him. It forced his eyes wide so it could peer out of them like windows from where it held sway in Viktor's mind.

The entrance to the cave was empty. Abbuv's bedroll lay discarded. Viktor felt invisible fingers pinch his eyelids into a squint, and he began to peer around. He wanted to struggle, but part of him was relieved the aggrieved was in control. He was tired of thinking.

--There.

Viktor's head swiveled. His eyes fixed on a tree. He let the aggrieved march him over to the tree. He stood in front of it, reeling like a drunk. He felt his arm cock back. His fist tightened. And he impaled the trunk. The blade slid through wood and bark as easily as it had slid through Ralad's fresh. He caught a flash of movement beside him. Tearing the blade free, he pivoted to face Keltin.

"Viktor," Keltin began, and went pale. Viktor felt his lips peel back. He bared his teeth in a feral grin. His vision swam in a red haze, and he knew Keltin was staring into eyes the rich, dark color of blood.

Keltin raised his palms. His hands shook.

"Viktor, you don't have to--"

Viktor went for his throat.

-23-

Keltin began his incantation in a shaky tone that rose in a scream. Viktor lunged at him, straining to reach him with the bloodstained tip of the sword. Keltin threw himself back, fighting against the instinct to throw his hands up over his face. His palms glowed and sprayed a mist of light that congealed into a luminescent wall. Keltin thudded to the ground and scrambled up. Viktor had crashed against the wall but had already regained his feet. He was still smiling that awful, savage grin. Keltin raised his palms again and muttered. The wall stretched to either side.

"Viktor, please. You have to let go of the sword. Just open your hand and let it--"

Viktor cleaved through the wall of light, parting it like a curtain. It exploded in a blinding flash. Keltin staggered back, blinking. Bright lights popped and burned across his vision. He heard a rush of footsteps through the grass and raised his hands again. Thin lines of fire extended from his fingertips and slashed at the air like whips. The tendrils would do no lasting harm; Keltin had tempered them to be just hot enough to surprise Viktor into releasing the blade. Once Viktor had come to his senses, Keltin would destroy it. *I never should have made it. This is my fault.*

He continued to walk steadily backward, blinking and listening for Viktor's screams of pain. His vision was returning, fading in like dawn breaking through clouds. The trees came into focus first, dark shapes against a lightening sky. He saw Viktor, and Viktor wasn't screaming. He weaved around the tendrils like a graceful dancer, pirouetting and pivoting. Coming for him. The sword--

--I am the aggrieved I will break you crack you drink your blood devour your flesh--

--flicked out in front of him like a tongue eager for a taste of flesh.

Keltin sidestepped, cutting the tendrils and drawing in more Talent. Sweat plastered his shirtsleeves to his skin. He spoke his next spell haltingly. A sharp gale of wind rose up from his hands, throwing twigs and dirt and loose grass. To Keltin's relief, Viktor ceased pushing forward. He was squinting against the wind, which had risen to a howl. He bent forward, one arm shielding his face, his bent legs pumping forward but sliding backward. His feet cut deep grooves in the earth.

Keltin felt the spell wavering. His arms trembled, and his head was growing heavy. With a shout, he closed his fists, severing the spell, and leaped at his friend with his arms thrown wide. Viktor waited until the last moment and leaped clear. Keltin hit the ground chest-first. Breath left his lungs in a whoosh. He lay there for a moment that stretched out into eternity.

In his mind, he scrambled to his feet and drove Viktor to the ground with a blast of raw Talent. Viktor dropped the sword; Keltin melted it down to mush, and the three friends left Strawbridge to start new lives in a new place. Perhaps they would go to Solomnia. Abbuv could finish his apprenticeship under the smithy and forge armor and blades--maybe not blades--for the king. Keltin would study under the royal magister, and, one day, take his place in court.

And Viktor. Viktor could do anything he wanted. He was so smart. His mother had known that, but had been in no position to offer her son the opportunity he needed to get away. Or, perhaps, had been too afraid to take action. None of that mattered now. In the capitol, Viktor could carve out any life he wanted.

Keltin smiled. It was a lovely vision. But it wasn't what happened.

-24-

Viktor saw red. Viktor He felt warm liquid splash against his face, and became aware of his muscles crying out for relief as his arms rose and fell, rose and fell, stabbing at something that had been hard at first but was soft and wet and squishy now. The motion of his arms slowed. He sagged to one side and breathed in the scent of damp earth.

--Rise.

I can't. Please.

Boiling anger filled him. He struggled to sit up. The aggrieved sent out waves of disgust and contempt, but Viktor did not rise to the bait. He couldn't. He was spent. After what seemed like hours, he sat up and looked around. He was in the woods. The cave was off to his left. Keltin and 'buv were in there, waiting for him. Viktor frowned. That wasn't right.

The aggrieved cupped his chin in an invisible hand and began to rotate his head around. Viktor wanted to resist. He thought about throwing away the sword and running into the cave, but abandoned all notions of resistance. Against the aggrieved, he was like a babe trying to push away a man the size of Ralad. Anger, he decided, was exhausting. Holding onto it sucked up all a man's energy like a drop of water on the dry, cracked plains of the Aribad Plains.

His eyes landed on Keltin, and then he did try to wrench his head free. As he predicted, the aggrieved held him in place with ease, forcing Viktor to see what it had done. What *he* had done.

Keltin lay on his back with his head arched back, his mouth open in a silent scream. His hands were claws. His chest had been cracked open like a shattered melon. Viscera and blood were splashed all over the ground and trees, and across Viktor's clothes and face.

He tried to close his eyes. The aggrieved permitted it, and preyed on it.

--Weak, it whispered in its dry and dusty voice. *You are weak, just as your father said.*

Rage spouted up in a geyser. He threw back his head and screamed. The sunny afternoon sky beamed back at him. His scream went on and on until his voice cracked and died, but his fury only grew blacker. Then, to his amazement, tears slid down his cheeks. His chest hitched in wracking sobs.

--Weak, the aggrieved said, only now it sounded worried. *Stop being a coward. Keltin deserved to die. Your father deserved to die.*

Viktor sobbed harder. The sensation of his grief colliding against his rage was like ice-cold water flooding a burning village: the water extinguished the flames, but ruin in its wake. He grieved for Keltin, his friend, a promising life that he had extinguished. He grieved for his mother. She had been poor and not the most beautiful of women. But she had been happy, fulfilled by a job she loved and a son gifted with a sharp mind, a kind heart, and an eye for beauty.

Viktor even grieved for his father. Ralad had sacrificed much to provide for his family, even if his provisions had left scars.

I forgive you, Father. I forgive you, and I'm sorry.

The sword slipped from his hand. Still sobbing, Viktor turned away from Keltin's remains. His mother would have been ashamed for him. He had known that, and ignored it. Worse, his anger had snared his friends like fish on barbed hooks. Keltin had paid for it with his life. There was still hope for 'buv.

Opening his eyes, he stood and brushed the dirt from his pants. He felt exhausted, but hopeful. He would go to the cave and get Abbuv. They would go back to Strawbridge together, and Viktor would confess his crimes.

The aggrieved.

He froze, remembering the sword. He needed to destroy it, to melt it down to slag. But he didn't think he could stand to touch it. Moreover, he didn't think he should. He had broken its hold on him, but he was in no condition to fight it off if it tried to take him again. Scanning the ground, he stooped over and gathered a handful of leaves. They would do as a makeshift glove.

As he straightened, the tip of the aggrieved burst through his chest and punctured his heart.

-25-

Abbuv wrenched the sword free from the hole in Viktor's back and gazed at it adoringly, paying no mind to the sight of Viktor crumpling to the ground in a heap. He had no mind for Viktor's death because *his sword was talking to him*, filling his head with all sorts of nice words. The sword praised him for creating it, and

Abbuv felt he deserved that praise. No one ever said nice things to him. Keltin and Viktor had, but they had only been pretending.

The sword made a suggestion. Timidly, asking him if *he* thought it was a good idea. Abbuv appreciated that. He'd never realized how bossy Keltin and Viktor could be. Always herding him this way and that, expecting him to go along with their plans. Abbuv had plenty of good ideas, too, but he had to give the sword credit: this was the best idea *ever*.

Turning away, he found his way to the main road and started toward Strawbridge. The sword had suggested that Abbuv go have a talk with his father. Abbuv smiled, listening to the birds sing at one another from their branches.

Yes, that was a fine idea indeed.

Digger's Lament
by Cameron Suey

In the night, the valley was so filled with smoke that Palta could not make out the dimmest guidestars. He had a dozen other ways to divine the time and his location, but it still filled him with a slippery dread, a feeling of being half-lost and pointed in the wrong direction. His tent, barely half the size of the reeves' tents and still stinking of the marsh crossing, seemed to close in on him like a fist as he tried to catch a few fitful moments of sleep.

He'd wet his scarf and tied a thin strip to his face, but the sharp stench of the burned town and a hundred cook-fires crept through, clinging to the soft tissue of his eyes and nose.

Outside, he could hear the 17th Expeditionary Host of Imperial Kattaka, the insectile buzz of a thousand men talking grimly by the fires, reeking of dismay and unease. He knew it wouldn't be long until they started to blame him for the men who'd died that day.

It'd been only a few half-drunk cavalry riders and their gida mounts in the front of column who'd been killed in the trap on the river crossing. But it was symbolic, a bloody nose they had not expected. It wasn't enough that they'd burned the little town without a name to the ground, and strung the surviving Selti ambushers up from the boughs of the fruit trees by the river. They would want someone else to blame, and sooner or later, it would fall to the man that had led them this far south.

Palta waited until the skittering anxiety was too much, and he flung back the woolen flap at the entrance of his tent. He drew the hood of his cloak up, and tucked his brown and gray hair back to don the black-lacquered mask. The entrance of his tent faced away from the Host, but he still scanned his surroundings with quick, birdlike glances. The holes in the black mask prevented his wide eyes from their full range of vision, but it would keep any of the men of the Host from seeing his face.

The mask, usually reserved for defectors or the Emperor's own most secret advisers, now kept his identity unknown from the fighting men. If he survived, and could show them the path over the godwall, he would be pardoned, all his years spent as a digger, criminal, and heretic erased. He could be just another Kattakan citizen. Palta would have accepted any terms that freed him from the dank stone cell beneath the Priory of Virtue.

He slung his wood and horn bow onto his shoulder, and donned the light pack containing his quiver of ceramic-tipped arrows and a short stone blade. The mask granted him theoretical amnesty, but feeling the seething need for retribution on the smoky air, he took no chances. He had to get out of the valley, to where the autumn air was clear and the stars were not silenced. He would sleep on the ridge, out under the stars, like the good old days.

He scaled the grassy ridge in silence, rising up through strata of stinking smoke, short legs unused to the rapid movement and uneven ground. The pain warmed him, reminded him of what liberty these few days of transgression would buy him.

He'd faced execution for his crimes. If he had not told the Emperor's Persuaders that he could lead them to the gap in the godwall surrounding the Southern Coastal Protectorate, where the dying god's magic had grown weak, and the gemstone solidity of the barrier crumbled, he would still be rotting in a cage. The freedom he bought would come with its own sort of death-sentence, as the hidden brotherhood of his former profession could accept no excuse for what he was doing. But the diggers were few and far away, and the Kattakan Empire was everywhere.

They were close. At the edge of the valley he could see the ivory godstone tower at the heart of the Southern Coastal Protectorate, glowing faintly in the night. Unlike the other Protectorates around the Empire, this tower still stood. It rose far above the clouds to unfurl into a delicate lattice of godstone; an impossibly immense tree that stretched across the entire Protectorate. Even now, red sunlight illuminated the lattice boughs, long after the sun had set on the ground below.

Once, when the gods first retreated behind the walls with their chosen people, all the Protectorates had towers like this, immense palaces that stretched through the clouds to touch the stars. But in the last few generations, the gods had begun to retreat and die; the structures had shriveled and cracked apart, raining sharp stone and the strange glass of the gods down onto the plains of the free peoples.

There were mosaics and engravings of in the libraries of Kattakan, depicting the Divine Protectorates in their former glory, but for several lifetimes, only this tower remained.

He looked out on the crystalline tower above the clouds, laying on the grass between two tall conetrees. The bed of needles beneath made his mattress, and the unease he felt in the smoky valley began to drift away on the fresh wind. Up here, he could almost forget what he was doing, forget his betrayal and impending freedom.

He'd almost fallen asleep when a something tapped at his foot, three times, then once, then once again. Something about the rhythm tickled the back of his skull, and he shot up at the waist, stone knife in hand. He saw nothing through the holes of the mask, heard nothing but the quiet chittering of tennabirds in the boughs.

"Palta," the voice whispered, the sound's direction lost beneath his hood. His blood froze, and he threw a hand to his face to confirm that the mask was still there.

"Who's there?" he replied, sounding cold and small. "You are mistaken, I am a tracker of the Empire, I do not know this Pa-"

The voice in the dark laughed, a throaty whisper of mirth. "You are Palta Qynes, and you are no man of the Emperor. You are a digger, and a criminal, and a betrayer."

He gripped the blade and tossed the mask, now a pointless impediment, to the side before he realized *he knew that voice.* A arm darted out from behind him, wrapped around his neck, and dragged his feet into the air. The knife dropped from a hand gone nerveless and limp, as two sharp fingers pressed into the points of his wrist.

The arm around his throat squeezed, almost lovingly, as he inhaled a familiar smell of sweat, leather, and denwood oil, and exhaled a heavy sigh.

"Ananda..."

She released him with a push, and they both leapt away, out of arms reach.

Ananda Khorae leaned back against the conetree. Her dark face, so gaunt and sharp now, curled up into an arrogant grin beneath hooked nose and piercing green eyes. Her hair was shorn nearly to her head, all trace of the sun-bleached honey color gone. A cloak covered her left side but he could see that her ragged old hideplates were gone, replaced by a magnificent breastplate of stiff and embossed leather, with bracers and pauldrons to match.

Although there were no signs of rank or affiliation, Palta knew Seltmade armor by sight, the same as the insurgents swinging from the trees in the valley below. She did not carry a Selti ceramic blade, but still held her old sword: tens and tens of sharp teeth, chips of blackrock embedded in a wooden bat. She made no comment on his Imperial attire, or the black mask. She only grinned at him.

"You made this easy for me, Palt," she whispered. "Thought I'd be down in the valley slitting throats one at a time 'till I'd found yours."

"What do you want?" he hissed, her easy calm amplifying his anxiety.

"To save you, Palt. When you reach the godwall of the Protectorate, this whole Host will be destroyed. I'm here to give you the opportunity of not being with them."

He fought for breath, a hundred bubbling thoughts bursting in his mouth unsaid. It had been nearly two years since he'd seen Ananda, when she'd dissolved their partnership and vanished from a roadside public house returning from this very Protectorate.

She'd left him, one helpless half of a functioning whole, with no recourse but to try and sell the fruits of their digs in the Capital. He'd lacked the savvy and smarts that had let her make such a short work of that task, and soon found himself surrounded by the city enforcers, and wooden binders clamped down upon his wrists. It wasn't entirely her fault he'd ended up condemned, but seeing her brought all the blind rage back.

"...What?" he asked, realizing he'd been staring dumbly at her for a few heartbeats.

"I'm here to rescue you, you ass," she said, her grin splitting wider. "That cheap traitor's mask won't save you when every Selt that can wield a bow or a blade encircles the Host. They know where you're headed. They've been waiting. And they'll crush the Host against the godwall."

"How?" he demanded. "How do they know about the gap?"

"I told them, Palt."

Twin urges struck him, one to turn and flee into the night, and the other to lunge forward and wrap his fingers around her long, dark neck. She'd catch him if he ran, her long legs easily outpacing his, and if he tried to attack her, he'd be on the ground before he could make contact. So instead he sighed, and stared up at the sky and the sparkling guidestars.

"Ana, you godsdamned witch, what have you done?"

"The same thing you did, Palt. Traded our secret for my life. I need to get back across the wall, and if the Empire crosses and claims the Southern Coastal Protectorate after the god's passing..." She let the words hang in the night air. "There's only one punishment for diggers caught tampering in holy sites."

"Something I'm quite aware of, Ana," he spat toward the mask, cast aside in the grass. "I spent two years in a Priory cell because you left me holding the bag."

"Please," she said with a wry chuckle, "The way I hear it, you got caught because you were peddling artefacts on a street corner in the Capital, practically wearing a sign on your chest saying 'Digger'. You didn't have to do that. You could have buried the haul and waited for me."

"You left me!" he hollered. "I had no idea *if* you were even coming back!"

"There were some lovely pieces," she sighed, "and those two little discs of bronze. Priceless."

"Well, they're all property of the Emperor now, as am I, until I lead them back to the gap." Palta tugged at his hair in frustration. "They know the godwall has weakened, and that the god in the Protectorate is departing, and they *will* be there first. It's the last sealed Protectorate in the Empire."

Ananda said nothing, only turned to gaze at the luminous tower, thrusting upward over the horizon. Palta followed her gaze, and saw that the tower was pulsing in odd waves of colors, all the way up through the delicate lattice canopy. The sight took the fire out of him, and they let the glow of the god's fading domain become the whole of the moment.

"The Emperor is dying," she said as they watched. "And the Empress-in-waiting is not yet a woman. The chamberlain will rule in her stead. Messagebirds may meet the Host before they arrive at the godwall, but it won't matter. It will be a slaughter. The Selti have been waiting a long time for an opportunity to strike."

"Godsdamn you, Ana, why did you leave me?" The anger abated, and the wound of her departure now split wide. "I missed you."

She stepped towards him, her right hand raised and a whisper on her lips, when he heard the twang of a bowstring's release, and the whistle of the arrow. Something beneath her cloak glowed and twitched, a pale pulse of light, gone as soon as he saw it, and the ceramic-tipped arrow struck something in the air next to her head, and caromed off into the dark.

He dropped into a practiced crouch, leaping behind one of the conetrees. His muscles, stiff from the lack of use and confinement screamed at him, but he pressed through the pain. Another arrow slid past, and with a noiseless pulse of pale light, bounced off of *nothing* and clattered to the soil below.

Ananda merely stood, dropping the cloak to the ground, and raising the blackrock sword to point it at the darkened grove of trees, the source of the arrows. Her left arm, Palta could see now, was wrapped from shoulder to fingertip in black ribbon and hung, thin and withered at her side.

A third arrow arced out of the dark, and Palta saw the limp arm ignite with blue fire, a maddening labyrinth of searing lines that blazed through the cloth wrapping to illuminate the night. When the arrow connected with the invisible barrier, there was another flash of blue, sketching the outline of the ephemeral shield that surrounded her.

Palta looked and saw four Imperial freespears charging up the rise. A fifth man, an archer behind them, loosed another arrow, which clattered uselessly against Ananda's spectral barrier. Palta turned his own short curved bow towards the archer, and drew the string back to the corner of his lips. The waxed bowstring brushed his flesh, and he shivered in anticipation.

Letting fly, the first shot he'd taken in months lifted with his heart, and then arced downward to pierce the Imperial archer's wooden helm, with a sound like an axe splitting logs. The ceramic arrowhead punched through the top of his skull and exited the soft flesh of his neck, and the archer collapsed like falling water.

He put another arrow against the seashell nock and drew back again to pierce the tree trunk thigh of the freespear closest to him. The giant man stumbled and fell, wrapping one huge hand around the shaft of the arrow. He turned his gaze to Palta and shot him a look of raw hatred.

"Your mask cannot hide you now, traitor, I see your face!" he bellowed. Palta's third shot took him in the eye, the arrow exiting through the back of his skull and sliding to the grass below.

And here it was. A few heartbeats spent with Ananda and he had thrown away his freedom, the Emperor's clemency, and killed two men.

How he'd missed her.

The three other freespears had reached Ananda. Her blackrock blade leapt out, shredding through the first man's throat before he'd had a chance to strike. The other two circled around her, splitting her attention to flank her. Palta noticed with a shock, as he fumbled for his last arrow, that her weapon swung in her right hand, and it was *her swordarm* that hung limp and wrapped in a black shroud.

But her long right arm flicked out with the speed and grace that Palta had grown to know over a long and violent decade, as she wielded the weapon in her off-hand like it had been born with her. She swept the blade through space, and the freespear raised his wooden shield to block the blow. Where the sword met the shield, wood leapt up and outward into a cloud of splinters, taking a chunk of meat from the man's arm with it.

He howled and threw the wrecked shield to the ground, and lunged again with the ceramic spear. Ananda parried it with a swipe of her blackrock sword, and then turned to the last freespear who charged her from behind.

Palta already had an arrow nocked and drawn when Ana raised her black-shrouded left arm, the skeletal fingers spread wide toward the charging man. Her arm flared, the dizzying outlines beneath the cloth shining brighter than the moon. The black cloth rippled, as if the arm beneath had become a storm of lightning and wind, and a wave of undulating blue light left her outstretched hand.

Where the bolt of light struck the man, the leather plates of his armor broke apart into tattered rotting scraps. The flesh beneath dried, desiccated and split open, coiling into dark frayed threads, and the wet flesh of his innards boiled and steamed before crumbling to ash. He died without a sound, a gaping burnt hole spreading across his crumpled torso.

The last freespear stopped, wide-eyed and held fast by the display of black arts. Ananda lifted her sword toward him, but her face looked even more gaunt than before. Her left arm collapsed, limp at her side, and the black wrappings hung loose, the bare edges of the cloth smoldering.

If her arm had been unnaturally slender before, now it was skeletal, a child's drawing of an arm done in a single charcoal line. Her breath came in great gasps, and only her eyes held onto the former intensity of the moment.

"Diggerwitch!" the freespear hissed as he found his courage and lunged with the hardened tip of his weapon.

Palta took the shot without aiming, still stunned by what Ananda had done. The arrow leapt from the string, curving in flight to strike the big man in the hip, but it was enough. He dropped to one knee with a bellow of frustration, and Ananda sidestepped the falling spear to strike his neck with the blackrock sword.

The sharp teeth bit through flesh, digging into the soft meat and veins of his throat, and the heavy weight of the bat drove it deeper, tearing the man's head halfway from his neck. His last breath sent a spray of blood up into the night air, where it fell like mist on the grass beneath the conetrees.

Ananda slid to her knees. Above, the tennabirds took flight, chittering softly. Palta started towards her, but some primal fear held him back. The withered arm, the black wraps slithering aside, shone in the moonlight, the once deep brown skin now the color of a corpse, and the strange designs shot across the skin in midnight hues of blue. He feared touching the arm, feared the awful power he'd seen dancing beneath her flesh. He thought for a moment of running, away from the Host, away from Ananda and her strange, changed body.

"Run if you're going to run, Palt," she wheezed. "Otherwise help me up."

"What happened to you, An?" he said. But he already knew.

When they'd crossed the godwall, two years ago, and entered the strange chambers there, they'd filled their packs with everything they could find. They'd been legends already among the small brotherhood of diggers, the grave robbers of gods, but before they'd been confined to the older sites, where the gods had long ago fled. This Protectorate still had a living god, at least just a few years prior, and the artefacts and tiny fragments of metal inside were like nothing either had ever seen. The biggest score a pair of outlaws could hope for.

There had been a knife; a solid piece of opaque crystal with an impossible edge that he'd thought would be with him for the rest of his life. No doubt now it would be buried with the Emperor. There was a bracelet, a thin band that when worn kept him as warm as any coat. And the diadem, a circlet of pearly light that seemed to do no more than grant vivid, strange dreams when worn at night. Discovering what the strange artefacts did was half the danger. Ananda had liked to tell him the story of her last partner, who'd slid what looked like a length of chain onto his neck where it contracted like a muscle, and he'd died with bulging eyes and a swollen tongue.

All those things were gone now, some sold to the black market artefact dealers in the Capital, the rest taken by the Emperor upon his arrest. When Ananda had left him in the dead of night, she'd only taken one thing.

It was a lattice of fine blue fibers, so thin that it was nearly invisible. When laid out flat, they'd noticed that it had the vague shape of an arm, with a hand at the one end, and shredded cracked edges at the other. Like a sleeve, torn from the rest of an immodest and alien outfit, nowhere to be found.

And here it was again, grafted in her skin, beneath the withered flesh. He'd seen what it could do, could still smell the dry cooked scent of the dead man's exposed innards. He'd seen arrows bounce off of the air around her. And now he saw how it was eating her alive from within.

It wasn't just the arm that was withered, her whole body was drawn and stretched tight. Ananda had always been an imposing woman, a towering broad-shouldered swordswoman, a digger who flaunted her criminality and wealth. But the lattice had drained her dry, had eaten up her reserves in order to grant her the power it wielded. It was killing her even as it saved her.

He crossed the clearing between them in a few strides and offered her his hand. She looked up at him with sunken, hollow eyes.

"Thanks, Palt."

"You're going back," he said, "You're going back to try to get it out of you."

"That's the plan."

***

Ananda, it turned out, had been the one who'd attacked the Host's baggage train the day before they'd reached the valley, when only twenty seven of the aurok-drawn wagons arrived at camp. She'd been following them for a few days, tracking them out of the safe borderlands of Kattaka, and into the disputed territories where the Selti held sway. In addition to food enough to feed a dozen men, she'd come away from the raid with ceramic spearheads, sheafs of arrows, bowstrings, dry hard bread, clean water and salted aurok meat.

She ate nearly a quarter of the stores that night, as they hunched around a tiny fire, two ridges beyond the valley.

Palta watched in stunned silence as she sucked the meat from the bone, cracked it to scrape the marrow, and moved on to the next haunch. She ate enough to feed five men, and with each ravenous bite, the gaunt look in her eyes faded, and the withered arm began to thicken, the grey, pale skin returning to some semblance of normalcy.

She didn't want him to look at the arm, seemed almost embarrassed of it, a self-conscious emotion he'd never known her to fall prey to. When the skeletal limb had enough thickness to support the black silken wraps, she hid it from him, wrapping each finger individually, then sliding a leather glove over the hand and throwing her cloak back over her left side. But he could feel the heat pouring off of it, like a fatal fever.

"And I knew if the Empire was headed to the gap," she said through a mouth full of dry, hard bread, "that you'd probably been *forced* to tell them."

"Mm," he said, unsure of what she'd meant by the stress of the words.

"If they make it there, and take control of the Protectorate... I'll never get a chance to go back in. So I went to the Selti chieftains. Showed them a little of the arm," she said, wiggling her glove wrapped fingers in the firelight. "And told the big lie. Told them I was in direct contact with the god, and that it was their sacred duty to keep intruders away."

Palta held his head in his hands. "An..." he groaned, in a tone that felt unnervingly familiar. "You've thrown a spark into the most volatile frontier in the Empire, just to ensure that you can revisit an old dig?"

"To save my life. And yours."

"I'm only here because you left me!" he yelled. "And if you hadn't helped set up this ambush, I wouldn't even be in any danger!"

"Please, Palt. You wore a condemned man's mask. You think they'd have just let you walk?"

"They might have!" he shouted, but it felt heavy on his tongue. He tossed a handful of dust into the fire, watching the flames arc and spiral. "I'm a dead man now. The freespear scouts watching me wouldn't have attacked without sending word back down to the Host that I was consorting with a woman in Selti armor. I'm doubly godsfucked now."

"I had to find you, Palt. If I'm going to doom a thousand men to slaughter, and push a Selti revolution into motion, just to get a chance at getting back in the Protectorate..." she said, staring at him. "You're the one death I didn't think I could bear."

"I'm trying to figure out how that's self-serving, because it has to be." Palta ground his teeth, waiting for her retort, but she only stared at him, her green eyes wide and expressionless. The firelight danced across the strong planes of her face, and he suppressed a shiver.

In the distance, a horn boomed, and another answered from farther off. They'd called off the search for him, which must mean they thought they had a good chance of finding the gap without him. It wouldn't be hard, now that he'd gotten them on the right side of the circumference, and it would only cost them a few dozen deaths to find the right place. By trial and error, a few enlisted yeomen would hold their bare hands to the godwall and wait for their hearts to burst, but in the end they'd find it. If the Selti ambushers didn't kill them first, crushing them against the fatal barrier.

"I need sleep," he said at last, when she'd offered no defense, and he'd pulled the little woolen blanket she'd given him up to over his eyes.

"All right, Palt. It's good to see you again," she said.

"Chew rocks, An."

The feeling of cool air on his face, the longest he'd gone in the open without the mask in weeks, was marvelous, and he was asleep within the space of a dozen exhales.

***

Along with the stores from the wagon, she'd brought a pair of saddled and bridled gida from her ambush on the baggage train, the animals nervously tapping at the ground. When sun crested the horizon in the east, they were on the move, staying just below the ridge line, and moving slightly faster than the Host could. Palta couldn't remember the last time he'd been in the saddle, and not even the pungent smell of the gida's sweat could shake his joy.

He wanted to be furious, wanted to make her feel every moment of terror and despair that he'd suffered in the last two years. But there was something so primally wondrous about the freedom of being mounted and in control of his own destiny again, that the best he could do was scowl at her.

By the way she laughed at his dark expression, her short dark hair ruffling in the wind as she threw her head back and bellowed, he knew his heart wasn't really in it.

"Why are we in a hurry?" he yelled at her as the crystal tower loomed closer on the horizon, the lace canopy covering a quarter of the sky. "Can't you just wait out the ambush, and cross the godwall at your leisure?"

"Well, that would have been my hope, yes," she hollered back, over the pounding of the gidas' split hooves.

"Which means you made a mistake, somewhere," he said, sensing her hesitation and striking.

"The Selti took my divine commandment more seriously than I had expected," she said with grin wide enough to show the old gaps on the right. "I know the superstitions in the Empire are all but ornamental, unless you're on the wrong side of the law... The Selti are a little more... intractable in matters of the divine. I can't be sure they'll let me cross once the ambush is over, and thanks to my enthusiastic argument, they'll be watching the gap for some time."

"Why didn't you just go straight to the gap, then, ahead of the Empire? Why wait two years? Did you tire of the parlor tricks your new arm afforded you?"

"I'm not fond of your tone, Palt." Her voice was a syrupy growl, and if he hadn't spent a decade listening to her refine and practice it, it might have been intimidating.

"There's not much in this dung-choked situation that I am fond of, An. Find a way to make peace with it."

Her jaw worked and ground for a few breaths before she answered. "I didn't know what to do. It was hard enough just to keep it hidden and fed, but it took me till now to get any answers. I went to half the Protectorates in the empire, retracing our best finds. They're all dead, of course, but some of the gods left behind... echoes."

"Like the one that scared us so bad in the Kwyd Protectorate. The dumb thing that just kept apologizing in a dozen languages?" he asked.

"Sort of. Some are dumber than the others, but one of them, at the Protectorate on the shores of the Western Ocean? The dead god there left an echo there could still answer questions. It looked at my arm, and told me that only the god who made the artefact could help me. Told me the god here wasn't all dead, if I hurried"

"All right. But why start a war just to secure passage across? Why not just go back yourself?" She didn't answer, which was as good as a signed confession. Palta could only laugh. "You don't know where it is. For all your fearsome reputation, you can't even remember how to find the gap!"

"You were always a better tracker, Palt," she said, her voice quiet, slipping away beneath the pounding hooves.

"You selfish witch, you aren't saving my life, I'm saving yours! I'm just a godsfucked map to you. Tell me that's not the way of it. Tell me!"

She could not. They rode on in silence.

***

They spent the night in silence, in a stand of conetrees just a quarterday's ride from the Protectorate. The crystal spire towered above the hills, and the lattice canopy spread out above them to enfold the stars. They avoided each other's eyes, instead falling into the familiar camp business, the division of labors well understood. Ananda stripped, prepared, and ate nearly all of the plump hoofed rodent that Palta had felled with an arrow. When the bones were cracked and drained, they stared at the cook fire far into the night.

Sometime in the quiet hours, he awoke to find her eyes open, staring at him, her face as placid as a salt lake.

"What," he growled, "do you want?"

She stared for another dozen breaths, then turned to look away.

"Nothing," she muttered. "Sorry."

"For what?" he demanded, but she'd already turned away.

***

A small scouting party of Selti trackers found them before sunrise. Someone prodded Palta awake with a boot. He opened his eyes to see a ring of ceramic blades, dull and stained from generations of use, pointed towards him.

There was a time when not even the skittering beetles of the forest floor could sneak up on him, and he cursed the atrophy of long-honed skills. Three young Selti men crowded around him, the soft creak of polished leather the only sound they made. Night-dark eyes peered out at him from beneath the hoods of feather woven cloaks.

Ananda's father had come from the Selti, in the early days of their liberation from the Empire, and he saw the echoes of her sharp nose and features exaggerated in these deeply-tanned children.

Ananda was awake, arguing in Selti with the warleader of the small band, her pronunciation harsh and clunky. It had been a while since Palta had been far enough south to speak the Selti tongue, but he caught enough to understand.

He asked why a man dressed in Imperial finery was consorting with the self-proclaimed prophet of the god. They doubted her claim. The Imperial Host was certainly at the boundary of heresy, and would be dealt with, but they no longer trusted her.

"Good morning, Palt," she said, not taking her eyes of the warleader's knife-edged face, lined with tiny intricate patterns of scars. "Your pack, are you ready to grab it and be moving in just a moment?"

He looked around him, saw his light pack and quiver, saw that one of the Selti warriors held a booted foot on top of his bow. The warleader was hollering now, and the young Selts tensed, waiting for some unseen command.

"No," he said, feeling weary and filthy. "No I am not. I think I'd like to go back to the Priory, actually."

She laughed, a rolling, hearty sound. The warleader's voice rose to a staccato stream of roaring, as the veins on his forehead pulsed. The young Selts began to close around them, steeling themselves for the slaughter.

"Forgive me. Down, Palt."

The black-wrapped arm rose up at her side, towards Palta and his captors. The shrouded fingers burst into flame, and a writhing blue tongue of fire crackled out. She swung the arm, snapping the bright blue trail through air that suddenly felt charged and portentous.

Palta fell to the earth, legs gone slack with terror. The Selts, seeing an attack that defied experience, stiffened in place to answer with violence.

The line of fire passed through flesh and armor with no resistance, like an oar through water. Bodies parted and opened, leather casings split and singed. A hot gust of steam billowed out into the chill, dry air, and Palta's guts heaved at the sudden fecund smell. There was a sound of meat, slippery and wet, like a butchers cart overturning on the forest floor.

One Selti hunter still stood, and he stared blankly at the smoking, charred wreck of his arm and shoulder. Then he turned and ran without a sound into the conetrees.

The warleader fell to his knees in the dirt, blood already pooling to make black mud beneath him, supplicant before Ananda. She stood above him, face drawn tight and pale. Cold sweat stood on her brow, and he saw the desperate leaping of her heart, pounding out on her long neck.

The warleader begged for her forgiveness, sang songs of praise and whispered prayers for deliverance. Ananda placed her smoldering hand on top of his head, and Palta saw him tense and whimper in anticipation. Ananda's eyes were clouded, her lips thin and bloodless. Light began to dance beneath the shroud on her arm.

Palta heaved up his pack and bow from the soiled earth, leaving his blanket behind, and drew his small ceramic knife. On the pommel, there was a polished stone, a deep midnight blue orb, and he cracked the heavy rock on the back of the warleader's head. The savage blow sent the man to the muddy earth, boneless and limp.

Ananda stood still, her smoking left hand still hanging in the air, her breathing labored.

"Enough, An," he said, one hand reached out to touch her, but when he neared the flesh of her luminous, spindly arm, he drew his hand back from the heat. She looked up at him, her jaw set.

"Yes," she said with a slow nod. "I've made some mistakes, Palt."

He wanted to laugh, but his eyes kept sliding back to the corpses, split into too many pieces, as they twitched and shuddered in the rising sunlight.

***

They pushed the gidas hard, crossing the distance between them and the godwall with feverish anticipation. Palta thought to delay finding the gap, to pretend that he couldn't remember the exact location to stretch out Ananda's discomfort. But she was hardly able to stay upright in the saddle, her skin gray and damp in the morning light, and he found he didn't have the heart for the deception.

The Selti ambushers had travelled light, no rations or meat amongst them, so Ananda drained all their canteens. The bitter mineral water within seemed to do her some good, but she still held the freshly-wrapped arm gingerly at her side.

By the time they reached the wide plain where the godwall had decayed, the Host of the Empire was just behind, a plume of dust from the old roads over the next forested rise. Somewhere in the trees, a force of hidden Selti fighters watched the Host march by.

When the men of the Empire reached the wall, the Selti would emerge to encircle them. The Empire, even this small detachment on the borders of the world, had numbers on the side, but they would fight with their back against the godwall, unable to retreat without dying instantly. Before the sun was at its zenith, one of the two armies would surely be destroyed.

Palta and Ananda had made it to the gap mere moments ahead of the Host and the Selti ambush, leaping from their saddles to approach the godwall on foot, but it hardly mattered.

For the gap had healed.

***

Palta had seen the domains and Protectorates of the gods all across the world, had made it his life's business to know the subtle signs that distinguished one god's work from another, and to read the age of a god's passing from the strata of what had been left behind.

He had seen a dozen godwalls in various states of collapse, but he always knew the signs. The slick, opalescent godstone of the walls fades. The material weakens, and it loses its translucence. It turns to something more solid, and earthly. After the god dies, its divinity bleeds away from the world.

Palta had been to Protectorates so long ago abandoned that the godwall had already crumbled into dust. A few gods, far outside the Empire still lived, their Protectorates unbreached, the chosen people inside still hidden and protected.

No one knew what a functioning Protectorate looked like from inside. Free men outside the gods' reservations could only guess and tell stories. But when a god died, and the walls fell, the first diggers over the wall usually got to see the best indications.

Palta had seen the insides of a dozen protectorates. Each was its own special madness. Some were shining cities made of gemstone, some were vast preserves of untouched land, and others were so obscured and inhuman that no coherent narrative could be attached to the structures and things inside.

But most were filled with corpses. Where gods died, the chosen people of their Protectorates die too. Perhaps gods take their people with them into death. Or perhaps without their subjects, the gods no longer have a purpose, so when the people of the Protectorate die, the gods depart the world.

In the Kwyd Protectorate, Ananda and Palta had almost certainly been the first inside when it became known that the god was dead. They found a vast mechanism for elimination, an organized, refined engine of death. Divine structures, cleverly constructed for the efficient extermination of life stretched from horizon to horizon, side by side with immense, dust-choked mausoleums where the desiccated dead were stacked like paving stones. The god there had deliberately killed its people before dying itself, leaving only echoes, little dumb ghosts manifesting as rolling spheres of colorless light, and they haunted the charnel fields of its Protectorate, begging forgiveness.

Here, in the South, two years ago, Palta and Ananda had found the gap before anyone had any suspicion that the god was dead. Ananda just had a feeling, something they'd both learned to trust, and they'd found the gap, the subtle signs of the weakened wall that only they would notice. There were no corpses inside, no echoes of gods. Just wild and unkempt plains, a few strange structures, and an underground chamber that seemed waiting for them. The chamber had held an embarrassment of riches, and this one find should have kept them in comfort and wealth for years. But instead it led them right back here.

To where a dead godwall had come back to life.

He stood, his mouth parted, and could only stare. He turned to help Ananda back into the saddle, but it was too late. The Host was upon them.

***

"This was not a well thought out ruse, Palt," Ananda said, her voice thick and phlegmy. The tapping rhythm of imperial drums shuddered in the air, and their gida departed, darting away from the thundering sound.

"I wish it were," was all he could say, his eyes frantically searching the same stretch of featureless *living* godwall, three manheights tall and gently rounded at the top. At the base of the godwall, there was a raised embankment where a riot of flowers and weeds grew, the fertile soil fed by the trickling stream of men and creatures who died when they touched the surface. He was still looking for some sign, when he heard Ananda release the clasp on her blackrock sword.

The Host slowed as it approached, spreading to encircle them. At the head of the march, a Greatreeve rode on a speckled gida, resplendent in the sunlight. On the nobleman-general's leather armor, a few ceremonial plates of bronze and iron sparkled, pressed so thin as to be like sheets of vellum, but the metal was a priceless display of wealth. His sword was the finest imperial blackrock, a single edged blade nested in a ceramic spine, as opposed to the hardwood and ragged teeth of Ananda's weapon. He pointed at Palta as he rode out ahead of the Host.

"Palta Qynes, you have abandoned your anonymity and turned your back on your homeland," he bellowed out, in a voice born and bred for statecraft. "In the name of the most wise and august Emperor of all Kattaka, Rhenan, seventh of his name, and son of Rhenan, sixth of his name, I hereby rescind your royal pardon on the grounds of *treason*." He cantered forward with this word, letting it hang in the air, until he stood just a few heights away. "You have taken our Emperor's gift of clemency and ground his generosity underfoot, wast-"

A rock sailed across the short distance and smacked into the Greatreeve's gem-studded ceramic helm with a hollow thud. He stopped, looked at them with an almost puzzled expression, before opening his bearded mouth to begin again, starting the formal charge from the beginning. Ananda scooped up another rock from the loamy soil and let fly, striking him in the same spot and dislodging a pair of sparkling blue gems. The nobleman went red, his face bulging with rage and he began to roar.

"The penalty for your crimes, diggers, is no less than th-"

A third rock, thrown by Palta, collided with his mouth and lips, sending chips of his teeth down his bellowing throat. He heaved forward to gag and spit, and then spurred his gida into movement, back around to rejoin his army, unable to look back. He waved some savage hand signal to the Host, and the men of the front line locked wooden shields, pointed fire-hardened spears toward the diggers, and began to advance, chanting a battle song as they approached.

Ananda tossed one more rock into the front lines, and then turned to Palta.

"I'm sorry for all of it Palt. I'm too weak to use the arm. It would kill me." She loosened up the wrist of her right hand to swing the blackrock sword in a few shallow arcs, and braced her feet into the dirt. "It's my fault you're here," she said.

"I know it is, An," he said. "I know." He had one sheaf of arrows still from the stolen supply cart, the rest strapped to the fleeing gidas saddle, and he brought the first shaft to the string. He took aim at the tall crested helm of the Greatreeve, now safely behind the front line of the advance, and prepared to let the arrow loose. He was unlikely to kill the man, but he could make his embarrassment all the richer in these last moments.

The Selti war cry washed over them, a deep, mournful chord, created by hundreds of throats vibrating in harmony. It was uncanny and alien sound, and it rolled out of the conewood trees and tall grass as the ambushers revealed themselves, dashing to encircle the Host from behind. The Imperial soldiers panicked as rear guard became the front line, the mounted cavalry trapped behind the infantry. The reeves of the Host tried to maintain control, but as the Selti drove forward to envelop the Host, Palta could see that the Imperial position was doomed.

Turned backwards and trapped between the living godwall, and the fury of the Selti, the Host was forced into a retreat. Their ranks bunched, squeezed into a dense clump of pressed bodies that left many of the fiercest warriors trapped by their own companions. They tried to move back to reorder their line, and with a shriek of atavistic terror, the first yeomen of the Imperial Host touched the wall. Then another. The wall became a chorus of screams.

Ananda and Palta found themselves surrounded, not so much fighting the panicked Imperial Host as swimming through it. The cavalry tried desperately to break through their own line, urging their gida to advance, and swinging the bludgeon end of their lances into their countrymen. The Selti had no mounted men and a far smaller force; the Imperial cavalry could break their advance, but the ambush had been well planned. Generations of grievances for atrocities under Imperial rule transmuted into a moment of righteous fury, and the Selti cut down the unprepared rear lines of the Host like stalks of wintergrain.

In the killing zone against the godwall, a barrier of corpses now protected the living from its fatal touch. Now, they only had to contend with the crushing press of the other soldiers. They saw Ananda, her Selti armor clearly marking her among the Imperial colors, and they boiled and frothed around her.

Ananda danced, the blackrock sword sliding through cloth, leather and flesh. She leapt from one foot to the other, extending her fatal edge into the sea of panicked soldiers. Palta caught a glimpse of her face, ashen and drawn, short hair slicked in sweat and blood. The shrouded arm trailed behind her like a lifeless piece of rope. She did not have the reserves of strength to use its magic, but she fought with her sword in her offhand like Palta had never seen.

He had known Ananda to take on a half dozen men by herself, in the days before her cursed arm. He'd seen her brawl in public houses, too drunk to stand straight, but still smashing noses and cracking arms with easy grace. He'd seen her in single combat with martial champions, when they had once thought to make easy money in the tournaments at harvest time.

He watched now, her body half-useless and drained, as she dealt death to a crushing wave of freespears and yeomen. As each blow maimed or cut short a life, she was already spinning the path of the sword into the next foe. She bent, long limbs and body curving like a stalk of grass, to gracefully step beneath the swing of a bludgeon, and then sidestep the thrust of a spear. Her eyes seemed unfocused, but her motions were like the flowing of water over the earth.

It was a thing of beauty, a war trance. Palta drew his bow back to the his lips, again and again, arrows lancing into flesh wherever he saw someone approach Ananda from behind, but each man he killed would have fallen beneath her blade a heartbeat later.

The Imperial Host found themselves beset on all sides, by the Selti marauders, the killing godwall, and this elegant, whirling witch with a blackrock blade.

The Selti encircled the Host, rendering the Imperial's numerical advantage a liability, and what had begun as a losing battle became a slaughter. The air rang with cracking wood, stone on flesh and the screaming of the damned. Palta felt dizzy and drunk.

Ananda arrested her arm in mid swing, a river of blood flowing from the blade. She looked up to catch Palta's eyes as she fell to one knee, and he saw he'd been wrong. She had been hurt, a constellation of wounds spread across her body. She had taken blow after blow, but never stopped, never called out.

Now she stared into him, a final apology in her eyes. He had no more arrows, but in the chaos of the Imperial defeat, they were nearly forgotten.

In the thrashing chaos of the slaughter, as the Selti tightened the net, and the last of the Imperial cavalry was dragged down into the blood-soaked ground, a ball of fire streaked across the sky, bathing the world in light like a second sun. From behind the comet came a roar, a cry of fury from the throat of a god.

The killing stopped, as men of both armies craned their necks to watch its passing, transfixed as the fist of flame left a smoking trail through the clouds. It came out of the East, and punched through the lattice treetop canopy of the godstone tower, sending arcs of light and jagged white splinters tumbling outward and away. The fireball passed in front of the sun, and arced downward, a halfday's ride to the northwest. When it touched the horizon, a flash of brilliant white flared and then faded. Then, there was only silence, punctuated only by the fearful, awed whispers of a thousand men.

From the distance, where the fiery comet had struck the world, there came a sound of rolling thunder, a drumbeat of muffled blasts. For a single breath, the battleground was still, and all knew that they had witnessed a divine omen.

It took a few heartbeats for the Selti to see the sign as evidence of their divine favor. Buoyed by the support of the gods, their voices rose in song as they drove forward, crushing the last scraps of Imperial resistance. Somewhere in the distance, hollow thumps heralded the impact of the shattered canopy.

Bodies, living and dead, pressed against them, smashed them together, bloodied flesh to bloodied flesh. He wrapped his arms around her, felt the feverish heat of her body and shrouded arm, and he held her close.

She whispered to him, something lost beneath the cacophony of death, and pressed her forehead to his.

Then, before he could stop her, she lifted the cursed arm. As it ignited in a ripple of blue light, Palta screamed for her to stop, but it was too late.

The wave of arcane fire washed across the remnant of the Imperials, turning bodies to dust, and splashed against the godwall. The living stone shuddered, the luster fading as it grew opaque in the azure heat. And then it cracked, collapsed inward, creating a gap the size of a man.

Palta hooked one arm beneath Ananda's sword arm, hoisted her limp and burning body over his shoulder and launched himself towards the gap, kicking out at an Imperial yeoman who thought to escape with them. The wall already began to heal, the godstone flowing back to cover the wound like luminous flesh.

He slid through as it closed behind them, the godstone awakening and igniting with fatal light, but they were safe. He was inside the Protectorate on a vast, wild plain, with Ananda by his side.

Her face was corpselike, skeletal, her closed eyes sunken deep into the hollows of her skull. The black shrouds lay in flaming tatters around an arm that was nothing more than scorched leather, bone, and the geometric labyrinth of blue light streaming from beneath ruined flesh.

He held her, and as the mad cries of war on the other side of the wall faded into a Selti victory song, he let his world become the quiet sound of her shallow breath.

***

Two years ago, they'd found an underground chamber just a few hundred heights from the gap. Now it was gone. He held his dying friend on his back, her strong right arm and charred left wrapped around his neck, and dragged her towards the base of the tower. Ananda rose in and out of consciousness, whispering in a voice like grains of sand shifting on a beach.

He found a small trickling stream emerging from a cluster of granite boulders, and they drank water that tasted unlike anything he could recall. Shining fish flitted in the shallows, schools so dense that he could reach in and grab them, again and again. He propped her up, still unable to stand, and they feasted on the vivid red flesh of a dozen little fish.

It took them two days to cross the plains, as he dragged her towards the tower. He didn't know where she'd expected to find the god, but he could think of no better plan. They passed small villages, domes made of the same pale godstone as the walls, but saw no inhabitants at first.

One night, as Ananda snored noisily around the fire, by the light of the moon, Palta saw a figure watching them. It looked like a man, but he would have sworn the gracile shape was covered in a light sheen of fur, and giant saucer eyes reflected the firelight back at him. He waved, and called for help in a few tongues, but the figure vanished, slinking away into the grass and gloom.

They made it to the base of the tower at noon of the third day. Ananda had not woken that morning, but she was muttering to herself in her sleep, foul curses the only words he could hear. He looked up, at the lattice canopy, where he saw that the wounds caused by the passing of the comet worsened, the material around the cracks bending and crumbling away. A few chunks had fallen to earth in the morning, impacting into the wild land around them with a low distant sound. He laid Ananda in the grass, her eyes still shut, and walked a circle around the base of the tower. There was no entrance, only the smooth and featureless texture of godstone. He kept walking.

When he arrived back where he started, a quarterday later, the sun was sinking. Ananda sat cross-legged in the grass, drinking from a Selti waterskin. She stared at him with tired, hollow eyes, and nodded. He could only raise his shoulders in a gesture of defeat. She smiled, a silent assurance, and stood to approach the tower.

She placed her withered corpse hand, the black shroud all but gone, upon the surface of the tower. The labyrinth of light beneath the desiccated skin ignited, and the tower's flesh melted away. A narrow passageway appeared, like a mouth opening. She turned back and grinned at Palta. In her smile he saw another black space where she'd lost a tooth in the battle at the godwall.

"Tell me," he said wearily, "Did you let me walk the whole circumference, knowing that was all it would take?"

She turned her palms upright and frowned theatrically, even as her eyes sparkled from their sunken pits.

"You godsdamned witch," he said, with a raspy echo of a laugh. She turned, and he followed her inside the tower.

***

They didn't have to go far. The aperture closed behind them, but the walls glowed with a comforting yellow aura, and soon they found themselves in a wide and cavernous chamber carved into the living godstone.

At the far end of the chamber was a figure, a long and spindly shape three times the height of a man, made entirely out of luminous godstone. The face was a featureless plain, a mirror that reflected Palta's sudden dread. It strode towards them like a surge of river rapid, the motion both breathtaking and horrifying in its inhumanity.

The figure raised smooth many-fingered hands and placed one on each of their foreheads. Palta didn't have the strength to resist. The figure held perfectly still, its warm appendage laid gently on Palta's flesh, he felt an implied question in the air. He could only nod, giving his assent.

There was a wave of sudden sensation, too intense to be anything but pain, and his skull felt a maddening pressure. Then it was over, and he looked up to see the figure had withdrawn its hands. Features extruded from the blank face, the impression of a nose, mouth, and two eyes that glowed warmly.

"Forgive my intrusion on your minds," the god said, in a voice like the creaking of an ancient tree, emanating from the shallow mouth pit on his smooth face. "But it's far easier this way, when your tongues are unknown to me."

"Please," Ananda whispered, "I come to you in great need-"

"You came to me before, when you thought me dead," the god said, the light of the chamber darkening with its voice. "You took pieces of my history. I could have stopped your heart then, would you prefer I do so now?"

Palta heard a sound, an unfamiliar hitching in Ananda's breath, and he realized she was crying.

"No," she said, through wet breaths. "I want to live."

"I see no reason why you should not. The thing you have taken inside yourself is a part of me, and it was not intended for you. You want it out." She nodded, the bones in her neck popping. "I cannot," the god said. "It would kill you. For better or worse, it is a part of you. I am a part of you, now."

Ananda didn't move. For a horrified moment, Palta thought she was about to lunge forward and attack the god, but her body held no reserves of motion.

"I can alter it," he said, "I can train it not too eat your body when it needs nourishment. It will still need to be fed, but I can show you how to do so without having to gorge yourself on marrow and meat."

Palta held perfectly still and watched. The god reached out and held Ananda's shattered limb. The blue design pulsed and glowed and then began to swirl, unwind and remake itself. The flesh of her arm, gray and chapped, began to flush and swell. Ananda's sobs became gasps, not of pain, but of a sensation nearly as intense. She still looked mere steps from a corpse, but the old glow of life and energy crept back into her skin.

"It is done, thief," the god said.

"Thank you," Ananda murmured, her eyes locked on her hands.

"You will find that blood, now, from any source, will provide you with the strength to keep it from devouring your own flesh. You will need to learn how to control it, but that is your concern."

Palta blinked, wondering if they'd come all this way just to doom Ananda to a life of drinking blood, but she seemed to accept the solution with a stiff nod. The god rose up and stood tall above them.

"And now that I have made right what you did to yourself, you will hear me."

They waited, supplicated by exhaustion.

"We are dying," the god said, in a tone that could almost be called sad. "One by one, the oldest of us are slipping away. The Protectorates, established hundreds of thousands of cycles ago, are failing. Your ancestors that chose to stay and walk amongst the gods, will be left to die with their protectors. But that fate is preferable to your own."

"You vermin on the outside, you headstrong madmen, you think you're unaffected by our passing. We have not only protected those who chose to remain inside our walls. We have been protecting all the minds of the world. But there are not enough of us left, and it is too late."

Palta found he wasn't breathing, waiting on what prophecy would unfurl from the god's lips, like some divine flower of madness.

"Dominion has returned, riding a derelict of iron down from the stars. We exiled it, so long ago, in the war, but it is back. It fell to the earth a few days ago."

Palta thought of the streaming comet overhead, tried to picture it as pure iron. How much had fallen to the world? He thought of the tiny fragments of lesser metals they'd found amongst the spoils of dead gods. The most valuable material in the Empire, as much as any magic artefact. A finger of iron could make a man wealthy for life. And somewhere there a was a mountain of iron, smoldering on the open ground.

"Dominion?" asked Ananda.

"It was the greatest of us, and became the worst. It listened to songs from the stars, and it grew mad. It loathes thinking minds, and it will begin its crusade again, as if the aeons of exile in the void had not happened. Only now, there are so few of us left to resist him."

"What can we do?" Ananda asked as she stood, flexing her arm. The blue tattoo on her left arm stood out on flesh as healthy and as warm brown as her right.

"Nothing," said the god. "Know that your end is coming, and prepare. Dominion does not hate life, only minds, so know that the world itself will survive, just not you and your kingdoms. You can tell your kings and emperors, or not. You can march right into to Dominion's wake to salvage the iron that he brought back with him, if your desire for wealth outstrips your sense. Beyond that, there is nothing I can do but tell you the name of your death."

Palta realized that his mouth hung open. He closed it, dry lips cracking. The god stared at them in silence. Ananda worked her jaw, lost in some private spiral of thought.

"I have absolved myself," the god announced, as the aperture opened behind them, and cool night air spilled in. "Return to the wall, and I will allow you to pass. You will not return while I live."

And it was gone, the long luminous limbs splitting into fine threads as it poured away into the walls, mist vanishing on a warm morning.

***

As they walked back to the wall, they talked about nothing of consequence. They told jokes, and sang songs, and slept long into the warm autumn mornings on the wild plains of the Protectorate. Several of the long limbed and wide-eyed people of the Protectorate tracked them, watching from distant hilltops with curiosity, but never approached.

At last, when the godwall was in sight, Palta could take in no longer, and asked the question that squirmed around his head.

"What now?"

She paused, looking up at the treetop canopy of godstone above the clouds, and at the wound of the iron comet's passing. Then she looked north, to where it had fallen to the earth, the chariot of a mad god.

"Our days of raiding Protectorates are done," she said, with a sly twinkle.

He grinned, knowing exactly what she would say now. She returned the smile, and looked down at the glowing tattoo on her arm. There were wars coming, and there were fortunes to be made.

"I'd say we're in the iron business now, Palt."

They crossed the wall, and headed north, toward the column of smoke on the horizon.

Flames of Madness
by Jonathan Shipley

The knock at the door awakened Lisbet out of sound sleep. She rolled over and stared groggily around the dark room.

There's been another skirmish, she thought, pulling her cloak over her night dress. They need a Healer.

She stopped as she realized this wasn't the infirmary. The siege and all its misery lay far to the south. And she was supposed to be a simple traveler, not a Healer. Ignoring a growing pounding at her temples, she opened the door and peered at the innkeeper holding the lantern in the corridor outside.

He began fidgeting. "A thousand pardons, Mistress. I must put you out of your room."

"Why?" she demanded sharply, feeling a sudden dread that news from the siege had finally caught up with her. She had been running ever since the Citadel defenders had broken the stranglehold of the Imperial legions on their stronghold. Fighting was still fierce, she knew. Every Healer, every Mage, every Acolyte was needed to contain the enemy, but she hadn't stopped running until she was safely away from the battlefields. She wanted nothing to do with this new war of the Archimage. She'd seen too much death in the last campaign. And the one before that.

"It's not my doing, Mistress," the man sighed. "It's more notables from the capital coming through. They need all the rooms . . . immediately."

Lisbet felt a surge of disgust. How typical of the Imperial burcaucracy. While people were dying to the south, the lordlings kept on requisitioning whatever they wanted for their own comfort. If she had dared, she would have put on her Robe of Rank and thrown their requisition back in their face. But she didn't dare, not after deserting the siege.

The innkeeper stepped closer and murmured in her ear. "It's Mages, Mistress. Don't ask me why they need all the rooms. I don't argue with magekind."

Mages. Downstairs. Her muzziness evaporated instantly. "I'll move at once," she said, turning to collect her things.

Halfway down the staircase, her headache suddenly worsened. Blinking back the pain, she realized the taproom was completely empty. She stepped toward the door only to have the throbbing in her head erupt with increased intensity.

Lisbet backed away until the pounding subsided to a tolerable level again. No wonder she was so groggy. Someone in the coach outside was broadcasting raw, unshielded energy.

Suddenly, the door banged open and a silver-robed figure strode in, cloak billowing around him. "Why are you still here?" he demanded.

Lisbet stared at the hue of the robe, the insignias, and realized this was a very high-ranking Acolyte, just under full Mage status. His mind was shielded but leaking around the edges in a very unprofessional way. She could sense his fatigue all the way across the room. Then her head began pounding again.

Suddenly he was framed in a golden glow, backlit by the figures coming through the door behind him. "No. Wait," he said, whirling around to face the two Mages.

"We can't wait any longer," one of them, a woman, replied tightly.

Lisbet barely heard the interchange. Her attention was seized by the glow of the other Mage. Even with a splitting headache she could sense this was no ordinary nimbus. Its texture seemed wrong somehow, warped in a way that pulled her. The need to heal overwhelmed her.

"Clear the inn!" snapped the Acolyte. "Now!"

Lisbet just kept staring.

"Move, woman!" the Acolyte ordered.

"He's in pain," Lisbet answered, barely aware of her own words.

The Acolyte took a closer look at her. "Healer." He closed his eyes and Lisbet felt a quick shock pass through her body. "Strongly talented," he added.

"Bring her, then," the woman Mage ordered. "Anything to get him sleeping again."

Lisbet found herself in tow of the three of them up the stairs. Her head throbbed. This Mage was leaking all over the place. That wasn't supposed to happen. People with that much raw power were supposed to know how to control it.

"Is he a war casualty?" she asked as the glowing figure was led forward to the bed. That was the only thing that made sense.

"We're on our way *to* the battle, not away from it," the silver Acolyte snapped back.

"Never mind--do something," the woman Mage added in voice barely above a whisper. At close quarters, Lisbet could feel a separate pain from her. She was on the verge of collapse.

"If you can hold on a just few more minutes," Lisbet soothed, stepping over to the bed. Already she was slipping into healing trance. Her head still ached, but she felt strangely relaxed. She was back in her element.

She pressed the palms of her hands against the glowing aura and concentrated. It was working, she realized after a moment. Moving through his mental shields, she felt almost no resistance.

She could feel the mind within now . . . a conscious mind in great pain . . . or at least, great distress. The thoughts were so chaotic that she couldn't distinguish one from the other. She focused on radiating a soothing, relaxing presence. And made contact--

The world seemed to explode around her.

When she opened her eyes again, she found herself lying on the floor a good ten feet from the bed. Her left arm ached where she had apparently landed on it. "What happened?" she managed to croak.

"He doesn't know you," the Acolyte said, helping her up. "Maybe he thought you were the enemy. He senses the battle, you know. She's going to need your help, Nemora."

The woman nodded and closed her eyes in concentration.

"It isn't going to work this way," Lisbet said. "All of you are too fatigued to do more than hang on with your fingertips."

"He has to sleep," Nemora insisted. "We can't rest until he does."

"Who is he, anyway?" Lisbet asked. "Is he injured?"

"That's not your concern," said the Acolyte sharply. "Your only concern is getting him to sleep."

Lisbet gave him her best professional stare. "I will. But I'll have to approach the problem obliquely."

"You seem to have started already," he snorted.

"Ensley, stop," said Nemora. "At this point, I'm open to all suggestions."

Lisbet saw the Acolyte drop his eyes and nod. They might be on a first-name basis, but there was no mistaking the difference in rank.

"What I propose," Lisbet said, "is channeling enough healing energy to you to banish the fatigue for a few minutes. Then maybe we'll have a chance. You'll need to disengage to do this. Can"--using his first name sounded a little too intimate--"can the Acolyte take each of your places for a few minutes?"

Nemora nodded. "He's trained to spell me."

"Let's start, then."

There was a moment when the room seemed to whirl. When it stopped, Lisbet saw that Ensley had taken Nemora's place at the side of the bed. He looked strained already.

"The next room," Lisbet said, leading the way.

"I need to sit," said Nemora, collapsing into the chair inside the door. "Can you work from this position?"

"Yes, certainly." Lisbet walked over and picked up the three-cornered stool by the window. She placed it next to Nemora's chair and seated herself facing the Mage. "Standard healing energy transfer," she said. "A light trance would make you more receptive if you can manage."

Nemora nodded and closed her eyes. Then at the first feather-touch of contact the eyes flew open again. "Do I know you?" she asked suddenly.

Lisbet stiffened. "I don't think so," she said quickly. She certainly hoped not. Letting Nemora settle again, Lisbet sent out another careful probe.

"But you're not some backwoods Healer," Nemora insisted, coming alert again. "You've had training. When were you at the Schola Arcana? Have you campaigned with the legions?"

Lisbet felt cornered and had to fight to keep her detachment. "I can either talk, or heal. Not both."

"Of course. Proceed."

Lisbet tried a third time, expecting any second another round of questions. But this time Nemora's eyes remained closed.

Healing Mages was always risky, Lisbet reminded herself. She'd heard about spontaneous mind-to-mind links, and the last thing she wanted was to share her thoughts with a Mage.

A little skittish, Lisbet's contact remained uneven, but she held onto to it long enough to channel a bit of energy. "Do you feel any different?" she asked hesitantly.

Nemora opened her eyes, concentrated a moment, and nodded. "The fatigue is much diminished. Good work, Lisbet."

Lisbet managed a polite smile, then suddenly froze. She hadn't introduced herself by name. If that had come through during the healing, how much else had as well? Did Nemora know she was a deserter?

She strained for any echo of suspicion or veiled hostility, but caught nothing. That was hardly conclusive. This was, after all, a Mage.

She forced herself to keep calm as she followed Nemora back to the other bedroom. There was no sense borrowing more trouble. She would have quite enough coaxing the wild one to sleep without getting herself reduced to ashes in the process.

When she entered the room, Nemora was just finishing the exchange with Ensley. The Acolyte slumped as soon as he released the mental link and stumbled toward the nearest chair.

He may need some attention later, Lisbet thought distractedly. But most of her attention remained on the glowing figure on the bed. The psychic leak had been reduced to a minimum by Nemora's strengthened shields, but that wouldn't last. Using healing energy to banish fatigue was only a temporary solution.

"Any time you're ready," Nemora said tightly.

"Of course," Lisbet nodded, crossing the remaining distance to the bedside. She placed her hands against the glowing shields.

Chaos. She was swimming in chaos. But no explosion.

She tried to orient herself. She'd been sucked into a mentality she couldn't begin to fathom. But she could still focus, send out a soothing healing to lull the chaos to dormancy. At least according to the plan. But the force of the link made her wonder about the outcome. This mind, this Mage, far exceeded Nemora's power. Nemora and Ensley in tandem could barely contain him.

A doubly powerful Mage? Lisbet's concentration faltered as she realized she had linked to one of the Empire's half-dozen High Magi. And of the six, it wasn't hard to guess which one it had to be. Even in the provinces there were tales of Old Urlich. The Mad Mage. She remembered hearing that it took the Archimage himself to subdue Old Urlich at his worst. Where did that leave her?

In a close mental link with a madman, she told herself. And if she didn't pull herself together, she might not get out intact. She gathered her will, concentrating on filtering out the flood of wild images bombarding her senses. She could almost recognize some of the faces but steadfastly refused to be drawn along that path. Her purpose was to soothe, to help. She couldn't afford to let anything upset her.

The palms of her hands grew warm as she pushed the healing energy through them, through the shields. She could feel the heat, used it to center herself more firmly in her own body. The images receded into riotous background noise as she pulled back from the link, reclaiming a feeling of herself as an entity apart from the chaos. She could almost see the room again, though not clearly.

She sent another surge of energy through the open channel and the room became slightly clearer. The figure of Nemora was now visible on the edge of her vision. The form on the bed was glowing only slightly under her fingertips. She heard his slow, regular breathing and knew she was close to success. Just a little longer.

A hand on her shoulder jarred her like a slap in the face.

"Enough," Nemora told her. "He's asleep. It took a while, but you did it."

"How long?" Lisbet asked thickly. Her voice sounded as if it hadn't been used in days. Her whole body felt odd, out of step with itself.

"Two hours."

Lisbet took a deep breath. That was too long for a healing trance. She was trained to break contact every quarter-hour or so in intensive work, but this time she hadn't even been aware of the passage of time.

"I already sent Ensley to bed," Nemora continued. "I need to sleep as well. Can you sit with him for a few hours? Make sure he stays asleep until one of us returns?"

Lisbet started to shake her head, then realized she didn't feel half as depleted as she should have after that long a healing. Tired, yes, but not exhausted. "I can do that," she said. "And in case of emergency?"

Nemora gave a thin smile. "If it comes to one of his fits, Lisbet, you won't have time to worry about it. Keep him asleep. At all costs. I think you understand why."

Hardly reassuring words. But Lisbet had understood the danger the moment she recognized her patient as Old Urlich. "I hope that--"

The coachman walked in with something under his arm.

"Set it up by the bed," Nemora told him. "Something to help with the long vigil," she told Lisbet. "Believe me, I've been there."

Lisbet nodded as the coachman's bundle resolved itself into a portable camp chair. A nicely cushioned camp chair, she noticed. She hadn't seen anything so comfortable in years.

"And the horses?" Nemora asked, leading the way to the door.

"Attended to, Excellency," the coachman answered. "But we'll have to spare them tomorrow after pushing them so hard--"

Lisbet gave a sigh of relief as the door closed, cutting off the rest of the conversation. She moved herself into the camp chair, found it every bit as comfortable as it looked, and settled in for the duration. It was going to be a long night. Or morning, she corrected, glancing at the already graying windows. Maybe she could coax a pot of tea from the innkeeper.

A sudden pounding in her temples was all the warning she had. Leaning over the bed, she struggled to link again, to soothe the waking Mage back into sleep.

A riot of images flooded her mind at first touch, but this time they were sharper, more recognizable. Fire. She barely recognized the bright green light as fire. And people, some chanting, some screaming. Faces, many faces--

--a blast of intense mental pain jolted her out of the link.

She opened her eyes and found a pair of watery blue eyes inches in front of her face. There was a sudden stench in the air, like burning refuse, but she couldn't tear her eyes away from those blue ones.

"So," cackled Old Urlich, "you think I'm mad."

Lisbet tried to pull back from the compelling stare, but felt herself being drawn closer instead.

"I said," Old Urlich whispered, "you think I'm mad, don't you?"

Lisbet groped for an answer. Nemora's parting warning kept running through her mind. "I'm a Healer," she managed to say. "Let me help you sleep again."

Old Urlich's eyes grew round with displeasure. "Sleep! I spend too much time sleeping as it is. If you were truly a Healer, you would help me awaken from the horrible dreams."

"Dreams?" she echoed. "What kind of dreams?" She stepped back from the bed while he appeared to mull that over. If she could just find a way to keep him preoccupied long enough for her to reach the door.

"Dreams and dreams and dreams." He gave a long sigh. "I am mad, you know. I can tell that when I'm awake. The rest of the time--" He shrugged.

"You mean, the madness comes and goes?" Lisbet asked. "How can that be?"

"The ancients, they knew. They had names for these fits of mine. Yes, they come and go. Just as the lucid moments come and go. What does the Healer make of that?"

Lisbet shook her head. "My Talent is to heal the body. I've never dealt with the mind."

Old Urlich started laughing. Loudly, uncontrollably. Lisbet began edging toward the door once more.

"Stop!" he ordered. His mirth ceased abruptly. "I never gave you permission to leave. Ah, the irony, woman, the irony. And such secrets my mind contains. Shall I tell you some?"

A chill raced up Lisbet's spine. She shouldn't be hearing this. Mad or not, this man was a keeper of the innermost mysteries. There were Mages who would kill to know such things; Mages who would kill to keep the knowledge from a provincial Healer.

"Don't say anything more," she blurted out. "I don't want to know. I just want to heal."

He leaned closer and raised his eyebrows. "You don't want to know the great secrets of the High Magi?" He fell back, cackling wildly.

Lisbet bolted. The room wasn't large--only a few steps to the doorway.

Some sixth sense screamed and she dropped to the floor. A bolt of fire whizzed over her head. The door frame sizzled and the room suddenly smelled of wood smoke.

Recharge. The thought popped into her head from nowhere. He would have to recharge.

Lisbet scrambled forward and pelted into the corridor. It seemed to have a hundred doors, a hundred options. She threw open the nearest door and stumbled into a darkened room. "Help me!" she cried.

No answer.

She bolted across the hall into the room directly opposite. "Is anyone--"

"You won't steal my secrets!" cried Old Urlich from the corridor. "You'll burn--just like the rest of them. Burn, witch, burn!"

"What the--" A globe of light flared into existence as Ensley, still fully robed, stumbled out of the bed in the corner.

"He woke up," Lisbet gasped. "Can you--"

"Aha!" Old Urlich loomed in the doorway. "Thought you'd escape my wrath, did you? Hiding won't save you, you foolish child. To the fire with you! A new and brighter tomorrow will come. You'll see, you'll see."

"Do something," Ensley hissed in her ear.

Lisbet blinked in confusion. What was she supposed to do? She was running for her life.

"Oh-ho, a tricky one," continued Old Urlich. "Still a little fight left to you, eh? Watch him, guards! Can't you see he's trying to get away?"

"Does he even see us?" Lisbet whispered to Ensley.

"He sees us as someone else. But he's very much aware of two people in this room with him. Don't make any sudden movements."

"Can you signal Nemora?"

"Not directly--not without drawing his fire. And I can't handle a direct attack."

Lisbet already assumed that. And she knew that there was nothing she could do at this distance, that she was dead if she moved.

"Do something," Ensley urged again.

"I'm just a Healer," she hissed back. "You're the one with the spellcraft."

"I don't mean challenge his power, fool. Talk to him. You've been inside his mind. You know how he thinks."

No, I don't know, Lisbet wanted to protest. What she'd seen of his mind was pure chaos. She couldn't speak to that. Actually, he seemed more coherent now than she'd seen earlier. Not at all rational, but he seemed to be reacting consistently to whatever reality he was seeing.

She dug into the images she had gleaned from his mind. What was Old Urlich seeing? A high tower, fire, guards. A glimpse of Old Urlich struggling with someone--was that the Archimage? The scene froze before her in vivid detail. It *was* the Archimage, his face contorted in a grim mask as he drove the flames into Old Urlich's mind, shattering his resistance.

"The flames," Lisbet blurted out abruptly. She had no idea what the scene represented, but it just might be the leverage she needed. "The flames that destroy the mind."

Old Urlich paused in his tirade.

"How can I help?" she asked. "Should I call in more guards?"

"More guards?" Old Urlich's unfocused eyes swept the room. "No, fewer guards. I'm trying to escape . . . but I never escape. Help me!"

Lisbet edged forward until she was almost at the door. "Yes, I'll help you escape this time."

"Yes," he breathed in almost childlike wonder. Then his eyes suddenly focused on her with terrifying intensity. "You see it, too. You know. The wars, the slaughter--it is not I who am mad. I keep trying to warn them but they don't listen."

"But now there is someone to listen," she soothed. "Your part is done. You can rest." She gingerly brought her hand into contact with his. It was hot to the touch, like a warming brick. "Rest," she repeated, sending him healing energy as fast as she could channel.

"Together we can . . . escape . . ." Old Urlich's voice faded to a whisper. He touched her forehead lightly with his finger.

Lisbet felt the tingling. The next moment she was supporting all his weight.

Ensley rushed forward, helping her carry the old man over to the bed. But he kept giving her suspicious glances. She had some serious explaining to do, she could tell already.

"I'll keep watch here," she said hurriedly. "You still look exhausted. Take his room and try to get what rest you can in the time remaining."

"What was that about escaping?" demanded Ensley. "You seemed to understand what he meant."

Lisbet shook her head. "I caught a few images from his mind, but the rest was guesswork." She could tell he didn't quite believe her. "Maybe we should discuss this later when Nemora is awake," she added. "I'm too spent to think about much of anything right now."

"All right." Ensley waited a moment more. "He's one of the Archimage's most powerful weapons. His very madness makes him unstoppable on the battlefield." He moved toward the corridor.

Lisbet gave a small sigh of relief as the door closed behind him. She leaned forward and checked Old Urlich one last time. Still in deep, deep sleep. He wouldn't be waking until--

She probed more deeply, startled by what she was reading from him. The mind was more than quiescent--it had changed. The power was gone.

She touched her forehead. Old Urlich's power signature pulsed faintly, but unmistakably in her own head. He had somehow transferred his terrifying abilities to her.

Shuddering, Lisbet sank down on the bed. Why had he done it? So she could return to the capital and confront the Archimage? Redress wrongs and stop the wars?

But she felt no compulsion to do any of that. She couldn't even be sure what the chaotic images of the Archimage meant. They could merely be distorted memories of the last time Old Urlich had gone on a rampage.

Why? The question remained. But whatever the answer, Lisbet recognized her cue to disappear. Nemora and Ensley would be relentless in their questioning tomorrow when they discovered the change in Old Urlich. Sooner or later, they would know the truth and bring her before the Archimage.

But not if she could not be found. She rose and headed for the door, eager to be gone before it all came to pass. As she touched the door handle, she felt the energy. The door had been spelled shut-- Ensley's final good night, no doubt.

Lisbet stared at the door. With time, she could perhaps unweave the spell, but she had no time. Power, however, she did have.

Stepping back, she gathered the memories of Old Urlich's attack. She closed her eyes and willed the energy to come. Power rose within her and exploded, leaving behind the scent of charred wood.

When she opened her eyes, a gaping hole greeted her. The door, doorjamb, and half the wall had been reduced to fine dust. Another stretch of wall was charred to the timbers and looked ready to collapse at any moment. The realization that she had done this thing unnerved her, and she quickly shouldered past the wreckage into the corridor. Surely such power was never intended to be wielded by any single person. Perhaps that in itself had driven Old Urlich mad over the years. It wasn't a comfortable thought.

As she descended the stairs, the inn seemed quiet. Deathly quiet, she thought grimly. The perfect backdrop for a desperate escape.

Escape.

She paused, then with sudden clarity, she saw. The Mad Mage had finally made his escape. Without his power he was useless, just a crazy old man who could die in peace. Through no intent of her own, she had provided him with the ultimate healing. And had come away blessed--or cursed. Only time would tell which.

As Lisbet stepped into the gray dawn, the faintest suggestion of an old man's chuckle echoed in her mind.

Book of a Thousand Tales
by Diana Whiley

Kaleda materialized in a salon. The emerald cat at her side growled.

"Control your pet," the book, Illustra, intoned as its pages opened. The cat ignored it, muscles bunched to leap.

A swirl of dark inkiness shot up from the book's pages.

Kaleda moved forward, dodging underneath its fountain of black droplets, evading all but one. It hit her eye and turned it into a blackened mess. Fighting the pain, she drew her dagger, and aimed its point at her dissolving iris, prepared to plunge.

The blackness paused, then reluctantly receded, and she was made whole again. The cat licked a burn on her leg.

"Shazade, come," Kaleda said, and this time the cat obeyed, going back into the gem on her sword's pommel.

Kaleda reached the book, venting her frustration and fatigue at the book's show of control. She saw a finely detailed map of three tributaries spilling into one great river to a city called Dohavar. Water collected and stored in five holding tanks. Beside the largest, a figure knelt, hands outstretched.

"The Keeper," Illustra said.

"And?"

"He seeks the wisdom of the river Gods. They will instruct him to name the five who will compete for the succession of Maharaj. Watch and learn." And so saying, she became witness to the Keeper's divination.

He selected five bowls from the alcove set above his workbench and set them upon the floor in a wide circle, each filled with different crystal shards. He then selected the ceremonial knife of his ancestors and cut his skin. Blood welled, and he turned and placed a drop of it into each of the five bowls. He placed a cloth around his arm to stop the bleeding then sat down, closing his eyes. He concentrated on the chakra of his body and built within himself a flame. It grew, intensified, and he focused its inner light on the crystals.

One by one, a small flame rose within each and he spoke the words of lore of the Keepers, of the rivers, the blood and tears of the kingdom, and waited.

And five souls came to him. Five who would face the will of the Gods; each linked and held within each flame. He noted them, named them, and was greatly surprised by the last.

A small intake of breath stirred the room suddenly and he nearly lost concentration, then tightened his will. He finished the ritual and was not surprised to find Anhara in front of him when he opened his eyes.

"Is it time?" she whispered.

He drew her close and felt the apprehension stiffening her body. "Not yet."

"But he is dying – is he not?"

He drew back, gripping her arms. "Anhara. You must never speak thus."

Her eyes widened, then she looked down at his hands. He let go abruptly but did not apologize. "Do you understand?"

She hesitated then nodded. "And remember,'" he said sternly, "it is the River God's will, the naming, not mine, and their choice of who will eventually rule." He moved to the bench where a scroll was unwound ready for the naming. He handed her a quill, eyes softening as he said. "Shall we begin?"

She nodded and began to write. He tried to ignore the trembling of her hand when the last name was written. She controlled it, then blotted the ink, folded it and tied it with red and gold thread. Red for blood, gold for the sun and a reminder of its influence over water.

"Thank you, daughter." She shivered and he dropped a kiss on her head. "Your task is done. Be at peace. The naming has to be sanctioned first."

She began to speak, but he put a finger on her mouth.

"I must go back to the palace. Do you wish to accompany me?"

She looked surprised, then fearful. "No. I'll clean up here for you."

"So be it," he said, and picking up the scroll, left the room.

The Keeper's form wavered and diminished until it was once again part of the page, and Illustra spoke.

"The five candidates so chosen now travel from their indentured city toward the tributaries. Each youth carries within him a link to the ruling families of Dohavar. You will need to find the one who is the white pearl."

"And a way to identify him?"

"Your task. They are travelling by caravan, here," the book said and red dots appeared, marking their progress. Two of the groups were ahead slightly. She nodded. These she would target first.

No sooner had she thought it than she was there, mouth instantly dry, skin breaking out into a sweat. She reached for the water skin and sipped, squinting against the glare and heat haze to a distant swirl of dust. Her target.

Beyond it, a smear of darkness heralded the river's edge. She felt the whisper of its magic along her skin, and Shazade materialized. She stroked the great cat's sleek body.

"Soon my lovely," she said, then started walking down the sand dune.

The smell of camel and salt-tanged sweat hit as she neared the group. She moved to a position midway between the four stationed guards. As the fifth member of them, the men were already aware of and used to her, a past familiarity with her woven into their memory.

Ahead, palms clustered and ran ahead toward a rising rocky landscape. The caravan was at its most vulnerable once they entered that territory. Tension ran through the men. Glances met and she moved closer to the group around a youth dressed in white cloth. Light bounced off it like pearl lustre and she paused, then looked deeper and encountered a spell of deflection. It was strong but it took only seconds for her to twist and inveigle the spell so its wielder would not know it had been penetrated. Underneath she met another spell. This one perpetuated by the youth himself. That gave her pause. She cursed under her breath; cursed Illustra from keeping this from her. Did all the youths have sorcerous ability? She had to assume so.

She withdrew a little to think, and to avoid the youth's notice. Or so she'd hoped, but coffee coloured eyes turned and looked at her with an uncommon wisdom and simplicity. That stunned her. She wondered about the true nature of the city of Dohavar.

Her skin prickled. After participating in a hundred tales, could her search actually be over?

"Geon, let the Lady approach," she heard suddenly and looked up, realized she'd drawn closer to the youth and his armed manservant.

She moved; a blur as she jumped off the camel to the ground, sword out and a spell at the back of her throat. It was unnecessary. The manservant had not moved to engage.

"I am Tazar," the youth said. "I have been expecting you."

No sooner had he finished speaking than a maelstrom of wind and dirt descended. She spun faster and faster into darkness, then silence.

She stood on a dune. The caravan below marched toward a river town. Shazade appeared. She leant down, touched her sleek form.

"Soon my lovely," she said then stopped dead.

"By all the powers," she muttered angrily then ran at great speed once again through sand and dust to the heart of the caravan.

The youth in the centre was different from the other, but still cloaked in spells. She easily stripped them away to the hidden symbol within, a blue lotus.

Not the one she sought.

The next instant she fell back, as a sudden whistling and thwaak saw three dark arrows embedded the youth's chest. Chaos descended. Guards and camels shot every which way trying to determine the threat.

Kaleda turned toward the direction and angle of the arrows and saw … a thin magical thread. She swore and strengthened the barrier of protection around herself and ran to the youth. His manservant stopped her. "He is dead. Do not touch him."

He looked down. The body was already decaying, flesh drying and shrivelling.

A very strong spell.

She looked up to speak to the manservant but he was striding away. Her eyes narrowed. His back looked familiar and she swore again. The book had decided to oversee her activities. It had not done so for a long time.

There must be more at stake here than she'd imagined, but what? And the magic used here, who had sent it?

One of the other Families, or Illustra itself?

She decided the former. Illustra had been too close. Which meant … *she* may have caused the youth's death. She'd stripped his spells without immediately protecting him. A mistake, and one she would not make next time.

Abandoning her post she raced back the way she'd come and found the link to the second youth. He was on the tributary some fifty leagues east of her. Drawing her sword, Shazade appeared. She climbed onto her back and the cat set off, faster than any other living being.

Two days later, the dunes descended to a land of shrub and rock, then to richer soil and the tell-tale silhouette, of palms. She called a stop and Shazade returned to the sword. Kaleda walked a league along the river bank to a small village and purchased a raft.

Once on the river, she navigated a series of turns and falls to a widening canyon, mustered the wind, and by day's end came in sight of a wharf. Several small craft surrounded a larger boat and beyond it, a sprawling town.

The sun set and she eased the raft into reeds running along the foreshore away from the wharf. After tethering it, she waded up the bank, found a path, and walked to the western edge of the town.

Keeping to the shadows where lantern light did not penetrate, she passed shop fronts until she found the first Inn.

She watched and waited as customers arrived. Most were traders. A perfect place to hide the youth in plain sight, but first she had to be sure he was there, identify him then decide to delay or join the group.

After reviewing what she'd seen in the book, it was Anhara's reaction that had given her the clue. The last youth named to the succession had been familiar to her and…beloved.

Her gut clenched.

No. she would not think of he, whom she did not name ... And moved toward the back of the Inn.

Slipping into the steam shrouded, busy kitchen she grabbed and donned an apron. At the same moment, a curse and dropped plate drew everyone's attention. She took the opportunity to step up to the side table and started cutting vegetables.

Once the broken pieces were cleared, work resumed and she added the vegetables to the pot then walked toward the pantry. As soon as the hanging pots concealed her, she nipped over to the swinging doors and peered over them.

The Inn was crowded, the three trestles in the middle overflowing with raucous heavy drinkers. None were young. She checked in the corners, right side first and nearly moved on but part of the area appeared smudged. She took a closer look. And yes, there was a spell of misdirection but it covered several figures, not just one.

Clever.

If the spell were lifted it gave the bodyguards a chance to retaliate before the target was identified. It appeared this family had taken added precautions.

"Move. Oaf," a waitress said glaring at her, then pushed past her into the main room. Kaleda adjusted her stance, flung off the apron and followed her; a glamour instantly in place. She too looked like a waitress with tray in hand. But she had but taken a few steps when she felt a shift in the air and threw the tray. It collided with metal. Three men had erupted from the side table, swords out.

Kaleda dissolved the glamour and drew Shazade. A green light immediately flashed toward her. She rolled and came up, crashed into a patron trying to leave, flung herself to the opposite side as that patron screamed, face burning.

When she stood, the swordsmen and sorcerer were gone. Men ran to get buckets. Others turned to look at her with angry faces. She made a hasty retreat.

Outside, she ran. Without asking, Shazade ran with her. Kaleda saw a flash of cloth before it disappeared and she hurried to the street corner, then stopped abruptly. A trail left by the sorcerer had diverged. Had he taken the youth and was shielding him?

Shazade growled and took off down the street toward the wharf. Kaleda did not hesitate but followed her friend's nose, alert for attacks from behind.

None materialized. She ran on and had almost reached the end of the street edging the town when the *youth* stepped out in front of her.

She slowed, eyes on him, while her senses darted back and forth. He was alone. She suspected a trap and readied a spell.

"What do you want, warrior?" he said, lip curling.

"A word only," she said calmly.

"And would that be *white pearl?*"

"Perhaps," she said, and ran straight at him. But was pushed back by a wall of wind and dirt; dirt that became slivers of steel. She parried with her sword. Deflected ten that embedded themselves in the buildings nearby. Saw the shadow encroaching just in time and swung around, plunged her sword into the ballooning stomach of a Djinn. It popped and matter splattered everywhere.

She turned and the youth sent fire. Her readied spell sent it back. The youth as quickly defended himself with a sheet of ice. It soon melted. The youth then conjured a dark cloud formed of noxious poison.

Kaleda increased her protection and sent it back with her own wind. The spell dissipated and he readied for another, but had not counted on Shazade. She hurled herself into him, knocked him flat and pinned him.

He struggled but could not get up. Kaleda advanced, shaking her head. "You should have expected the *unexpected.* Shazade is immune to your spells."

She stopped when three swordsmen appeared at the end of the street. Their swords were sheathed. She looked quickly to her right and an older sorcerer stepped out, body shimmering protection. "He has learnt his lesson, you may now desist."

She stared back. "I am not part of this game."

"Are you not, Sword Mistress Kaleda?"

She swore then bowed. "My payment?"

"Named and accepted."

She nodded, then disappeared in a warp of air and materialized on the other side of the building, furious.

Illustra *had* duped her.

She hurried toward the shore. Leapt onto the raft then set it adrift, revisiting the map of the river in her head.

Ahead lay the convergence of the tributaries into the one great river. She checked, could not feel any of the other youths' presence ahead. Time enough then to get to Dohavar first and work out what, if anything, of the book's scenario held truth.

The whirlpool when she reached it nearly took her life, so powerful was its churning. But aided by Shazade, balancing the raft as her spell counteracted the water's fury, she shot out the other side. Drenched but still afloat, the raft sped along and so too her thoughts.

Anhara's importance was a ruse. Illustra knew she'd consider the girl a threat and it *had* clouded her judgement. All aspects of the book's tale were now suspect, especially the names of the chosen.

Illustra had been there when the first youth died.

What if the opposite of what she'd been told was true? That all the youths had been contracted to die. But the last youth had survived. Or had he?

She'd been angry and left too soon. Normally she would have gone back secretly to check. Why hadn't she?

Could she be… a catalyst?

No. She couldn't be …and whipped out her sword, swung it out in a wide, fast arc then plunged it deep into her stomach.

Shock froze her body then blood splayed out in a fan of… *black drops*.

"No," she shouted and fell to her knees trying to force the blade through further but it was yanked out.

Staggering pain took her breath. Sweat broke out and salted the wound to terrible new heights before suddenly, it was all gone. No pain. No blood, and her sword back, sheathed.

She fell then and curled up into a ball. All her threats had been for nothing. The book would forever keep her alive to do its bidding.

A wet tongue on her face roused her. She sat up. Shazade stepped back slowly, eyes holding hers, not judging. It was enough. Kaleda stood and reached for the pole and sliced it through the water.

The sun sank. Night starred a universe of the deepest blue. The moon cascaded threads of silver and she parried them in a deadly dance swung, cut, swung; not stopping until dawn.

Exhausted but more at peace, Kaleda finally sheathed the blade. Shazade remained on deck; she'd not be relegated back to the gem. A silent pact they'd made during the night.

The morning scents on the wind announced the presence of a caravan; dust and camel, sweat and perfume. It was time to leave the river; to mingle and find out what was happening.

Securing the raft to a clump of reeds, she climbed the high bank and emerged to witness a great gathering of many caravans and a tent city. Around it and through it swirled tell-tale signs of sorcery, all open to detection.

Her guard went up. She felt a seeking. Carefully increasing a spell of misdirection, she joined a group of camel herders swinging in to water their stock and listened in on their conversation.

"Our Jamil is the favoured one, you know that."

"Ha, not so," said another, older. "Nemir is the one who carries the blood of the eldest family."

"But does he carry the black star?"

"He will."

"And by some miracle has he become friend to Sorcerer Tazar?"

Kaleda's hand clenched.

The older one blustered. "His attendants are cousins to…"

The others snorted and the older protested as Kaleda left them and circled the tents, weaving her way through camp fires.

The whole set up smelled of intrigue and deception. Hoping, yet not really sure she was undetected, she aimed for the largest tent. It had no guards. She slowed. The youth Tazar appeared and looked straight at her. She kept walking. He nodded and re-entered the tent.

When she stepped inside a wave of spells streamed over her but did not strip her own. She frowned.

"I have circumvented time, so Illustra cannot hear us,' Tazar said sitting crossed legged on a cushion.

Kaleda stiffened. How did he know?

He waved an arm and a web of spells rippled into existence, gossamer thin and complex.

"It is I, who is the catalyst."

She shook her head remembering the black drops.

"Illusion," he said. "And one working on your greatest fear. I, on the other hand *want* to be the catalyst."

"Why?"

"Because I can and do affect outcomes. And this time I knew you would be pushed."

"And the succession?" she said sharply not quite believing, yet.

"Real and taking place today. I test and name the five."

"I don't understand. Do you not mark the chosen one with a black star?"

"This time they will *all* carry the mark."

"To keep them alive?" she said softly, seeing in him a deep sadness.

"Yes."

"And the Keeper?"

"His ritual will reveal the same."

"But why the other deaths?" she mused.

"To make you doubt."And she realized that was true.

The night on the river, Illustra had controlled her mind. Fooled her.

Never again.

"So why now. What is so important?"

"Illustra must not prevail this time."

"You know what he wants?" she asked

"Yes. To destroy Dohavar.'"

"How? Wait. Through Anhara?"

"Yes, she harbours a secret. Get her to reveal it to you."

"And then?"

"Prevent the catastrophe she'd cause."

"'But why is that city of concern?"

"Chaos feeds the book, and this city's holding tanks hold more than water."

"And when the book understands what I've done?"

"I can protect you."

"Because … I saw you?"

"You will always see me, when you have need."

She clamped down on the feeling that *that* stirred. "Then I must go to Dohavar."

"Yes, but stay tonight and get a sense of what awaits the youths."

She nodded. It made sense, and touching Shazade's head she exited all too aware of Tazar's eyes on her back.

The cat slipped off into the night and Kaleda mingled, helping where it was needed then ended up drinking with the guards.

She came under a lot of scrutiny being the only female, but her confidence and understanding of a working caravan eventually satisfied them.

Readying for bed, the night sky lit up with a comet and behind it, five trails of flame.

Coincidence, or a show of Tazar's power?

The latter most likely, and she wondered if it was that power held him to his position. It would not her. Nothing would induce her to stay trapped in this endless cycle of fighting and servitude.

On that determined note, she bedded down and closed her eyes. Set her internal clock and rose again at midnight to relieve the watch.

Back facing the fires, she extended her awareness out through Tazar's tangle of spells and past them to the open space beyond. Met the taste and weight of ancient hills and deep wells familiar yet new, their difference offering a way to reinvent her magic. And that ability had at least stopped the monotony.

So what could she draw from the land this time?

The river, she thought, swinging back on a wide curve. It called and sang a melody both sweet and fierce.

She had not heard it yesterday, dimmed most probably by Tazar's spells. She concentrated and listened to its story unfold, of centuries giving life, changing the land's face and making connections to mortal beings.

The Keeper and Marahaj had developed a link to each other and the river. A clue to how Anhara could destroy Dohavar?

It was worth investigating.

She gathered what she could of the spirit of the water and drew back to the encampment. Morning stirred fires and hunger. A guard came to relieve her and she went to eat and listen to the murmur and texture of talk.

There was distrust as well as joy and anticipation. A heady mix exuding energy and hints of the other sorcerers placed among the groups. Their spells entwined with Tazar's in such a manner that they had no idea he controlled them.

But not her spells. That confirmed Tazar's claim he *had* expected her, and prepared accordingly.

The ten youths, heirs to their families, gathered with their mentors and armed guards on the edge of camp. Once the ritual circle had been laid down and consecrated, the testing would begin.

Kaleda studied them, surprised to find that five of the youths had already been marked. She looked quickly about to see if anyone noticed. No-one reacted. She waited then, committing the faces and magical aspects of the five to memory. She made her way out of the camp.

Taking the path beside the river, she strode briskly past scattered brush and boulders, half expecting Illustra to turn up. The book didn't, but she remained alert.

A league further on, Shazade finally joined her. Noting the cat's easy lope and bright golden eyes Kaleda relaxed a little. She was the best barometer of Illustra's presence.

At day's end they'd reached the point where the river looped and continued on between low lying hills. They would take the shortest route due south and reach Dohavar in three more days. The party with the youths was using the river.

Day three, she came upon the tail end of a caravan, once again beside the river. Barges floated downstream toward a growing line of white buildings and a great wall.

Nested alongside the mighty river, it spread back and out in a dazzling white sprawl from an arched gate covered in the symbols of water and life.

Symbols embedded with spells of detection and protection.

Shazade reluctantly returned to the sword. Kaleda hoped it would be for the last time.

She entered through the gate and immediately felt energy sizzle through her. Her spell had not prevented detection. She moved steadily but with pace around the edge of the square to the main thoroughfare beyond. Slipped into the shadows of the buildings, avoiding sellers and buyers as best she could.

After cutting into alleys she wound left then right. She had a rough idea where the Holding Tanks were; she'd glimpsed the water's sheen from the summit.

The first magical attack came as she turned into an alley of warehouses. A bubble of glittering energy enveloped her. Tightened. She pushed back with her own spell with just enough impact to pierce the spell. It collapsed.

The second attack came immediately afterward. Two swordsmen and a sorcerer emerged in front of her.

She'd already felt their coming and rushed the first swordsman gutting him quickly. Whipping around she clashed swords with the second, all the while counteracting the spells sent by the sorcerer.

For ten minutes she fought before losing patience, then furiously dispatched her opponents. Panting she looked around. No energy signature. She blew hard then set off at a loping run back toward the main thoroughfare where she should have stayed.

Amongst the crowd, the sorcerers would be less likely to cause a scene. And so it transpired. She walked unmolested, blending in with the dark haired, honey skinned inhabitants. But after a time the street diverged and she stopped. Going this way she'd be further away from the Tanks.

She retraced her steps and strode back out of the city. The river was her best course. She should have thought of it before; its magic was likely to disguise hers.

But first, to get into the river. She could not afford to be seen. That proved difficult with so many people travelling the road. Then a group of traders with their families came along, children rushing back and forth close to the banks.

Kaleda moved when mothers moved as if helping to gather them. Saw an opportunity once they passed higher shrubs, and ducked out of sight.

She quickly climbed down to the water, sliding into its tingling coolness, then dived, creating a bubble of air around her as she swam underneath along its course.

When she emerged within the Holding Tanks she was exhausted. She hung onto the steps carved into the stone wall until her breath eased.

It took some minutes and she used that time to listen. Footsteps regularly trod a path some distance away, and her body felt a jolt. It was the Keeper. It meant she was within the main tank. She carefully climbed the steps to the wall's top and peered over the rim. Two guards stood on either side of tall gates; the entry and exit to buildings beyond. The Keeper walked the length of the tanks spreading a fine powder over the water, his words igniting a reaction. The water stirred.

Kaleda stepped down a rung and hugged the wall, dribbling a spell of camouflage, grew still. The footsteps drew near and words whispered, yet clear to her, "River God, I have heard you and see, feel your offering, whose name is Kaleda."

Listening, Kaleda nearly lost her control then tightened her spell as the Keeper continued. "Sacred one, who was sent, I will shield you. My daughter," and he paused here, spoke louder as he flung dust flung over her head. "Bless the waters and gift it with the essence of our ever, grateful souls." Then softer. "Anhara, my heart, is Keeper in waiting but is torn. I fear she will make a terrible decision. I seek your guidance lest all she is or can ever be is unravelled and with it the river's course. I await with undying gratitude," and stepped away

Kaleda hung, suspended between disbelief and a quiet rage for a long moment then moved to look above the rim.

The Keeper was keeping his word. He'd sent one guard away, the other he was leading to the further end of the Tank.

She acted quickly, climbed up and over the wall then sped across the ground to the gate and entered a courtyard. Facing her stood a wall and archway. She strode through. Beyond it lay an avenue of trees and shrubs to the palace.

She moved within their leafy cover and made her way forward, knowing where to go courtesy of a map placed in her head by the Keeper.

That ability alone had convinced her of his intentions. But did not ease her frustration and concern.

It seemed every moment the rules changed. Who was pulling whose strings? Had Tazar got it wrong? Had Illustra wanted this all along?

Only one way to find out. She had to speak with Anhara and get her to reveal her secret.

To that end she followed the Keeper's directions, careful to avoid the wandering guards, and found the side door in the palace wall.

It led to corridor and another door, the back of the Keeper's workroom.

Here lay all his trappings of service; benches covered with crystals and stones, shelves filled with herbs, and to the left a barely discernible alcove. Instinct took her there. The Keeper had not provided that detail, so it must be important. And so it seemed. Its walls held masses of tightly rolled scrolls, bunched together and held by a great spell.

She moved closer and tentatively reached out with her power and encountered a complex binding; so complex, she knew it would take hours to unravel. Too long. She had only one day until the nominated arrived.

She left the alcove then exited the workroom

Entering Anhara's room she moved around it getting a sense of who she was; tidy, methodical, yet here and there touches of wild colour in small vases and odd carved figures.

A river stone on a side table polished to the sheen of glass, and evoking the impression of movement. Here evidence of her connection to the river. And an alcove where she stored inks and scrolls bound neatly but with less complexity than her father's.

She was about to inspect them when a sound warned her, and she'd already turned to grab the knife aimed at her back. Pushed the girl back.

"A nice try Anhara." The girl jerked. "Yes, I know you."

"How? Who are *you*?" she demanded, staring at Kaleda's emerald eyes.

"One who means you no harm. In fact, one who was sent by the River Gods," and eased back.

"You lie," she said, but dropped her arm, a flicker of hope running across her face.

It reminded Kaleda of how young the girl was. "I do not lie," she said, and mentally blasted all liars alike.

"You carry a sword," Anhara said.

"Yes. And it carries a secret," she said, and saw the girl flinch. She ignored it and whispered to the gem and … Shazade appeared, sleek, beautiful, golden eyes like a new sun.

Anhara fell to her knees and Shazade moved forward.

"I always dreamed…" and put an arm around the cat, quite unafraid, laughing, amazed.

Kaleda felt her punch in the gut, had an inkling…shook off a coming grief she knew she could not afford to indulge.

Anhara drew back and rose. "Sword Mistress, how is it you can be…"

"A warrior? Because it has long been my calling," and saw that hope again. "I believed and it came to pass."

"Not here in Ghyryn province."

"No. But where I come from there were obstacles to females in this role."

"But a sorcerer accepted you?"

She nodded. The girl was attuned to the life that gave a sorcerer ability, along with her clear link to the river. Interestingly, it was the river that had given her another aspect of her….ability.

"You are….the River God's servant," Anhara said and closed her eyes, then opened them. "I…there is something I would ask…" She stopped as the door opened and a guard stepped in. He eyed Kaleda suspiciously.

"A trusted friend, Fahar," Anhara explained, "visiting from… Nehre."

The guard frowned, eye going to her sword, where Shazade had returned. "I see." He coughed and looked, saying formally, "You are summoned by our most beloved Marahaj Senjii to appear before him."

"As he wills, and my guest also," she replied firmly.

Fahar nodded and waited as they preceded him from the room. His gaze bored into her back as they walked the corridor.

Kaleda hoped the Keeper's shield still held.

It did. As she entered the throne room, every guard eyed her. She returned their stares with one of her own as she followed Anhara past all those gathered; five individuals standing out, their elaborate turbans proclaiming them heads of the five most powerful families. Every one of them radiated a lust and greed for power.

It sickened her, and she wondered what lay at the heart of such…then realized their presence meant the nominated had arrived, and earlier than she expected.

She stopped walking when they reached the front. Anahar continued on to join the Keeper to the left of the throne. The Maharaj watched her take her place then turned his gaze to her –a long and penetrating look before he turned to the Keeper.

A long silent communion proceeded, then a nod.

Throughout the exchange, she felt their bond and it was strong, yet weakening on the Maharaj's side. He was obviously ailing and it explained both the drought and the reason for the succession.

On other side of the throne, three sorcerers eyed her with sharp attention despite the shield. But before they could probe further, the announcement of the nominated drew all eyes to the five youths as they appeared. All carried the mark of the black star and a rush of confusion ran through the crowd.

Kaleda saw the quick intense look pass between one of them as each youth moved to stand in front of the Marahaj, who named and accepted them.

No advantage had been given.

Rage replaced confusion.

The Keeper moved forward to speak. "The River Gods have spoken. This time, the successor will be tested by blood and by the river's hand. Do any here wish to contest their will?"

A long, taught silence fell.

Kaleda sensed many a desire to speak, Anhara among them, but when she looked at her the moment passed. No others spoke up.

"The blood of the named will be taken to the womb of life to await the River's judgement," The Keeper said. "On the morrow, only the successor's vial of blood will find the right stream and emerge within the fountain of Aymun. So it is proclaimed."

And no sooner it had then the five families converged on the Marahaj to vent their frustration and unease.

Kaleda could not believe he allowed it, but then again, he *did* need their support.

Anhara took the moment of chaos to slip away. Kaleda had a fair idea where she'd gone and looked quickly to follow, but first eyed the Keeper. He was watching her. She nodded and he turned back to usher the youths from the room.

Kaleda had made her escape from the Palace and remembering that inner map, made for the menagerie; all rulers seemed to have one.

Anhara loved animals. She assumed it would be the first place she'd go to be alone, to think. And there she was, watching a great giraffe curl its tongue around leaves.

"I'd let them go if I could," she said turning. Kaleda nodded. She abhorred cages. "Let's walk."

Anhara joined her. The silence stretched then the girl spoke. "I know who the successor will be."

"How?"

"I see his black star."

"Only his?"

"Of course, why would...Oh, they were all marked?"

"As a safeguard even now against trouble."

"I have not told anyone."

"Good," then felt the hairs on the back of her neck prickle. She stopped and looked around and saw....a retreating back and one familiar. She cursed.

"What's wrong?"

"Do not mention his name. Just tell me this; what troubles you?"

"I cannot be Keeper," she said and shoved a scroll into her hands then rushed off.

Kaleda cursed. Her hands tingled. The scroll was bespelled and she recognized its wielder, the Keeper. So. Here was the secret.

She quickly unrolled it and was stunned by its content. Understood why Anhara was torn.

Did Illustra know and was counting on her interference?

If chaos were his objective so it would be but...how to counteract it? And what about Tazar's conviction she should not be allowed a choice? Had he, too, been duped ?

She put the scroll into an inner seam of her tunic and walked back toward the main Holding Tank. Maybe an answer would come to her, or a way to get the information she needed.

The water's vitality did revive her and that within her, the new link through the river magic gave her a way, a way of seeing, for an afternoon she would be the Keeper.

The blood collected. The Keeper began the lengthy process of preparing the gifts. In each vial, he placed the special powder that preserved the blood, sustained it for at least a day before it lost its potency and started to poison.

Once there had been another powder that preserved blood for much longer, but that formula had been lost. It had been said that the first Maharaj's blood was still inside the stone womb, still preserved. He would dearly love to study it properties.

By keeping dead blood alive, could the living also be sustained?

No. The River Gods would have told him.

He put the idea aside and concentrated on keeping each vial pure. Wove threads of colour around each of them in the colour of the youth's Family House.

Once completed, he made his way to the temple of the Gods. Behind a recess in the stone wall he pressed a symbol. It opened and he travelled a corridor to a chamber and the great well. A rope ladder provided him with the means to climb down. He secured the bundle of vials and made the descent into darkness.

A hundred steps down, he stopped and placed the vials on a small ledge carved into the stone. "Bless these offerings," he intoned, then ascended.

In the morning, water would rise and take the vials into its embrace and be tested.

As he left the temple, Anhara emerged from her hiding place, a vial of blood in her hand.

Kaleda returned to herself. She had to reach Anhara. Leaping into a run, she thought of all the possible outcomes. What could be right?

Later, the Keeper managed a brief word and she answered truthfully. "I have interceded and Anhara knows her mind. You will not be disappointed."

He nodded tightly and carried on. He had much to organize.

Kaleda spent the night in reflection, in the room assigned her. Knees crossed, she imagined finishing her duty here and being released.

It was a fantasy but she needed it. Fell asleep finally, a lone tear running down her cheek.

In the morning, the crowd built to thousands. Drums beat. Tambourines shook. Dancers threw lotus blossoms onto the edge of the fountain's pool.

The Maharaj sat atop a throne built especially for the ceremony. His face, lined and yellow was impassive. Only his eyes hinted at the grim struggle for life.

The fountain sprayed out from one of its streams to disgorge the awaited vial. The Keeper dipped his hand in the water and brought out ...two bound together with red and gold thread. Brahen's family colours; the other...and Anhara stepped forward, grabbed it and stated. "I too claim the honour."

The crowd surged forward.

The Marahaj's sharp command split the air. "Guards."

"No," the Keeper said, and turned to see guards moving to surround them.

Suddenly, Shazade appeared at Anhara's side all glittering facets of emerald. She growled and grew to twice her normal size. The guards hesitated. Bahren took that moment to quickly move forward, braving Shazade's stare, and was let through to stand with Anhara.

The Marahaj stared at the tableau, face made of stone. He gestured. A barrage of spells erupted from his three sorcerers only to be deflected by a barrier of interlocking pattern of golden threads.

They tried again and were thwarted. Immediately afterward, the sorcerers of the four families unsuccessful sent their spells but also failed. Instead of weakening the barrier, the spells seemed to strengthen them.

Kaleda stepped out, not ten feet from the Maharaj. No magical assault occurred. She was too close.

"Great one, should you not at least listen to what these two have to say?" pointing to Anhara and Bahren.

"Why should I?"

"If you would read this," she said and produced a scroll. It vibrated and they both stiffened, both hit by the Keeper's terrible, inner anguish.

"Give it to me," Senjii said hoarsely, and she passed it to him.

He read of the history of the first Maharaj and his bride, who was also the first Keeper. Continued down the family tree, down in a line to... his own Keeper, and Anhara . He closed his eyes then opened them and met *his* Keeper's eyes.

"I could not destroy it," he said.

"No. It *is* the foundation of who we are," he said, voice harsh, eyes flashing before he stood. "Hear me all. I, Marahaj Senjii do proclaim these two both sacred and nominated. I humbly ask the River God's for a sign of approbation."

And he was answered. The fountain erupted five magnificent streams, water cascading over everyone.

A deep roar welled up from the crowd. Kaleda heard another roar, Illustra's. But it could do nothing against the tide of faith and joy.

The Keeper embraced Anhara then went to Senjii and fell to his knees, and was as quickly lifted up to stand at his side. Together; bonded still the future was set in motion.

Kaleda took the opportunity to slip away, heart aching as she left Shazade behind. Anhara needed her more, and she had known that one day Shazade would no longer be hers.

She strode back to the main gate and passed through its spells of protection to the crisp heat outside, half expecting to be summoned back into Illustra's presence. Instead, Tazar emerged from the tree lined road carrying a small cub.

"I know a place where she can be trained. A safe place for both of you for awhile," he said, his spells whirring black dots into oblivion.

Illusion perhaps, but it was enough - for now.

About the Authors and Cover Artist

David L. Craddock lives with his wife and business partner, Amie Kline, in Canton, Ohio. He writes short and long fiction, nonfiction, and grocery lists. His nonfiction book, Stay Awhile and Listen - Book I, which chronicles the history of Diablo and WarCraft developer Blizzard Entertainment, rose to the #1 spot on Amazon's "Video & Electronic Games" category within 24 hours of its release in October 2013. His young adult fantasy novel, Heritage, will be published by Tyche Books in summer 2014. Follow David online at www.davidlcraddock.com, www.facebook.com/davidlcraddock, and @davidlcraddock on Twitter.

Jennifer Crow's short fiction and poetry have appeared in a number of print and electronic venues, including Mythic Delirium, Strange Horizons, and DAW Books' Ages of Wonder anthology. She's received several honorable mentions in the Year's Best Fantasy and Horror and Year's Best Horror anthologies. A collection of her dark folk tale and fairy tale poetry, The First Bite of the Apple, was released by Elektrik Milk Bath Press in November. Ms. Crow lives near a waterfall in western New York, and when not writing she can be found hunting for fossils and doing various crafts. She's active on Twitter and Facebook, and is always happy to hear from readers.

Aaron J. French (a.k.a. A. J. French) is a member of the Horror Writers Association. He edited Monk Punk, an anthology of monk-themed speculative fiction, as well as The Shadow of the Unknown, an anthology of nü-Lovecraftian fiction. His latest anthology Songs of the Satyrs will be published in 2013-14. Aaron's article on Thomas Ligotti appeared in issue #20 of Dark Discoveries, where he is an associate editor. Aaron's fiction has appeared in many publications including Dark Discoveries, Black Ink Horror, Something Wicked, After Death, Bedlam, Beware the Dark, and The Lovecraft eZine. Look for his zombie collection Up From Soil Fresh from Hazardous Press, his metaphysical horror story collection Aberrations of Reality from Hydra Publications, and his novella The

Order in the Dreaming in Darkness collection about a Lovecraftian secret society. He is the Reviews Coordinator for Hellnotes.

Lon Prater has worked in the Reactor Compartments of USS Enterprise, edited the military's textbook on arms deals, and kept things safe in the produce and laundry industries. He lives, writes, and games in Pensacola, Florida. Visit www.LonPrater.com to find out more.

Rie Sheridan Rose has been writing professionally for over ten years. She writes most genres and is willing to try anything else at least once. She has contributed to numerous anthologies, including Reloaded: Both Barrels, Nightmare Stalkers and Dream Walkers, In the Bloodstream, and A Bubba in Time Saves None, with several more in the pipeline. Her website is www.RieWriter.com

Multiple award-winning author **Jacqueline Seewald** has taught creative, expository and technical writing at Rutgers University as well as high school English. She also worked as both an academic librarian and an educational media specialist. Fifteen of her books of fiction have been published to critical praise, including The Inferno, The Drowning Pool, The Truth Sleuth, and Death Legacy. Recently released in hardcover is her co-authored mystery The Third Eye. Her short stories, poems, essays, reviews and articles have appeared in hundreds of diverse publications and numerous anthologies such as The Writer, Pedestal, Surreal, Library Journal, After Dark, and Publishers Weekly.

Jonathan Shipley is a Fort Worth, TX, writer and active SFWA member with speculative fiction stories published in magazines and two-dozen-plus anthologies, including Sword & Sorceress Volumes XXV through XXVII, Weird Tales, and Dragon Magazine. A complete bibliography of his publications is available at http://www.shipleyscifi.com/publishedworks.

Cameron Suey is a California native living in San Francisco with his wife (who can occasionally be convinced to edit his work, as long as it's not too gross) and daughter. He works as a writer in the games industry, and his work has appeared on the Pseudopod Podcast, several anthologies including A Quick Bite of Flesh and Historic History, and will be featured in the upcoming magazine Jamais Vu: The Journal of Strange Among the Familiar. He can be found on the web at thejosefkstories.com, where he writes about writing, horror, and other influences.

DJ Tyrer is the person behind Atlantean Publishing and has been widely published in anthologies and magazines in the UK, USA and elsewhere, most recently Cthulhu Haiku and Other Mythos Madness (Popcorn Press), Sorcery & Sanctity: A Homage to Arthur Machen (Hieroglyphics Press), All Hallow's Evil (Mystery & Horror LLC) and Strange Lucky Hallowe'en (Whortleberry Press), and the well-received, sold-out limited-edition release novella, The Yellow House (Dynatox Ministries). DJ Tyrer's website is at djtyrer.blogspot.co.uk/ The Atlantean Publishing website is at atlanteanpublishing.blogspot.co.uk/

Jason M Waltz believes in heroes and in the need to believe in heroes. He believes everyone should be able to read and be inspired by heroic deeds. To that end, he writes and publishes heroic adventure. His Amazon Author's Page /www.amazon.com/Jason-M.-Waltz/e/B003SPIO7U/ lists a few of the places his words can be found, and he operates Rogue Blades Entertainment, found at roguebladesentertain.wix.com/roguebladespresents under the byline: Putting the Hero back into heroics! Except it's not just a byline for him.

Diana Whiley, inspired by music and art, writes mainly fantasy and has had short stories published as well as book covers. She enjoys teaching Creative Writing and Art, in the Community and at TAFE colleges. She also moved into songwriting for a time and had 5 CD's produced. She is currently doing a final edit of her fantasy novel while exhibiting her art. Visit her online at www.dianakwhiley.weebly.com.

Jay Wilburn lives in the swamps of coastal South Carolina with his wife and two sons. He left teaching after sixteen years to care for the health needs of his younger son and to pursue writing full time. He has recently taken up archery to prepare for the apocalypse, but isn't quite zombie-fighter ready yet. He has written a wide range of stories in horror, science fiction, fantasy, steampunk, and many other genres. He has written the novel Loose Ends: A Zombie Novel and the novel Time Eaters. He has a piece in Best Horror of the Year volume 5 and is proud member of the Horror Writers Association. Follow his many dark thoughts at JayWilburn.com and @AmongTheZombies on Twitter.

Cover artist, **Luke Spooner**, a.k.a. 'Carrion House', currently lives and works in the South of England. Having recently graduated from the University of Portsmouth with a first class degree he is now a full time illustrator for just about any project that piques his interest. Despite regular forays into children's books and fairy tales his true love lies in anything macabre, melancholy or dark in nature and essence. He believes that the job of putting someone else's words into a visual form, to accompany and support their text, is a massive responsibility as well as being something he truly treasures.

Find him online at http://www.carrionhouse.com.